For the Love of the Bull Rider

Sam E. Kraemer

Kaye Klub Publishing

@Copyright

Their story:

What happens when a little lost cowboy brings a professional bull rider and a software designer together? First comes utter contempt. Second comes judgment. Will understanding and attraction soon follow?

Matthew Collins has spent far too many years away from his family, competing on the professional bull riding circuit. When his marriage hits the skids, his wife leaves him and takes their three-year-old son with her. Matt finally gets his son back some three years later, only to realize he has no idea how to care for a six-year-old boy.

One day, Matt loses track of the boy while ordering supplies at the farmer's co-op, and a handsome man with gorgeous eyes and a protective stance helps the boy search for his father. Matt meets the man of his dreams... though he doesn't know it.

Freshly graduated from college, Timothy Moran returns to a rural area of southern Virginia to spend the summer before embarking on a job search. Tim wants to repay his aunt and uncle for their kindness after a tragic loss, but some of the chores at Katydid Farm are more than Tim ever imagined himself doing in a lifetime.

During a perusal of the local farmer's co-op, Tim encounters a little boy with a big cowboy hat who's lost. When he assists the young boy in finding his father, Tim meets... The Bull Rider.

This original work of fiction is the first book in the "Love & Cowboys" Series. It is approximately 90,000 words in length and ends happily without a cliffhanger.

Contents

Chapter One

Tim Moran stood in the aisle of Southern States Farm Supply looking at a whole lot of buckets when he felt a tug on the hem of his T-shirt. He turned to see no one standing next to him, so he continued weighing the merits of the five-gallon feed bucket versus the shorter, rounder, five-gallon grain bin. His Uncle Josh had sent him to the store with the farm credit card and a list. Unfortunately,

Josh wasn't one to provide many details, so Tim wasn't sure what the hell he was supposed to choose.

He felt another tug to his T-shirt and a pinch to his thigh, causing him to glance down to see a little boy—six, maybe—dressed in full cowboy gear, right down to the ten-gallon hat. "Whatcha doin'?" the boy asked, his cute face showing confusion.

"I'm looking at buckets for my uncle. What are you doing?" Tim asked, smiling at the adorable little boy.

"Lookin' for my daddy. Are you lost, too?" the boy asked.

Tim must have had a stupid look on his face even a child could recognize as a clear sign he was out of his element. Though, he doubted the boy was lost in the same way Tim was lost.

He couldn't hold the chuckle. "Yeah, but for a very different reason, I'm sure. Let's go to the service desk and have them page your father."

"*Ryan Earl!*" The boy turned to the sound of the shouting, so Tim followed his line of sight, seeing a bona fide stud of a cowboy spinning nervously at the end of the aisle, clearly searching for someone.

The man was tall, dark, and handsome with broad shoulders and muscular thighs that were almost busting out of the Wranglers he was wearing. There was an old wheat-colored, straw cowboy hat tipped back on his head, and as Tim continued to scan his body and enjoy the view, it ended with a pair of beat-up cowboy boots. His ensemble was a sure sign the man didn't play at being a cowboy. He was the real deal.

Of course, Tim's dick got hard... well, as hard as it was going to get in the jeans *he* was wearing. He was adorned in hand-me-downs from his late cousin, Shane, who had been in the Marine Corp.

Tim was eight years younger than Shane and a lot shorter than his cousin in the pictures that hung on the walls of his aunt and uncle's home. Those pictures of Shane were from when he'd finished boot camp, having traded his cowboy clothes for camo gear. Thankfully, Shane's clothes from middle school fit Tim well—and he was damn grateful to have them.

When Shane was killed in Baghdad, it hit Tim's aunt and uncle hard, but every time he wore one of Shane's shirts, his Aunt Katie would smile and hug him tightly as if she was hugging her son again. It made Tim somewhat uncomfortable, but he'd never say a word because he loved her and owed her more than he could ever repay.

"Over here, Daddy!" the boy yelled back, waving his small hand in the air. Tim heard a faint, "crap," guessing the boy next to him might be the Ryan Earl in question.

Tim stared at the attractive brunet barreling toward them and observed the man appeared extremely worried and somewhat pissed off.

"I *told* you to stay by the water fountain while I went to the men's room. I came out, and you were gone." The man knelt in front of the boy, pulling him into his arms so forcefully, the boy's little cowboy hat fell off.

"Daddy, I was there like you said, but then Tommy Morrow came in with his dad, and we was talkin' about the horse show tomorrow. He needed me to help him pick out new spurs, and when I got back to the water fountain, the bathroom door was open, and you was gone."

The man reached up to dry his eyes with the back of his hands, which surprised Tim, but who was he to judge? He didn't have kids, but if he were in the cowboy's boots, thinking someone had taken the little boy, he'd be worried too.

The man in question picked up the boy's hat and replaced it on his head. "I'm sorry, bud. I worry about ya. I haven't had ya back long enough not to worry yet, okay?"

Ryan nodded and touched the side of his father's face. "I'm okay, Daddy. I missed you while I was gone too."

Tim was cemented to the spot—because he was nosy by nature—and based on their conversation that he was straining to hear, he was intrigued. What had separated the two of them for any significant length of time?

Of course, the cat had his tongue enough that he didn't speak but looking into the sky-blue eyes of the good-looking man in front of him, Tim wasn't surprised that his brain had shut down.

The cowboy stood and took the boy's hand, holding it tightly in his own large one. "I'm Matthew Collins. This is my son, Ryan. Thank you for drawin' his attention so he'd stay in one place where I could find him. You're Josh Simmons' nephew, right? He told me about you the other day when I came over to shoe that bay gelding, Chester, for you to ride," the tall man stated.

Tim swallowed, knowing it was his turn to speak. "Yes, sir. I just got here Wednesday afternoon, myself. I graduated from Penn State, and Aunt Katie and Uncle Josh got me a U-Haul van so I could bring my stuff with me when I moved down. I didn't have much because my apartment was furnished, so it was just my clothes and books and stuff. I'm here this summer to help Uncle Josh at the farm while I start my job search." Tim was babbling nervously, certain he was making an ass of himself, but finding it very hard to shut up.

The cowboy chuckled. "I'm not really old enough to be a *sir*. What'd you study in college?" The lopsided grin on the man's handsome face was nearly more than Tim could handle.

"Computer programming and network security." Tim's was surprised he'd been able to answer because he was mesmerized by the man.

The cowboy's grin grew into a full-size smile, which nearly brought Tim to his knees. "So, you're a computer genius?"

Tim felt the blush begin at his neck and work its way north. "I don't know if I'd say that, but I can hold my own, I guess. I'm at the Katydid to help Uncle Josh modernize his operations. I'm here because this is where he shops and aside from getting everything on this list, I need an idea of the things he uses so I can set up an automatic inventory and order system. Once that's done, he won't have to... Well, it's kind of boring, but I'm excited about helping him. How about you?" Tim was eager to hear more about the handsome man in front of him.

Tim supposed it was his way of torturing himself by asking about the details of the cowboy's life, but at the end of the day, the man was fucking hot, and Tim was dying of curiosity for any information the guy would volunteer.

"Well, aside from doin' some farrier work for a few close friends, I own a cattle ranch. Instead of college, I chose to ride buckin' bulls, first in the amateur ranks on the rodeo circuit, then on the professional circuit in the PBR. I retired from it, and I'm settled down with a son, so I breed and sell cattle." Matt placed his hand on the boy's shoulder protectively. The resemblance between the two was uncanny, right down to the blue eyes. Tim genuinely wondered what the mother looked like.

Ryan pulled his dad's hand, so the man leaned down and listened to the boy's whispers. When he was finished, the father smiled and nodded as he stood in front of Tim in all his six-plus-foot glory. "Me and the boy, here, we'd like it if you'd come out to our place sometime. Maybe you could come out and look at the business if you're lookin' to do a little freelancin'. I'm sure you could come up with ideas to update my operation and make it run smoother. If you have the time and any interest, ask Josh to give ya my number. I'd be happy to have ya take a look."

"Uh, sure, Mr. Collins. Maybe next month? I'm still kind of getting settled with Uncle Josh's operation." Tim was overcome with nerves at the prospect of being alone with Matthew Collins. But then again, any red-blooded gay man would feel the same if they got a look at him.

The hot cowboy laughed. "Mr. Collins is my daddy. I'm Matt. I hope to hear from ya when you got the time." He turned to the boy and smiled. "Let's go, Ryan. Tell—I forgot your name." Matt's cheeks turned pink, which only made him more handsome.

Tim stuck out his hand as his late mother had taught him to do since he was a little boy and offered his name. "Timothy Moran." As he shook the man's hand, Matt smiled, and Tim melted. Matt Collins was too gorgeous for Tim's own good.

"*Timmy!*"

Tim was in a hot barn with a bandana over his mouth and nose because the smell of horse shit made him nauseous. It always had, and he feared it always would.

Every chore on the farm wasn't a cakewalk—especially cleaning the horse stalls. Tim *hated* cleaning the stalls, though he did it for his Uncle Josh because, truth be told, he'd do anything for the man.

Over the years, Josh had developed a way of talking Tim into doing things he'd never imagined he'd do. This particular *thing* involved shit—actual horse manure—and cleaning the horse barn just because Josh said it needed to be done.

Tim stuck his head out to see Uncle Josh and Hank, the foreman at Katydid Farm, standing at the end of the barn by the sliding doors. "Yeah?" Tim walked out with a pitchfork full of manure, dumping it into the manure spreader in the hallway.

Cleaning those stalls seemed to show the cowboys on the Katydid that Tim was willing to work alongside them for the betterment of the farm, so they didn't give him any trouble about being Josh's nephew, or so Tim believed. He'd determined before he could get down to business regarding automating the archaic operation, he needed to understand how everything fit together. It meant Tim needed to learn all the jobs, regardless of the unpleasantness. Uncle Josh seemed proud of Tim for taking the bull by the horns, or so he'd heard Josh tell Aunt Katie one night when he was coming downstairs for dinner.

In all honesty, Tim thought himself lucky because it was early summer, and Uncle Josh had about ten head of his own horses out on pasture. It was a breeding/boarding/training/selling operation, and there were only eight in the barn at night. They were board horses, or horses Josh was training, so the hands took extra, special care of them because they supplemented the income at the Katydid, as well as the money made from the sales of the American Quarter Horses Josh bred and trained.

"You 'bout done?" Uncle Josh asked.

Josh had a white-blond crew cut and lots of freckles from too much sun on his pale skin, along with a crooked nose from too many face-plants from the back of a rank horse. That being said, there was no denying Josh's caring disposition made the man someone that everyone wanted to know. He was the kindest person Tim had met in his lifetime. That was something no one would dispute.

Uncle Josh... Well, he and Aunt Kathleen were exceptional people. They didn't give a shit about the fact Tim liked boys, and Aunt Katie had tried to find him guys to date the few times he'd visited during college, even though he begged her to let it go.

Eventually, she gave up, and Tim was genuinely grateful. Being at their place in Holloway became his haven. They took him in after hell broke loose with his folks, and they let him know every day he was loved and a part of their family.

"Just about finished. What's next?" Tim was ready for anything Uncle Josh had to throw at him, especially since the man had saved him from his father who wanted to beat Tim to death because of his sexuality.

His dad, Harold Moran, had beaten the crap out of Tim before his mom, Sherry, returned home from work. After she saw the damage done to her son that night, she called her brother, Josh Simmons, who drove from Holloway to Pittsburgh to help them. Josh also made sure Sherry got the hell away from her abusive bastard of a husband for all the good it had done.

"Matt Collins called your Aunt Katie. He's havin' trouble with his computer, and he asked if you'd be able to come over and take a look. Claims you two ran into each other at the feed store."

Tim had mentioned meeting the man the afternoon when he'd returned to the farm. He'd tried to be nonchalant about it, ignoring the fact that he'd been jacking off to the memory of meeting Matt Collins for weeks. He was so damn good-looking that Tim couldn't help himself.

Before swallowing his tongue, Tim coughed to buy a little time. "Sure. It's probably nothing." He finished filling the spreader without looking up for fear of giving away the excitement at Matt Collins' call for Tim's help. It wasn't Tim's job to empty it, so he didn't waste time in the barn once it was done.

"Where does he live?" Tim followed Uncle Josh toward the house. He sure as hell needed a shower because he smelled as ripe as the barn, but Tim wanted to hurry so he could see the handsome cowboy again.

He *was* trying his damnedest to play it cool because he didn't want Uncle Josh to know he was infatuated with the hot bull rider, but it wasn't easy. Acting like a giddy fanboy was going to give him away pretty damn quick.

Josh gave Tim the directions and sent him to the house to get cleaned up so he could head over to the Collins' place. After Tim dressed in Shane's jeans and a shirt with snaps up the front and on the pockets, he pulled on the pair of boots bought with his first paycheck at the Katydid. The boots weren't fancy, but they were becoming more comfortable with every wear.

Tim combed his blond, wavy hair, making a note to get it cut soon, and splashed on a little of the aftershave his aunt had bought for him one birthday. As he looked in the mirror, he was grateful he had his mother's hazel eyes and looked nothing like his worthless father.

If he had to look into a mirror and see the man's face every day, Tim wasn't sure how he'd have survived after the evil bastard had killed his mother. The nightmare was never too far from his mind, but he no longer cried out in the middle of the night. It was definitely a sign of progress.

Tim walked downstairs into the kitchen to get a drink of water, surprised to see Aunt Katie at the counter, wrapping a pie. He judged it was apple, based on the amazing smells in the room. She looked up and smiled brightly at him as she usually did when Tim walked into a room where she was busy.

"Take this with you, please? Little Ryan likes apple pie, and I made two of them today. Sit for a minute, will ya, hun?"

Tim couldn't turn down Aunt Katie for anything either. She'd been so unbelievable to him when he didn't have family left. In his mind, the universe brought Katie Simmons into his life to keep him from wasting it because Tim was headed down the road to just give up.

He'd sincerely thought he had no reason to really exist, so Tim considered ending his life. After Kathleen Simmons got ahold of him and took him into her home, any thoughts he'd had of an early out fled.

Katie had encouraged him to go to college to make something of himself. Tim speculated she'd likely have tanned his dead hide if he followed through on his death wish, so he backed off those thoughts and buckled down in school to make her and his uncle proud.

"Sure. What can I do for you?" Tim asked her.

Kathleen Simmons was a beautiful woman, not looking her age at all. She had dark auburn hair, attributed to her O'Hare heritage. Katie had bright, green eyes and was a little round, but Uncle Josh loved her like the stars loved the moon. It showed on his face when she walked into his line of sight.

He'd get a smile, and he'd walk over to her, regardless of when or where they were. He'd pull her into his strong arms and kiss her like they'd been apart for years. She'd eventually pull away, breathless, and she'd giggle and gently slap his chest. It gave Tim comfort to see people who actually loved each other demonstrate it. It hadn't happened in his own family.

In fact, it had been quite the opposite. After Sherry and Tim relocated to New Jersey for his senior year of high school, Sherry filed for divorce. For a while, things were calm, and Tim and his mother had a decent life in Trenton.

Unfortunately, Tim's dad tracked her down after he was served with the divorce papers and acted out a murder/suicide scenario, though not successfully. Sherry was dead, but his father was in a coma.

At the end of the day, Tim's grandmother, Joanne, was the one to pull the plug on the son she didn't like. Of course, she was less than happy to find out her grandson was queer after her son was dead, so Tim was nothing to her. He didn't want anything to do with the bitter old woman either.

"Before you go over to the Collins' place, I should give you a little background. Matthew is one of the most sought-after bachelors in the county. Unfortunately, he has some baggage that puts him off the idea of any kind of relationship, I suspect. After Matt graduated high school, he started ridin' bulls full-time during the season. He'd done the amateur circuit during high school, and he was good at the task, so he advanced to the professional ranks after a few years, and he did well for such a tall guy, or so Josh tells me.

"Matt started seein' a girl from town when he was home after his third season in the pros. He'd done well over the years, but he was yet to rank above the top fifteen in the world, so he wasn't exactly famous. However, Matthew was on his way to becoming a world champion in the not too distant future, and he was only twenty-four.

"The girl's name was Bertie Stanford. She was fresh outta high school and worked as a waitress at Pete's Place. The girl had always been bad news from what I heard around town, though I try not to listen to gossip too much, Jeri, Matt's momma, didn't have any kind words for her.

"When Matt came back to recuperate after he broke his arm on a devil bull that season, Bertie saw her shot at hookin' up with a cowboy—*permanently*. In the process, she got pregnant and demanded that he marry her."

Tim got it. Matt was straight. It wasn't a surprise.

Katie continued. "Matt, bein' the kind of man he is, did the honorable thing and married her, even though we all speculated he didn't love her. He bought 'em a place outside of town with a cute white farmhouse and a fair piece of land, and in the off-season, Matt apprenticed with Old Ed Marshall, the blacksmith back then. When rodeo season came around again, Matt went back to bull ridin' and left Bertie at home to have the baby with his mother lookin' after her.

"Long story short—when Ryan was three, Matt quit the circuit because Bertie complained about bein' a single mom. She got mad at him because his quittin' wasn't what she had in mind. She wanted to go on the circuit *with* him and leave Ryan with Matt's momma. It was more important to him that the boy should have a normal life with a mother and father at home, so Matt quit rodeo. Bertie didn't take it well, so to punish Matt for spoilin' her dream of bein' a buckle bunny, she took Ryan and ran off. Matt looked for the two of 'em for three years."

Tim was surprised someone would go to such lengths as to take away a child to punish their spouse for a change of vocation, but Matt's comment at the co-op about just getting Ryan back made more sense.

"She'd call Matt demanding money, and he'd send it every time, but she never stayed in one place long enough for him to find her. All he wanted was that little boy. She finally brought the boy home six months ago for no reason anyone's ever heard, and Matt gave her divorce papers. Supposedly, Matt wrote her a big check to sign 'em, and she left town after the papers were filed. As far as I know, nobody's seen or heard a thing from her since." Aunt Katie stopped to take a breath.

She took Tim's hand and squeezed it as she looked into his eyes. "Son, Matthew was hurtin' somthin' awful until that little boy was safe at home. He's a good man, sweetie, but he's in a mess right now as he's tryin' to figure out a life for the two of 'em."

Tim took a deep breath. "Aunt Katie, I'm not going to corrupt the hometown hero, I swear. I'll go over and try to figure out his computer problem, and I'll be home for supper."

She smiled and laughed. "I'll keep you a plate."

With that, she left him alone. Tim had no idea what the hell she thought he was going to do with Matt Collins, but Tim wasn't one to hold out the vain hope he would be bumping into Matt at a local gay bar—if there was such a thing. The bull rider was hot, and Tim didn't believe that the man would give him the time of day, even with the baggage Aunt Katie had just explained. Matt had a computer-related problem, and Tim was a techie. Nothing more, nothing less.

Chapter Two

Tim drove up the long, gravel driveway to the house where Matt and Ryan Collins lived. He saw a large barn to the right and a lot of cattle in the pastures. The house was a white, two-story clapboard with a large, wraparound, front porch, hosting a two-seater swing and blooming flowers in white window boxes. There were hanging baskets with lazy petunias of many colors across the front. He could see it was a home for a family, and he smiled.

He walked up to the back porch and knocked, as people were known to do in the country. When little Ryan opened the door, he gave Tim a thousand-watt smile. "Hi, Mr. Tim. Come on in. Daddy's cussin' in the office.' The boy shook his head, which brought a grin to Tim's lips.

Tim laughed as he picked up Ryan, unable to resist for reasons he didn't understand. "Okay, cowboy. Show me where to find the office."

Ryan pointed down the hall, and Tim followed his directions, slyly taking in the house to see it was clean and comfortable. It wasn't a designer anything; it was a simple home. It was the best kind of home to have.

The two of them continued down the short hallway and turned into a room which seemed to be a den. The cowboy-in-question was sitting behind an oak desk in shorts and a T-shirt with the Professional Bull Riding Association emblem on the front.

"Mr. Collins, I heard you were having a problem with your computer." Tim carried Ryan into the room and deposited him on the floor next to the desk.

The drop-dead, gorgeous man looked up and sighed. "I should have known better... Well, don't open emails from people you don't know, but the subject line read that there was interest in one of the bulls I've advertised on an auction website. When I opened it, the whole computer went crazy, and I can't even get the damn calculator or calendar to work, much less everything else I have on here. This thing has all my financial records, along with all the information about the cattle for sale and my address book," Matt complained.

Tim held the laugh as he witnessed the man's hands flailing at his sides before pointing to the offending laptop. He turned to Ryan who looked equally as upset as his father. "Can you get me some water?" The boy nodded, hurrying out of the room and down the hallway, little feet scurrying over the hardwood.

"I need to check if someone attached a virus to it. The sooner I know what it is, the faster I can fix it. I won't bore you with the details, but it's not my first time at *this* rodeo. My roommate in college used to download shit on his computer from porn sites all the time. I used the example of his computer situation as my senior project before I graduated. Kenny ended up going to Hollywood to work as a production assistant at a porn studio, or so I heard. Go figure."

Tim slowly walked around the desk and stood next to the chair where Matt remained seated, appearing to be confused. His eyes grew bigger as Tim got closer to the device, so Tim stopped.

She was foundered when those women dropped her off, but Hank's been trimmin' her hooves every week. Josh thinks she's gentle, and he wants to put shoes on her," she explained with a roll of her eyes that brought a chuckle from Tim.

A little while later, Tim saw a small cowboy hat through the glass panes on the office door, reminding him about his babysitting appointment with Ryan Collins. Aunt Katie had been reading the paper on her phone when the boy knocked on the door, and before Tim could say a word, Aunt Katie jerked it open and knelt in front of him, opening her arms for a hug which the boy gave freely. "Hello there, Ryan Collins. How are ya, sweetie?"

After the two separated from their hug, the boy reached up and took off the little straw cowboy hat, holding it by the brim in his small hands. "Hi, Miss Katie. Gramma Jeri says hi. She's havin' a barbecue and a swimmin' party on the holiday, and she wanted me to ask you if you and Mr. Josh would come. She wants Mr. Tim to come, too, 'cause she wants to meet him."

Ryan walked over to the desk and stuck out his hand. "How you been? Mr. Josh said maybe you could lead me around on Betsy? Daddy won't let me ride her by myself yet, but when I turn seven, I'm gonna get my own horse.

Papa Marty promised me." Ryan leaned against the desk as he spoke, reminding Tim of a little grown-up.

Ryan was dressed in jeans and a T-shirt with the logo for the Circle C on the front. Tim didn't know what the Circle C was, but the boy looked cute. Just a mini version of Matt, right down to those sparkling blue eyes.

He chuckled. "Sure, Ryan. Aunt Katie brought down some muffins and chocolate milk. You hungry?" Tim picked up the boy and put him in the large desk chair. Ryan scurried up to his knees and leaned his elbows against the desk, looking at the computer screen with interest.

Tim opened the thermos and poured Ryan a cup of chocolate milk before he refilled his own coffee cup. He got them a muffin and small paper plates Aunt Kate had included in the basket, along with napkins. Tim heard the office door shut behind them, turning to see the back of his sainted aunt as she walked out of the office and turned toward the house. He was on his own with the kid, and she was likely enjoying Tim's lack of confidence in the situation.

Tim pulled up the wooden side chair and sat down next to Ryan. "You ready for school?"

The two of them dug into the muffins, and there wasn't much conversation between bites for a minute. "You miss breakfast?" Tim thought Ryan seemed awfully hungry so early in the day.

The boy took a sip of his milk and wiped his mouth with the napkin before sheepishly looking at the desktop. "Nope, we had it. See, Daddy can't cook so good. He tries, but he's not good as Gramma. This mornin' he made eggs, and they was burned, so I pretended to eat 'em till the phone rang and he went to answer it. I shoved 'em in the trash under my napkin and pretended I ate 'em while he was gone.

"I don't wanna hurt his feelin's. He's tryin' hard to take care of me, and I know how much he missed me when I was gone, so I just eat around the burnt. It makes Daddy happy when I have a clean plate. Can you cook like Miss Katie?" the boy asked.

Tim was terribly concerned about the kid. Ryan was small, and if he wasn't eating well, then Tim decided he needed to talk to Aunt Katie. "I thought your grandmother brought over food?"

"She just brings over supper. Daddy told her he could feed me durin' the day, and we do okay, just us bachelors. He says Gramma Jeri has enough to do without feedin' us. She works for the school in the office. She just went back to work, so she doesn't have as much time as she did during the summer. When I get taller, she said she'd teach me to

cook, so Daddy don't kill us before I get to high school."
Ryan released a little giggle before he shoved the last piece
of muffin in his mouth.

Ryan had given Tim a lot of information to chew on...
as he munched on a muffin of his own. He watched as the
little cowboy finished his milk and wiped his mouth again.
The mini-Matt was the cutest little guy Tim had ever met.

"You want another? You can take it with you while we
go fetch Betsy. I think Hank let her out in the pasture this
morning while the boys were cleaning stalls. Uncle Josh
has apples in a bucket in the hallway, and I bet if we took
one with us, we could catch her easy."

Ryan hopped down from the chair with a glowing
smile. "That's a good idea. Can we take a muffin to Daddy?
I don't think he ate his eggs neither," the boy asked. Tim
could only smile. Ryan Earl Collins was a special little boy,
and clearly, he loved his dad.

Tim grabbed the basket of muffins and a clean cup,
filling it with coffee. He'd have to apologize to Matt for
the taste of the black sludge, but Uncle Josh and the
farmhands liked it that way, and Tim wasn't going to make
waves on the farm. "Let's go," he told Ryan. The boy
opened the office door and let Tim out, closing it behind
them.

Uncle Josh's laughter was heard from the barn hallway, so Tim turned to see him talking to the handsome cowboy who had been the star of too many of Tim's dreams for the last ten weeks since they'd first met. Tim knew the night he went to Matt's place to fix his computer—the night the man had kissed him—it had freaked out Matt Collins. Tim damn sure wasn't going to make a big deal out of it. Hell, it was a meaningless kiss...just like every kiss he'd shared with the few girls he'd dated in high school while trying to figure out his shit. Those kisses didn't mean anything, and the kiss from Matt Collins didn't either.

Ryan slowly walked down the hallway in front of Tim, obviously having been coached about running up on a horse. Even though the mare was staked tightly, Matt was in a vulnerable position with his back to the mare's head as he worked on the right, front hoof. Her hind leg could easily come up and strike him on the head. Thankfully, Princess was a gentle mare used to a pedicure, so Tim doubted she'd startle easily while Matt was working on her.

Tim could see the large F-250 King Cab truck parked outside the entrance of the barn with a small trailer hitched to it. The firebox on the trailer was glowing red-hot from the blazing fire inside. There were metal cabinets on one side, and tools attached to the other side. It looked custom-made and very old. Tim was instantly intrigued.

They walked to where Uncle Josh was sitting on a bale
of hay in the hallway, watching Matt work. "Hi, Mr. Josh.
Tim said he'd lead me around on ol' Betsy. Where's them
apples?"

Matt glanced at them and smiled until his eyes met
Tim's. Matt's face turned red, and he lowered his base-
ball-cap-covered head to continue his work without comment. "If it's okay with you, Mr. Collins, I don't mind
catching Betsy and leading Ryan around the round pen for
a while. Would that be okay?"

Tim really hated himself for putting the bull rider on the
spot since he seemed to be trying to avoid Tim in the first
place, but hell, the man had kissed Tim first. He just kissed
Matt back.

In Tim's mind, he wasn't pining after Matt—not much,
anyway. Tim damn well wasn't stalking Matt, but they
were going to have to be able to speak to each other because
it seemed the families were good friends, and the two men
were bound to run into each other from time to time.

If they reacted strangely when they saw one another,
people would begin to ask why. Tim didn't want either of
them to feel they had to offer an explanation or a lie.

Matt gently lowered Princess' hoof to the sawdust-cov-
ered floor of the barn and turned to look at Tim as he gently brushed his hand over the mare's side. "Please, call me

Matt. It's good to see you again. My laptop's workin' fine since you fixed my problem. Thanks again." The sincerity in his voice was easy to recognize.

Tim smiled at the man. "No trouble at all. That's what we do for our neighbors. Is it okay if I take Ryan for a ride on Betsy?" Tim asked the question again as the boy handed Matt a muffin from the basket.

"Damn, where are my manners. Would ya like a cup of coffee?" Tim offered Matt the mug from his hand.

The taller man slipped off leather gloves and accepted the coffee and the muffin. "Thanks. We were a little light on breakfast this mornin', weren't we, bud?" The gorgeous grin as Matt stared at his son made Tim's heart skip a beat.

Ryan giggled. "Sorry, Daddy. I ate some of 'em."

Matt let loose with a belly laugh, totally blowing Tim's mind. There was no such thing as love at first sight, as Tim had learned over the years, but that laugh and the love in Matt's eyes as he gazed at his son? That might have been the thing to tip Tim over the edge. He was going to be a sad case of a lovestruck fool for a very long time.

"S'okay, bud. We're still learnin' together. Anyway, if Mr. Moran doesn't mind leadin' Betsy, I don't mind you ridin' her. You just listen to Ti... him." Matt gestured toward Tim.

Tim nodded and left the basket of muffins with his uncle and the handsome cowboy. He took Ryan's hand and led him down the hall to the tack room where he grabbed a blanket, a bridle, and a lead rope.

He pointed to the bucket of apples, and Ryan grabbed three. "We don't want the other horses to think we don't like 'em, too." When the little cowboy's hands were full, Tim laughed and grabbed three more.

The pair walked down to the pasture where the horses were grazing on the late summer grass. Uncle Josh had two cuttings of premium hay from it earlier in the summer, so he was leaving the third cutting for the horses to clean up. The baled hay was in a barn the size of a gymnasium across the road on the other parcel of land Uncle Josh owned, ready for winter feeding.

The Katydid had put up nearly five thousand bales of hay, which was more than enough to get the farm and its inhabitants through the winter. Uncle Josh's view on it was if any of the neighbors needed hay, he was more than happy to load up a trailer and deliver it himself. He lived the Golden Rule every day and set a good example for Tim.

Ryan climbed up the plank fence and latched onto Tim's shoulder as they looked out at the pasture, taking in the sights. Tim never thought he'd be one to fall in love with the country life, but he had. Watching the horses lazily grazing or galloping through the fields brought a peace to his soul. Looking out at the grand vista reminded Tim of a postcard. How could anyone be unhappy with that view?

"*Betseyyyy!*" Ryan didn't waste any time hollering for the mare.

Tim turned to see the old mare under a large oak tree near the creek. She looked up, and when she saw Ryan waving his little hand in the air with an apple, she leisurely strolled up the hill to where they waited at the fence. Tim was glad they didn't have to walk down that hill to get her.

A few of the other horses started following her, and Ryan giggled. "Glad we brought extras." He climbed down and picked up another apple.

Tim tossed the saddle pad over the fence and hooked the bridle on top of a post, taking the lead rope with him to the gate. "You stay on this side while I get her. Some of these horses are new boarders, and I don't want you getting hurt, okay?"

"Okay, Mr. Tim," the boy answered.

"Just call me Tim, Ryan. We're friends now, so you can drop the mister." Tim stepped through the gate.

"Sure thing, Tim," the boy answered as Tim walked a few feet to meet Betsy.

The mare stopped in front of the gate and waited while Tim clasped the lead to her halter. He led her over to the gate and let the two of them through it while ensuring the other horses didn't follow.

Tim looped her halter around the gate and walked to where Ryan was standing as the other horses walked up to investigate their visitor. The little cowboy held an apple on his flat palm through the fence to a new gelding Josh had just taken in for boarding. The horse was gentle, or so Tim had been told, but he didn't feel too comfortable with Ryan feeding the horse without assistance.

"Here, Ryan, let's get you up here where I can keep an eye on the horses," Tim told the boy as he lifted the little cowboy to rest on his hip. He took the apple and put it on his flat palm with Ryan's hand beneath to guide it to the horse, for the sake of safety. When the horse took it, Ryan giggled. The two stood at the fence feeding apples to the horses until they ran out while Betsy waited patiently.

After he placed the saddle pad on the mare's back, Tim gently swung the boy up before he grabbed the bridle, feeding the bit into her mouth. She chewed it around until it was comfortable, and she whinnied softly, letting the pair know she was ready to go.

Tim handed Ryan the reins. "Hold these with one hand and hold onto her mane with the other. We don't have a saddle small enough for you, and I don't want you to fall."

Ryan reached forward to take a handful of mane and nodded. "I'm ready, Tim." With that, they were off.

Instead of leading the mare and boy to the covered, round pen, he led them around the upper pasture. Tim and Ryan had a grand talk about the boy's expectations for first grade. "I thought you'd be going into second grade," Tim made the mistake of voicing.

"I didn't go to school last year. We didn't live anywhere long enough for me to go, so I'm startin' now. I'm smart enough for second grade because Daddy and Gramma work with me on numbers and letters and stuff, but I don't wanna skip a grade. I'll be the oldest boy in my class," Ryan stated proudly.

Tim smiled and nodded at him. "I get ya. All the other boys will wanna hang with the big kid, ya know? You're gonna be a good leader for the littler kids." Tim hoped he hadn't made Ryan feel bad about starting school late. He'd have to ask Aunt Katie about it.

"And I'm not gonna be mean about it, either. I went to daycare for a while when Momma was workin' for a doctor one time, and the big kids who came after school were mean. I didn't like 'em." Ryan was adamant about not being a bully, which Tim was happy to hear.

The computer nerd inside him nodded in understanding. He'd had his share of bullies in life, but it had only been harsh words. Well, except for his father.

Thankfully, nobody knew the real story when Tim showed up in Holloway after he'd graduated high school in New Jersey. Aunt Katie came up with a fabrication about his father being in the military. She said Tim's parents were in Japan but wanted him to stay in the States for college. That was why Aunt Katie and Uncle Josh took him in, or so they told folks back then when it was all too fresh and too painful for Tim to think about.

"Do you like to ride horses?" The question pulled Tim from the horrible memories rattling around in his head.

He loosened his hold on the lead rope and let Betsy continue meandering around the pasture with him walking by her side. Tim moved behind her head to place his hand on Ryan's leg. The boy's boots caught his attention because they were little roughouts, and they looked awfully cute on him.

"I ride Chester every once in a while. I didn't grow up around horses, but when Uncle Josh and Aunt Katie let me come live with them, I learned how to ride. I'm not very good at it, but I can keep myself from falling off. You seem to have a good seat on the back of a horse," Tim told the little cowboy as they continued to walk around the upper pasture.

"Gramma Jeri takes me ridin' with her on her mare, Lucy. We ride double. We check the fences on Saturdays at our place, and then check her fences on Sundays 'cause they live up the hill from our place and we run cattle on their land, too. You ever check fences?"

"When I came here to visit during college, I'd take the four-wheeler we used to have and check the fences. I didn't really have much interest in riding horses back then. I was scared, I guess. When I graduated from college and came back home, I decided I was gonna learn how to ride, and Uncle Josh worked with me. I'm not great, but I'm not scared anymore." Tim was being honest.

They walked around the pasture for an hour, and Tim led Betsy slowly so Ryan didn't lose his place on her back. Tim had the lead rope over his shoulder and his hand on Ryan's leg, so he didn't slide around. The mare seemed to know she was carrying precious cargo because she didn't stumble one time.

Ryan and Tim talked about all kinds of things, from books and movies to sports, and it was one of the better conversations Tim had had recently. Aunt Katie and Uncle Josh weren't big on unnecessary discussions, and he'd adapted and became a man of few words as well.

Ryan, however, seemed to enjoy talking. Tim listened and answered a few questions the boy had asked about the horses or computers or how Tim thought first grade might be. It was a joy to listen to how Ryan's mind worked. He was a very intelligent kid.

Tim felt a vibration in his pocket, so he pulled out his cell phone, knowing it was either Aunt Katie or Uncle Josh. Nobody else had his number. "Hey."

"Timothy, can you bring Ryan up to the house? Josh convinced Matt to stay for lunch after he's finished with Josie. Your uncle is still determined to put shoes on that damn thing. He's asked Hank to bring Ethan over tomorrow to try to ride her." It wasn't a surprise that Aunt Katie was exasperated with Uncle Josh's fascination of the jenny.

The female mule, which was called a jenny, was about three. With the right stallion, she'd likely throw cute foals, Tim was sure. He had no idea why they wanted her shod.

"Okay. We're gonna turn Betsy back onto the pasture, and then Ryan and I will come up to the house. We'll hurry," Tim told his aunt.

Ten minutes later, they'd returned Betsy to the pasture and watched her trot down to the creek for a drink. Tim hoisted Ryan up on his shoulders before he gathered the saddle pad, bridle, and lead rope.

He trotted a little and both laughed as they made their way up the hill. Once the pair reached the barn, Tim hung the horse blanket over a gate to dry out and placed the bridle and lead on a hook in the tack room.

Tim started galloping toward the house, causing Ryan to giggle. Tim reached up and pulled the boy's hands down to clasp under Tim's chin.

"Whoa!" Ryan announced as they approached the yard.

The boy walked up the steps, stopping to clean his boots on the mat before he opened the back door and walked onto the screened porch. He pulled off his boots and placed them on the tray Aunt Katie insisted they all use.

They walked into the kitchen where Uncle Josh and Matt were sitting at the table with sweet tea. Ryan removed his cowboy hat and placed it on the bench by the back door, next to his father's baseball cap.

Matt's hair was slicked back, and Tim wondered if it was sweat or water. He truly wanted to bury his nose in that beautiful mop to take in the scent from the source.

"Come on, bud. Let's go get you washed up before Miss Katie sets the food. Did you have fun?" Matt rose from his chair.

"I'll take him. I need to clean up myself," Tim offered.

Ryan didn't hesitate to take Tim's hand and follow him down the hallway to the powder room. Tim hefted Ryan up and helped him wash his hands and face before doing the same.

Ryan took the towel Tim offered to dry off, and then he used it himself. Tim reached into the little cabinet to the side and pulled out a comb. "Hold still, dude," he told the boy as he combed the wavy, brown hair. He placed the comb back in the drawer and offered Ryan his hand, which he took with a grand smile.

In the kitchen, Tim helped Ryan into a chair where two phone books were waiting as a booster seat. "You okay?" He didn't want Ryan to fall, so when the boy settled in, Tim took a seat next to him.

"I'm fine, Tim. Miss Katie keeps these big books for when I come by. I like sittin' up high." Ryan picked up the plastic glass Aunt Katie put in front of him. He took a sip and smacked his lips, bringing a laugh from Tim, Matt, and Uncle Josh.

"Good lemonade, ma'am." Ryan was six going on sixty as Tim listened to him. It was so damn sweet, Tim felt a lump in his throat, wishing Ryan Earl Collins was his own son.

Lunch was an entertaining affair. Tim left Uncle Josh and Matt to talk between themselves as he turned his attention to Ryan because he knew he made the boy's father uncomfortable.

Tim didn't want to cause the man any distress, but he was sure Matt knew he was gay, and apparently, Matt hadn't settled on a team thus far. Tim remembered that confusion in his own life. Matt wasn't the first person he'd met who was so deep in the closet they just couldn't find a way out.

Chapter Four

As the group was finishing their lunch at the Katydid, after the Stallings' mare was put into her stall to await the vet, there was a knock on the back door. Uncle Josh yelled, *"Come on in!"*

Everyone turned toward the door to see a tall, strawberry blond guy who couldn't have been too much older than Tim. The guy looked a little sunburned, having more than a few freckles on his handsome face. He appeared to be assessing Tim, so he gave the guy the up and down in return.

"Hi, Mr. Simmons. I'm Cory, Melinda Stallings' stepson. She asked me to pick up Princess for her. I've got the trailer here. Is the blacksmith finished?"

Matt stood and extended his hand. "Matthew Collins, blacksmith. I've got Princess ready to go."

The cute guy reached into his T-shirt pocket and handed a check to Matt. "Mel said to tell you thanks for doin' it on such short notice. She and Dad are goin' on a trail ride with a large group this weekend, and she wants to take Princess. I'll be happy they're gone so I can have a party." Cory addressed the group with an easy smile.

Everyone laughed before Aunt Katie offered him something to eat and drink. He declined the offer of food but accepted the sweet tea.

Uncle Josh looked at Tim and gave a sly wink before he turned back to Cory. "I'll call Doc Grant to go to your place to check Princess, so you don't have to wait, Cory. Tim, would you take Cory down to the barn and show him Melinda's tack? Load up with some grain and five of the bigger hay bales. It'll save Melinda time when she's leavin' and should hold her over for the weekend."

Tim grabbed his and Ryan's plates, dumping the bones before he rinsed them and put them into the dishwasher, turning to his short friend. "Ryan, it was fun. Get your dad to drop you off some time so you and I can go riding again." Tim hugged the boy.

"I'll remind him, Tim. Thanks again. I had a lot of fun," Ryan responded.

Tim started for the door. "Hey, Tim, would you ever babysit Ryan for me? It would help me out if I gotta do somethin' and Mom's not available. I'd pay ya."

Should Tim be insulted or happy at the prospect that Matt Collins was asking him to babysit his son? Tim truly liked the boy and had enjoyed the time they'd spent together. In truth, he wouldn't mind babysitting if Matt was working late.

He would, however, draw the line at babysitting if the bull rider was going on a date or something similar. Tim didn't need to witness the man dressed for a date with someone else because he was sure his heart would shatter, though he really had no reason to feel that way.

"Well, I'm kind of busy around here but if it's an emergency, I'll try to work it out. Just call the house." Tim's response was half-hearted at best.

He turned to follow Cory out the back door toward the barn where the truck and trailer were parked outside the front sliding doors. Tim wondered where the rest of the hands were, but he remembered Uncle Josh had given them Saturday afternoon, Sunday, and Monday off for Labor Day.

"So, you live here in Holloway?" Tim asked Cory, trying to make some sort of small talk which he wasn't great at. He was trying for the sake of Uncle Josh's business.

"I'm just here for the summer since I finished my masters' degree. You're Mr. Simmons's nephew, I guess. Melinda's mentioned how cute you were based on when she's stopped by to ride. I can see she wasn't wrong," Cory explained with a bright smile. *That* was unexpected.

"Yeah, well, I just got back here myself not so long ago." Tim then explained his project to modernize the farm to make life easier for his aunt and uncle. "I was an IT major. How about you?" Tim led Cory to the barn where the tack room was located.

Cory smiled as he leaned against the doorframe. "You busy tonight? I'd love to have you come over for the party. We have a pool, after all. Clothing optional when the 'rents are gone." The hot guy added a wink that surprised Tim.

"Guest list?" Tim went into the tack room and carried out Melinda's saddle on the first trip, placing it on some hay bales in the hallway of the barn.

The second trip had his arms full of saddle pads, bridles, a few of their lead ropes, and a hay bag. Tim wasn't sure they'd need it all, but he was familiar with the supplies

Uncle Josh sent with boarders when they were taking a horse off the property.

"I went to UVA, so there are a few of my friends who are going to show, but my boyfriend invited some of his friends from NYU. You're a member of the *clan*, right?" Cory cocked flipped his wrist, which brought a laugh from Tim.

"You caught me. Aren't you worried about getting your ass stomped out here in the country? People in town aren't exactly accepting of our community."

"You'd be surprised what money can do, sexy. Bring your own condoms and lube. I'll have everything else. I can guarantee you a good time, Tim. I can already see a few of my friends falling on their knees for you. You are quite the yummy snack." And there was another wink.

In Tim's estimation, the tall guy was definitely full of shit because in keeping with the computer geek stereotype, he was on the thin side with very little definition along with his dirty blond hair. Since he'd started working in the office to implement the new system, he didn't get the physical workout he had earlier in the summer, and his once tanned skin had reverted to its usual pasty shade of antique white.

Tim was about five-nine and weighed about a buck-fifty, having his mother's and Uncle Josh's high metabolism. Nothing about him said *sexy*.

It wasn't often Tim thought anyone cruised him as Cory seemed to be doing there in the hallway of the barn. The guy had said he had a boyfriend, but Tim wondered how serious they were if he was studying Tim's ass as if it would be the subject of a final exam.

Tim loaded hay into the trailer and made sure there was enough grain for the long weekend. He also loaded watering buckets and a picket line for them to tie Princess outside when she wasn't being ridden.

After those things were safely in the trailer, the two men added the tack and saddle, and Tim went to get Princess from the stall where Uncle Josh had put her after she'd been shod.

"Hey!" Tim was following Cory and the mare toward the front of the barn. He turned to see Matt Collins trotting toward him with a pissed off expression. Tim waited for the cowboy because he was curious about why the man was chasing him.

"You need something? You're finished with her, right?" Tim asked, pointing toward the mare in the hallway. Cory continued down the long hallway and stopped outside the trailer to wait for Tim.

"Yeah, um, you're not gonna go to that party, right?" Matt seemed nervous.

Tim stared at the bull rider, trying to understand what business it was of Matt Collins' if he went to the party or not. Cory Stallings was a hot guy, and it seemed he thought some of his friends might be interested in Tim. That was enough reason to go to the party, as far as Tim was concerned.

Tim knew his crush on Matthew Collins was ridiculous and that he needed to find something else to focus on instead of the bull riding cowboy. The party sounded like just the ticket to help him maintain his sanity on two fronts—forgetting Matt and finally losing his virginity.

"It's a swim party. We don't have a pool, so I might go for a while to have some fun. It's hot here, you know." Tim slowly turned to head toward the front of the barn again.

Matt seemed about ready to protest, but then, Ryan ran out of the house yelling for the two of them. Ryan flew through the back doors of the barn, nearer where Matt and Tim were standing, and he jumped up, launching himself into his father's arms with an excited look on his face.

"I called Gramma Jeri. She said we can come swimmin' at her house tonight and stay over. She and Papa are goin' to Front Royal for a party, but they'll be back for the cookout on Monday. Can Tim come over?" The boy caught both men's attention with his excited demeanor.

Matt chuckled as Aunt Katie walked into the barn with a smile on her face. She had the cordless in her hand, and she handed it to Matt. "It's your momma."

He walked away so Tim headed toward the horse trailer, waiting for the horse and the hunk. Just before he was out of the doorway, Aunt Katie stepped in front of him, clearly having something to say.

He stopped, checking to see if Cory was paying attention to mayhem. When he was sure the man was busy talking on his phone as he held the lead rope for the mare, Tim looked at his aunt, warning her off of the impending tirade he could see brewing on her face. "Don't get mixed up in things of the gay variety. I'm not about to chase a straight man." Tim walked past her without waiting for a response.

Cory stood at the back of the trailer with the door open, so Tim led the mare inside and tied her close so there wouldn't be a problem hauling her back to the Stallings' place. He patted her on the back as he walked out of the trailer and closed the back door.

"So, what's the address? I'm not sure if I can get away, but it sounds like fun," he told Cory as he leaned against the trailer.

"Can I have your number? It'll be easier to text you the directions than to explain it to you, and I'd really like it if you'd come."

Tim took the phone to enter his number. He returned it to Cory, who offered another wink before climbing into the white Dodge Ram flatbed hauling the fifth-wheel stainless trailer.

As the truck and trailer left the driveway, Tim felt a hand on his shoulder. When he turned his head, he came face to face with Matt Collins' chest. The bull rider was quite tall to Tim's five-nine, but he'd never seen a chest so attractive. Even through the T-shirt the man wore, Matt's muscles were *right there* and enough to bone Tim up from zero to sixty.

After a sniff of the man, Tim swallowed the lump in his throat, finally able to speak without his voice cracking. "Can I help you?"

Matt's laugh was deep, which sent a tingle down Tim's spine. "Tell me you're not goin' to that party. From what I've heard 'round town, they shuffle from one partner to another, and you know you're better than that, Tim."

For a sexual first timer, it was more than a little intimidating to think of more than one partner in one night, though Tim knew guys who loved a good orgy. If what Matt was saying was true, it wasn't Tim's scene at all.

Matt stared at Tim for a moment before speaking up again. "Why don't ya come over to Mom and Dad's place for swimmin' and steaks. I think the three of us could have a good time gettin' to know each other better." Matt seemingly put Ryan in the picture so Tim didn't mistake his intentions as anything more than friendship.

Tim laughed and shook his head. "So, my choices are attending a hedonistic bash with what I'm sure will be a lot of hot bodies in various stages of undress as we drink ourselves into beautiful oblivion, or I spend the evening getting to know your son better so he'll feel comfortable with me when you go catting around town to find some girl to fuck? Wow, imagine my dilemma." Tim sarcastically moved his hands up and down like a set of scales.

Matt Collins laughed as he grabbed Tim's arm and led him back into the barn and over to the tack room, out of sight of anyone watching from the windows of the house. "I'm not invitin' ya so you'll babysit Ryan while I go out sometime. I'm asking you not to go to that party, Tim. Come with Ryan and me. The parties at the Stallings' place are notorious for turning into orgies, or so I've heard talk around town about 'em. You're a better guy than that, I can tell. You don't want your aunt and uncle to hear rumors about you when they go shoppin' or get pie at the diner, do ya?

"You know for a fact I'm not gonna be hookin' up with a girl. You've peeked into my world, and I think we should talk about it. I'll leave it up to you." Matt walked away, leaving Tim a little breathless.

Chapter Five

"Is this really necessary?" Aunt Katie was rushing around as if there were a fire only she could put out.

Tim had told his aunt he was going to Matt's parents' home for a swim and dinner, not to the Stallings' place for what would likely be a drunken carousing party. In the end, he determined having sex for the first time with someone he didn't know might be a letdown—a really big letdown.

He wanted his first time with a man to be with someone he cared about and who cared about him, but he didn't share that information with Aunt Katie. Upon hearing the news of Tim and Matt's plans for the evening, she'd begun cooking while Tim went to the barn with Uncle Josh to feed and water the stock.

"Jeri will have left dinner in the fridge or the slow cooker, but I have some things to contribute. Those boys need a little TLC, Timothy. I know you and Matt are just friends, but he needs someone to confide in, and I think the two of you could be good for each other. Jeri and I've talked about it. She's afraid he's becoming so bitter about the way Roberta treated him that he'll never consider another serious relationship. Just be his friend, please?"

Tim really wanted to pound his head against the brick fireplace in the living room, not stopping until he knocked himself out and hopefully suffered a fractured skull and brain damage to the point that he was no longer able to think about Matt Collins. What had he ever done to suffer in this way?

He was sure the handsome man would never come out of the closet, if indeed Matt played full- or part-time for Tim's team. In the back of his mind, Tim believed it was curiosity that led the man to browse gay porn to the point of downloading a virus to his computer. Tim also knew if *he* continued to allow his fantasies to feed the crush, it would only leave him a broken man when the bull rider started dating a woman in town.

Tim turned to his aunt, staring deeply into her eyes. "Aunt Katie, I can't be his best friend because..." He hoped to explain what a bad idea it was to have any kind of relationship with Matt Collins just as the house phone rang.

Katie held up her hand as she walked to the old green phone on the wall, answering it before her face quickly developed a worried expression. "Hi, Matthew. Oh? Well, of course, we'd like to have Ryan spend the night. I'll send Tim— Oh, sure. I'll pick him up in an hour at your house. Sure. Okay, I'll tell him. See you soon." She hung up the phone.

"Well, change of plans. I'm to pick up Ryan at the ranch. Matthew has an unexpected buyer coming by to look at a bull, and he says he needs the sale. It'll be easier with Ryan away so he can take the man to dinner. He said to apologize to you and ask for a rain check."

Tim exhaled because he'd suspected something of the sort would *pop up*, but he knew, intellectually, how important sales were to the lifeblood of a ranching operation. He nodded. "I can go pick up Ryan."

Aunt Katie smiled at him. "Naw. I'll go. I need to make sure the boy has clothes for tomorrow and a toothbrush.

Hey, maybe you wanna get that new stock tank outta the machine shed and drag it up here to the backyard? We can heat some water on the stove and have a little pool if Ryan wants to play in the water since he can't swim at Jeri's? I'll make sure to bring him some trunks." Aunt Katie's big smile told Tim she was set on her idea, so he'd do as she requested.

Tim didn't argue, nor did he show disappointment at Matt's retraction of the invitation for him to spend time with the two of them. The fact it came by hearsay pissed him off to no end, but he reminded himself he and Matthew Collins were nothing more than acquaintances.

"Sure thing. I'll get it ready and put pots on the stove. Can I help you with dinner? You need me to put something else out?" Tim asked her, hardening his heart to Matt's future actions.

The potential for a huge heartbreak was right there in front of him, but he was committed to guard against the temptation of the handsome bull rider. Tim knew he wasn't good at masking his feelings, so the best idea was to stay away from the man as much as possible.

Aunt Katie turned his way, a thoughtful expression on her face. "Maybe put some charcoal in the grill and light a fire? I'll pick up hamburger meat and hot dogs to grill out since I've already made skillet corn and baked beans. Get some of those mosquito torches out of the garage and put them around the back patio. I'll be back in a little bit."

With that, she grabbed her purse and headed for the front door before she turned around. "Thank you, Timothy. I appreciate the help."

Once she was gone, Tim reconsidered not going to the Stallings' house for the party—or the orgy—but in the end, he put it out of his mind because he didn't want to let Ryan down. There was also the little voice inside that reminded him how he'd never been to anything of the sort and the thought of it scared the bejeezus out of him.

Instead of dwelling on things he didn't like, he went upstairs to his room to change into cargo shorts and a T-shirt. He grabbed a pair of flip-flops before he went in search of the oval-shaped water trough delivered to the farm earlier that day. Tim had put two large pots of water on the stove to heat as Aunt Katie had instructed before heading to the machine shed.

As he was dragging the trough back to the house, he saw Uncle Josh laughing at him. "What the hell are ya doin', boy?"

Tim stopped and turned toward Uncle Josh. "Ryan Collins is coming to spend the night because Matt has a buyer in town, so I'm trying to set up a swimming hole for him. You could help instead of standing there laughing at me, ya know. Maybe start the grill?"

Josh continued to laugh, but he picked up the galvanized tub and carried it up to the patio by himself, surprising Tim with his strength. For as long as Tim could remember, the man had been solid as a rock.

Comparing himself to Uncle Josh, Tim determined he was a bit of a runt, really. He didn't work out because he didn't gain weight, nor did he develop much muscle, though since he'd moved to the farm, he had a little better definition. Of course, as he thought about it, he knew he was starting to lose what he'd developed because he was working in the office all the time.

Tim knew for a fact he wasn't as hot as the guys he saw in men's fashion magazines, but he had seen a few guys looking his way from time to time during college. He was thin and likely unattractive to someone as buff and masculine as Matt Collins—not that it really mattered what the bull rider thought of him. He was pretty sure the man didn't think of him at all.

After Josh and Tim settled the tub on the patio, his uncle turned on the garden hose and placed it in the large tub. "You got water on in the kitchen?" Josh asked.

Tim laughed. "Yeah, how'd you know?"

"Kathleen used to do this for Shane when he was a boy. I offered to dig a pool a couple of times, but she was insistent we wouldn't use it much. In the end, she was right, I guess. We'd make a little pool for him when he was a kid, and he'd splash around for a few days, then he was done with it. I guess I'm glad we didn't dig up the back yard after all."

Josh's gaze wandered off toward the pasture where the horses were grazing, lost in his own memories of his deceased son. Tim was sure the pain was still as fresh as when they were told Shane had been killed.

There was something Tim wanted to say, so he cleared his throat. "Uncle Josh, with what you pay me, I can afford to buy my own clothes, so I don't keep wearing Shane's. I know it upsets Aunt Katie when she sees me in certain things, and I don't mean to remind her of the pain of losing a son."

Josh chuckled and moved the hose deeper into the tub before he headed for the kitchen. "Come help me get these pots so we can put on more."

Tim followed along without question. It seemed as though the subject was officially dropped.

After they'd dumped the hot water into the makeshift pool, they put on two more pots. Josh grabbed a couple of beers, handing one to Tim. "When we found out Shane had been killed, I was afraid I was gonna lose Katie too."

That wasn't anything Tim knew. The fact Uncle Josh was opening up to him was surprising.

"When your cousin was born, your aunt had complications durin' the delivery that led to us findin' out Shane would be our only. We cherished every minute we had with him as he was growin' up, and when he graduated high school and decided to enlist, your aunt's heart broke. She wasn't gonna get to see him every day, and there wasn't anything she could do about it.

"Don't get me wrong, we were proud of him for choosing to serve his country, but she wanted him to stay home and start a family. He wanted to see the world, so in the end, after a lot of arguin' and prayin', we supported him."

Tim scrunched up his face, searching his memories for anything about that time. "I don't remember momma ever saying anything about it being hard for you and Aunt Katie."

"Well, at the time, your mother had married that son of a bitch, and you were just a boy. We weren't allowed to visit because Harold said we *lorded our riches* over him, the stupid mother... He was an asshole to everyone, but your momma loved him, and she and I spoke on the phone when he was workin'. It wasn't ideal, but it was what she wanted so I didn't push things with her much."

Tim nodded. He vaguely remembered his mother taking calls in the afternoon and sending him out to play, probably so he didn't accidentally spill the beans.

"Fast forward, and here we are. I'm glad you're here because Kathleen was ready to cash in her chips until Sherry started tellin' me about what was goin' on in Pittsburgh. I would have beat your fa... donor... to death, but your momma begged me not to because she said the day might come when you'd need me, and she didn't want me in jail. So, in honor of her wishes, I didn't. In retrospect, I shoulda done it, but here you are, and the way I see it, we've all saved each other.

"The heavens brought us together to help get each other through bad times, and now we have you back home where we need you to be. Now, we'd better start the grill or Katie will have both our asses," Josh joked. Tim grinned at his uncle before the two got busy creating a fun-filled night for Ryan Collins.

The two men poured in pots of hot water as the cold well water continued to fill their makeshift pool. Tim put charcoal in the kettle grill on the corner of the patio, so the coals were ready when Aunt Katie returned with the meat and their guest.

Tim ran upstairs to change into a pair of nylon running shorts to wear as swim trunks and grabbed a few towels from the linen closet to take outside. Uncle Josh brought out some old toys to play with in the water, which Tim suspected had belonged to Shane, but he didn't mention it.

When Ryan and Aunt Katie returned to the house, Tim chuckled as he saw the boy in a pair of shorts and a T-shirt. He was wearing sneakers, and he seemed to be happy about the scene Josh and Tim had set.

"This is so cool. We don't have big candles at Gramma Jeri's. They have those ugly lights around the pool," Ryan announced as he pointed to the torches around the patio.

Tim chuckled. "Well, you know Miss Katie well enough. She's always ready for a party. You ready to get into the wading pool?"

Ryan looked over the edge and giggled. "I can walk all the way around it. I can't do that at Gramma and Papa's house. I have to wear those stupid, blow-up floater things." The look on Ryan's face was priceless and made Tim smile as he lifted the boy into the pool. He'd ensured the water was warm, but not hot. It was a scorcher of a day, and the damn trough wasn't a bathtub.

"Uncle Josh found a basketball set in the basement. You know how to play?" Tim shed his shirt and climbed in with Ryan. Uncle Josh was in shorts, which surprised Tim, sitting at the patio table with a bucket of cold beer. It sure wasn't hurting Tim's feelings at all considering his sour mood from earlier regarding Matt Collins' behavior.

Tim watched as Ryan pondered his suggestion of basketball for a minute before the boy smiled. "I've seen basketball on TV when Daddy watches it, but I don't know how to play it in the water."

Suddenly, a beach ball popped into the pool, startling both of them. He turned to see Aunt Katie with a bright smile. "I bought it at the store. Basketball is hard to play with just two people, but you can play volleyball or even keep-away if your uncle gets off his lazy backside," Aunt Katie teased as she pointed to her husband.

Tim took Ryan's hand and pulled him closer, forming his hand so his index finger was sticking up and set the ball spinning on the boy's finger as though they were the Harlem Globetrotters. He had to hold Ryan's hand because he started giggling so much they were about to lose momentum.

Uncle Josh hopped into the makeshift pool and laughed. "Oh, that doesn't scare me. I'll take both y'all on. I used to play volleyball in high school gym class. Two against one and loser has to go lock up the barn for the night." He winked at Tim, issuing a challenge.

Ryan giggled as Tim popped the ball in the air with the aid of his finger. "You're on, old man."

They moved across the tub from each other, and Uncle Josh and Tim both knelt to volley the ball a few times. Tim helped Ryan pop it with his fist in front of Uncle Josh, so it made a splash, and everyone laughed as the man scoffed and wiped the water from his face.

Aunt Katie came out with a camera and ordered the three of them to pose before she demanded they get out of the water because she had burgers and hot dogs ready to go on the grill. Tim wrapped Ryan in a towel and sat him on a lounger next to Uncle Josh before he went inside the house to help Aunt Katie with the food.

"He's such a sweet boy, isn't he?" Aunt Katie said.

Tim assembled the potato salad while Aunt Katie offered instructions. "Yeah. It sounds like he and Matt are getting into a routine now that Ryan's back home. That little boy has so much personality." Tim carried out the sides. Aunt Katie followed moments later with the tray of meat, and Uncle Josh went to work on the grill.

After the group ate their fill, Ryan wanted to get back into the pool, so Tim hopped in with him. Aunt Katie and Uncle Josh cleaned up the dinner dishes and went inside, leaving the two of them alone.

"So, your dad had a meeting with someone who wants to buy a bull? That must be cool to watch them grow up from calves," Tim ventured.

Shamelessly, Tim was pumping the kid for information, but he couldn't help himself. Matt Collins might be the most amazing guy Tim had ever met, and he wasn't able to stop himself from asking questions. Yes, he'd promised himself he didn't care, but when push came to shove, he'd never tire of hearing what Matt was doing, regardless of how much it might hurt.

"It's only Lanny. He rides bulls like Daddy used to do, but he wasn't gonna buy anything. They were gonna ride Papa and Gramma's horses and they were gonna talk about the old days like always. Daddy said I'd be bored, and when Miss Katie agreed to let me come here, I was glad. Lanny don't like kids," Ryan told Tim.

Completely flustered at the news, Tim sat down on the bottom of the tub and tossed the ball to Ryan in order to keep him talking. "How long have you known Lanny?" Tim was sure Aunt Katie would likely wash his mouth out with soap if she heard him interrogating the boy, but she was inside, and Tim had a little time...

"I only see'd him once right after Momma brought me home to Daddy. He showed up at the ranch, and Daddy told him we was goin' to Gramma's house so he couldn't stay. Lanny was mad, but he left. Daddy talks to him on the phone sometimes. Lanny still rides bulls, and he tries to talk Daddy into doin' it again, but Daddy tells him he has more important things to do and besides, he's too old. This time, Daddy said he needed to have a talk with Lanny, so he called Miss Katie to see if she'd let me come here. I'm glad she did 'cause I like hangin' out with you, Tim. I'm gettin' cold. Can we go inside now and dry off? I heard somethin' about some smores," Ryan said, his face morphing into a cute little grin Tim couldn't resist.

The water *had* cooled off, and the little pool was in the shade, so Tim could understand the boy's eagerness to get out. He picked up Ryan and wrapped him in a towel to dry off and warm up a little before they went into the much cooler house to change.

Tim wrapped a towel around himself before the two of them sat down on a bench next to the house. Ryan had a bottle of water and Tim had a beer, wishing it was something much stronger.

He had an idea *Lanny* was a lot more than a casual buddy of Matt's, and he could hardly concentrate on what the boy was saying as he fought to keep the jealousy from overwhelming him. Nothing good would come of it.

After the s'mores were eaten, they all worked together to clean up the mess, and Aunt Katie took Ryan inside to shower and get ready for bed at nine o'clock. Uncle Josh and Tim covered the pool with a tarp and sat at the patio table with a couple more beers.

"What do we need to do tomorrow?" Tim asked him as he sipped a cold Budweiser. He was trying to keep his mind off the information about Matt rolling around his brain, making it a total mess. It was ridiculous to even consider there was a chance of something with Matthew Collins. If he was straight, Tim wasn't the right gender. If he was gay, he already had a boyfriend he wasn't willing to talk about. *No win.*

"Well, we're gonna load up some good horses and go over to Matt's house to help him move his cattle. I know you don't like to ride much, but I could sure use your help. Hank, Jared, and Charlie are gonna help out on some of the ranch horses, but truth be told, Chester is the best cattle horse I have, and he's used to you. All you gotta do is hold on, Timmy. He'll do all the work, no joke," Uncle Josh stated, a pleading tone in his voice that Tim couldn't resist.

Tim would have rather pounded a railroad spike into his head before he went to the Collins' ranch to help move cattle, but he decided to be the better man. He'd help out and keep a big grin on his face. Matt Collins would never know Tim would have sunk to his knees to worship his body if he'd only given a sign. It was something he'd keep to himself for the rest of time, but it didn't make his heart ache any less.

"If you say so, Uncle Josh, I'm on board. What about Ryan?" Tim tried like hell to keep his contempt for the boy's father at bay because his emotions were all over the place.

Josh laughed a little. "You're attached to the boy already, aren't ya?"

Tim hated to acknowledge it, but he was becoming more attached to the boy every time the two of them were together. "Well, he does tend to grow on ya."

Without responding, Uncle Josh opened two more beers, handing one to Tim—who didn't miss the serious look on his uncle's face. "Katie told me about Matt's company. Lanny Whitehead was his travelin' buddy when they were both on the circuit. He's bad news anyway you play it, Tim.

"While Ryan was with his momma, Lanny came to visit Matt a couple times. I noticed a black eye and busted lip on Matt a time or two when he came over to shoe horses for us, but when I mentioned it to him, Matt just laughed it off and blamed it on a wild calf. That was before he got Ryan back. Far as I know, Lanny hasn't been around since the boy came home, so I'm worried about why Matt wanted Ryan gone." Uncle Josh's face showed the concern he'd just voiced.

Tim wasn't an aggressive guy by any stretch of the imagination, but he'd learned how to take care of himself, out of necessity because of the beatings his father had given him. He'd stewed over those self-defense lessons he'd taken after he'd coaxed his roommate and blow job buddy, Kenny, into teaching him how to defend himself during an attack. He might not be the first line of defense, but he'd fight until he drew his last breath for anyone he cared about.

"Okay, maybe I should take a ride over to the ranch by myself to check on things?" Tim thought it was the best idea he'd ever had.

Uncle Josh gave him a drunken smile. "You know, I think you're about one of the coolest guys I know. You're good lookin', and you have a protectiveness about you when it comes to someone important in your life. You're like your momma with your tender heart, but Timmy, you're not really a fighter, and I don't think it's a good idea to go over to Matt's place. He can take care of himself. He rode buckin' bulls for a livin', but I appreciate the fact you're worried."

Tim laughed a little, feeling his cheeks flush at his uncle's kind words. "My roommate at Penn was a really sweet guy. Unfortunately for him, I was gay and out. I was living the life of a gay kid at college, which brought a lot of grief for Kenny from his soccer buddies. One night, they decided they were gonna teach me a lesson for not being embarrassed about being myself.

"They got Kenny to bring me to the soccer field under the pretense we were all gonna party together. I knew Ken was straight, though we'd had some pretty innocent fun together, but for him to want to take it outside didn't make sense. I knew I was being led into a trap, so I was prepared, or so I thought."

Uncle Josh sat forward. "I don't like the way this is goin', son. Why didn't you call me?"

Tim appreciated Uncle Josh's protective nature. "Hang on a minute. There were four of them who stuck around after I kicked the goalie in the balls. They had plans to tape me doing something to Kenny that I'd done before, just not for an audience. They attempted to hold Kenny and me down, but he got away from them and beat the crap out of a few of his teammates for trying to humiliate the two of us.

"Kenny taught me a few defensive moves after that in case I got cornered by another group, but they manipulated some of the pictures to make it look like something it wasn't and put them on the internet. It ruined our friendship, and after that, I didn't trust anybody. That's why I don't have any friends from college."

The pain in his chest was just as fresh as the day he walked into a computer lab to find the slideshow on a loop on all of the monitors showing images that had been manipulated to show him blowing Kenny. The laughter from his fellow students rang in his ears for a long time after.

Josh pulled him into a hug and whispered, "I love ya, Tim. I know you've gone through hell, son, but I hope to fuck we can change it since you're home. Your aunt and me, well, we've missed ya."

Tim swallowed down a lump in his throat and whispered back, "I'm so damn grateful to the two of you. You rescued me from something much worse than hell. You don't have to do anything else." By then, both men had tears leaking from their eyes, which Tim was blaming on his level of intoxication.

Of course, Uncle Josh just laughed as he wiped his eyes with the end of the towel on which he was sitting. "Now, that's not the truth, and you know it. After Shane was killed, your aunt needed someone to fuss over, and when you came to us, well, it was a godsend. Before we get down in the weeds, we need to take a little ride, I reckon," Josh suggested as he grabbed Tim's hand to lead him inside.

"Go change. I'll take care of the outside stuff, and I'll meet you here in five minutes," Josh ordered. Tim quickly thought about the scene that had just played out and wondered how prudent it would be for either of them to drive anywhere, so he decided to change the subject.

"Yeah, okay, but can I ask you something? What did you think of Harold Moran when you met him?"

The look on Josh's face had Tim cringing for even bringing it up, but it was enough to start a conversation as the two men took a seat at the kitchen table. After Josh told Tim what a no-good-piece-of-shit his father was, not that the younger man didn't know it, the idea of going anywhere was long gone.

After talking about the dead man for an hour—and two more beers—they agreed to go to bed. If Matt was spending time with an old lover, it wasn't Tim's place to bust it up... regardless of how much his heart wanted him to.

Chapter Six

Tim rolled over in his queen-size bed, feeling a little body nearby. When he opened his eyes to see Ryan Collins in bed with him, he was a little surprised.

Tim's mind raced, and he remembered the boy had been in the hallway when Uncle Josh and he decided to turn in for the night. Ryan was coming out of the bathroom, still half asleep.

After a quick shower to rinse off and a pair of sleep pants, Tim slid into his bed to find Ryan sound asleep, having gone into the wrong room. Tim was too tired—and too drunk—to move the boy, so he dozed off and left him there.

Tim slipped out of bed and went to the bathroom to take care of his morning business. After a quick piss, he shaved, and brushed his teeth. His head was suffering from a next-level hangover, and his hair was all over the place, making it impossible to leave the house. He stepped into the shower and gingerly washed his pounding head.

In all honesty, Tim wasn't used to drinking so much beer, but he didn't really regret the headache after he re-membered the discussions from the night before. Having Uncle Josh be frank with him regarding his feelings about Tim's parents and even the loss of Shane was more than Tim ever thought he'd hear. It gave him more insight into his family than he'd been able to gain before, and it left him feeling a lot closer to his aunt and uncle.

When he heard the toilet flush, he peeked out of the shower curtain to see Ryan standing at the sink to wash his hands. Apparently, Aunt Katie had a little stool available for him, and Tim thought it was cute.

"Morning, Ryan. You need a shower?" he asked as he rinsed the shampoo and soap from his body, thankful his morning wood hadn't made an appearance due to the drumbeat in his head.

"Miss Katie made me take a bath last night, but I'd rather take a shower when I gotta. I take 'em with Dad in the morning before we start our day, but he says when school starts, I gotta take 'em at night 'cause there won't be time in the mornin'. I getta ride the bus to school, and I think that's gonna be cool. You ever ride the bus?" The boy's questions came in rapid fire fashion as Tim turned off the water.

Tim reached out to grab a towel off the rack before he stepped out of the shower. After securing it around his waist, he picked up another to dry his hair. "We lived near my school, so I walked, but I always wanted to ride the bus." Tim ignored the feelings brought on by the memories of back in the day. No good would come from rehashing any of it in the bright light of day.

"My best friend, Tommy Morrow, lives down the road. He's a year older than me, and he rides the bus, so I asked Daddy if I could ride the bus. He said Miss Terri could take me to school with her little girl, Beth. She's in kinneygarden, and I don't wanna show up with a baby. Beth is really little, and if the other guys see me with her, they'll think she's my sister." Ryan sounded exasperated at the thought as Tim pulled on boxer briefs under the towel.

"Who's Miss Terri?" Tim asked as he went to his room with Ryan on his tail. He went into the closet to grab a pair of Wranglers and a gray *Bud Lite* T-shirt he'd won at a bar in college during a dart tournament. The shirt was a great reminder of a time when things didn't suck.

He walked out of the closet and tossed his clothes on the bed where Ryan sat, watching him carefully. "Miss Terri works in Daddy's office at the ranch. She's only gonna work in the mornings while Beth's in school, and she told Daddy she'd take me to school with Beth, but I wanna ride the bus," the boy repeated.

"How many people work at the ranch?" Tim didn't know anything about Matt's operation, but he was pretty sure a cattle ranch needed more than one or two people to run the operation successfully.

"Umm... Miss Terri, Papa Marty, Danny, Stevie, and Carl. Stevie and Carl only work in the mornin' and after school. Danny, Daddy, and Papa Marty do most of the work, and Gramma Jeri helps sometimes." Ryan held up his little fingers as he named people, which was too cute for words.

Tim wasn't sure who any of those people were except for the grandparents, but it sounded like Matt might have a few high school kids working for him part-time. However, Tim's biggest concern at that moment was Lanny White-head, Matt's former rodeo partner, so he was in a hurry to get to the ranch to check out the bastard. It was a judgment based on nothing other than his Uncle Josh's assessment, but Tim felt he needed to witness their interactions for himself to know if there was anything more between them.

"Let's get you dressed before we go down to the barn and help the boys feed the horses. We can come back for Aunt Katie's breakfast and after that, we're going to the ranch to help your dad move cattle," Tim told him as he finished dressing.

He took Ryan to the spare room and got him dressed for the day before the two of them went downstairs to find Aunt Katie at the counter making a batter. She smiled at Ryan. "Ryan, would you go down to the barn and tell Hank that Josh will be down shortly?"

Ryan grinned before he headed for the door without a word. After he was gone, Katie looked at Tim with a small smile. His head was still pounding, and an ass chewing wasn't exactly what he wanted that morning. "Aunt Katie—"

She reached into the cabinet and grabbed a glass, filling it with water before she opened a small package and dropped something inside which fizzed immediately. She handed it to Tim and smiled. "Josh is in the shower. I already gave him hell, but not too much. I'm glad you two talked last night. I know sometimes men need a little liquor to grease the wheels, so I'm not gonna say more than this isn't gonna be a habit with the two of you drinkin' all night. Drink this and go watch over the barn, please? Josh was standin' in the shower with his eyes closed. It's been a while since he's had a hangover." The smile on her face told Tim she wasn't exactly sorry about it as she pushed the fizzing glass closer.

Tim chuckled and nodded before he drank the elixir in one large gulp, heading out the back door after he grabbed his boots from the tray. He went to the barn and helped feed the horses and tack up the ones they were gonna use at the Collins' place. Ryan was in the hallway picking up twine as the others were breaking up hay flakes to feed the board horses.

Hank stepped out of the stall, so Tim walked over to him. "How many are we bringing with us to the Collins' place?"

"Uh, three... well, with you, four if you're gonna ride Chester. Where's Josh? Is he okay?" Hank asked as his son, Ethan, walked out of a stall.

Ethan was a good-looking kid of about sixteen. Tim remembered Aunt Katie complaining about Uncle Josh wanting to have Ethan ride the jenny to see if she was gentle, and as far as he knew, the Jenny was a sweet burrow with no problems at all. Ethan appeared to enjoy the animal, and Tim was glad. If they kept the jenny, Tim would need to add her to the list of assets at the farm for tax purposes.

Turning to Hank, Tim felt a little squeamish about the answer. "He, uh, he's a little slow moving this morning. We had a cookout last night, and Uncle Josh and I had a long conversation over a few beers." Tim figured that was all Hank needed to know.

Hank started laughing and pounded the younger man on the back. "Kiddo, I'm happy to hear it. He and Katie needed ya. Nothin' like a few beers to loosen the tongue. Everything okay?"

Tim swallowed. "Yeah. Fine. Tell me which horses I should catch, will you?" he asked as he headed to the tack room to start pulling out saddles, blankets, bridles, and lead ropes.

"Let's see. Um, get Chester, Lady, Pally, and Caesar. Oh, can you bring that Jenny up from the pen out back? Ethan's gonna work with her today to see if she's worth anything since Josh put shoes on her. Heaven help us if we start raisin' mule stock around here," Hank mumbled as he shook his head.

Tim laughed and nodded, making a mental note of the list of horses. After he had all the tack lined up the barn hallway and checked to be certain Ryan was okay, he grabbed the leads and walked out to the pasture where

Uncle Josh's horses were lazily grazing. Tim whistled, as he'd seen Uncle Josh do several times, and when they started coming up the hill, he tried to remember which horse was which.

Thankfully, they were easy to catch, and after a few miscues, Tim had the cadre of mounts tied to the hooks in the hallway. Ryan was sitting on a stack of hay bales, looking a little wounded so Tim stopped to ask about him as he tied Chester to the ring next to where Ryan was sitting. "What's wrong?"

"I was in the way, so Mr. Hank put me here. It's too tall to jump down to go to the house, and they all left me." Ryan motioned around the empty barn as his face wrinkled in anger.

It was easy to see the boy was upset, and Tim would make it a point to sic Aunt Katie on Hank for leaving Ryan in the barn alone. "Well, I'm glad you're still here. I could use someone to help me saddle all these horses. You know how to be careful around horses, right?"

The little cowboy nodded, so Tim helped him down from the hay and led him to the first horse, Lady. She was a four-year-old mare Uncle Josh used as breeding stock. She'd slipped a colt in the spring, so she wouldn't be bred back until she was completely recovered.

"Currycomb and brush," Tim ordered. Ryan went to the box on the outside of one of the stalls and grabbed the comb and a brush so they could groom the horses before they were tacked up.

The two worked together, Ryan handing Tim the tools necessary to make the horses comfortable for their day of work, and once they finished the grooming, Tim saddled the horses so they could be loaded onto the trailer when the crew was ready to head out to the ranch.

Just as they finished saddling Chester, Tim's favorite mount, the intercom squawked. "Timothy, bring Ryan up for breakfast." It was Aunt Katie's voice, and she meant business.

"Uh-oh! Ryan, we were too busy and forgot about food," Tim told the boy as they finished up with the last horse before they tied it to the side of the trailer.

"She won't be mad, right? Gramma Jeri gets mad if her food gets cold before we sit down at the table, and she swears she won't cook for us again," Ryan said as the two walked toward the house.

Tim reached down and swung Ryan up on his shoulders before he ran to the house, the boy squealing the whole way as Tim balanced him on his right shoulder and Ryan held out his hands like an airplane. It was a joyous sound that Tim was thrilled to hear. Ryan was an amazing little boy. He hoped Matt appreciated the kid as much as Tim did.

The large Dodge Ram flatbed pulling an eight-horse, stainless trailer drove up the gravel driveway beyond the white, clapboard farmhouse. Tim followed behind it in a small, rusty-red pickup with Ryan riding shotgun in a booster seat. Unfortunately, no one could miss the cop car parked in front of the house.

Matt was sitting on the front steps in handcuffs, while another man was sitting on the grass ten feet away, also in handcuffs. The short, sandy blond-haired man had a black eye and a busted lip, and to Tim, he looked really pissed off.

As the truck continued up the driveway, Ryan looked out the window. "That's Mr. Lanny. Why's he... Why's Daddy in handcuffs? Lemme out." The boy frantically tried to unbuckle the seatbelt to get out.

Tim put his hand on the boy to keep him inside the truck as he continued driving down the gravel drive toward the barn. When the truck stopped, Josh walked up to the driver's side and opened Tim's door. "Let's get to work.

We can get Danny to tell us where he needs our help. We'll worry about what happened later."

Tim turned to Ryan and smiled, certain the worry on his face wasn't hidden from the astute little boy. "Let's help get the horses settled. The grown-ups can figure out that other business. We have cattle to tend." Tim hoped to get Ryan's mind settled on anything other than the scene of his father sitting on their front porch seemingly under arrest.

"Yeah, but my daddy's up there," Ryan complained loudly as he opened his door, hopping onto the running board and heading toward the house at full throttle. Tim started after him, but Hank whistled, so he turned around and walked back.

"No use gettin' in the way. They'll sort it out. We got a job to do, so let's do it," Hank reminded as he herded Tim toward the barn.

All Tim could do was nod. He had no idea how to handle the situation, never mind that Ryan wasn't his responsibility really, so he refocused energy on the job at hand, moving cattle. It was why they were at the ranch, after all.

"We appreciate what you boys are doin'. As soon as Marty gets back from town, he'll help move those cow-and-calf pairs to that pasture behind our place for the winter, I promise," Jerilyn Collins instructed as she set up a table for drinks near the barn.

Josh and Tim cut out calves that were being weaned from their mothers so they could be tagged and accounted for in Matt's inventory. The rest of the hands on the ranch were rotating the leftover stock in the fields while separating the bull calves to be castrated.

Matt's breeding stock was amazing, from what Tim had learned by doing research. The ranch had Angus, Longhorn, Shorthorn, and American Brahman breeds. Marty explained how Matt bought semen to breed his Angus and Hereford cows for the best quality stock. He'd been making a name for himself in ranching circles with the excellence of the stock he had for sale, and Marty was clearly proud of him.

"It's okay, ma'am. Where's Ryan?" Tim hopped off Chester.

As they'd been working to cut out certain cows or calves from the herd, Tim concluded his horsemanship skills were sorely lacking as he watched the others. Thankfully, the horse made him look good in front of the real cowboys.

Tim knew he needed to practice with the horse so he could be of more help in the future. Hell, he had the best horseman in the county living under the same roof, but it was his pesky pride that kept him from asking Uncle Josh. At the moment, however, all he wanted to see was Matt Collins not in handcuffs.

Glancing at Matt's mother, Tim decided Jerilyn Collins was a very attractive woman. She was a bit taller than Tim, but her features reminded him of her handsome son. She was thin, no doubt, unlike Aunt Katie, who had lots of curves.

Much like Aunt Katie, the woman had an outgoing, easy-to-like personality. Her husband, Marty, was tall like Matt, and he had a little bald spot. He had that dark-brown-hair, blue-eyed look about him which could make Tim's head spin if he let it, just like it did when he saw Matt.

Looking at the older man gave Tim a clear understanding of how gracefully the bull rider might age, and he was heartbroken he'd never get to see it. It would be amazing to witness the changes over time, but the chances of it were slim to zip.

Jeri looked at Tim with a warm smile before she made a sad face. "Ryan's mad at me. He wanted me to take him out on Lucy so he could watch you boys, but I needed to get the food settled for when y'all broke for lunch. He went inside and I'm pretty sure he's in his room. Maybe you can get him outta his funk?" she asked Tim, her happy smile returning.

Nodding, Tim climbed back on Chester and guided the horse to the trailer to secure the gelding with the other horses. There was a guy with a bucket of water and a big smile.

"Agua?" The young man pointed to the horse. Tim knew about three Spanish words, but *agua* was one of them. He hopped off Chester and tied him to the hook on the side of the trailer with a nod to the cute guy with the bucket.

Tim walked into Matt Collins' house, seeing some of the same things he'd briefly noticed the last time he was inside to fix the laptop. It was a decent house, but it needed some personal touches to make it homier.

The house looked as if Matt and Ryan had just moved in, but Tim knew for a fact Matt had bought the house when he married Ryan's mother. It was missing the lived-in feeling and family history that Tim experienced at Uncle Josh and Aunt Katie's home.

Tim strolled down the hallway to find Ryan on his twin bed with his little cowboy hat over his face. Tim almost laughed but was sure it was a bad idea because Ryan's little-boy feelings were hurt and being teased wouldn't help.

"Hey. You're not getting out of the work." Tim sat on the side of the bed.

The boy pushed back his hat and looked up at Tim. "Why's my daddy in jail?"

Yeah, Tim was kind of hoping Ryan wouldn't focus on that part, but only honest answers would appease the boy, he was sure. "Buddy, I don't know, but that doesn't mean we don't have cattle to move. Come on. You work here, remember?"

"Can you get my daddy out of jail?"

Tim took a deep breath before he spoke, hoping he wasn't lying to the boy. "I'm pretty sure your gramma and grandpa have a lawyer doing all they can to get your dad home to you. In the meantime, you live on a ranch where the work never stops, and you know it as well as me. Let's go show the other guys you're here in your daddy's place, and you're dedicated to looking out for the stock."

Tim hoped the boy would take the bait. When Ryan rose from the bed and dried his eyes, Tim touched his shoulder, grateful to get the boy out of his funk, if only for the moment.

After a quick stop in the bathroom for Ryan to wash away the tear tracks from his cheeks, Ryan and Tim walked out of the house and down to where Chester was tied at the trailer.

"You think you can hold onto the saddle horn? Chester's a great horse, and I think he'll let us ride double to help with the work. I suspect your daddy will be home sooner rather than later," Tim said, hoping he wasn't lying.

Ryan nodded so Tim hauled the two of them up on Chester's back, and they proceeded to help with working the cattle. The group stopped for a quick lunch provided by Jeri, and after they were finished, they quickly got back to work. There was only so much daylight of which they needed to take advantage.

When everyone was prepared to leave that evening, Tim hugged Ryan and kissed the top of the boy's head with a promise he'd be back the next morning. He had no idea where Matt was, but he'd be there for Ryan until his dad was home, safe and sound.

Chapter Seven

Tim stood in the barn office, watching the cowboys out the window as they herded horses up the hill. Doc Grant was in the hallway for wellness checks on the animals as the Katydid prepared for the fall.

After Matt Collins got out of jail, he thanked Josh and Tim for their help moving cattle but declined Tim's offer to help him out with Ryan. He wouldn't allow Ryan to visit the Katydid when Aunt Katie called to ask at Tim's urging. The boy was missed, but Tim was sure Matt's embarrassment at being arrested was the driving force behind the disappearing act.

Aunt Katie found out from Jerilyn Collins that Lanny and Matt got drunk and then got into a fight over an old girlfriend they had in common, which ended in a brawl. Apparently, when Danny, the ranch foreman, showed up that morning for work, the two men were shouting at each other loud enough that Danny called the sheriff after hearing a gunshot.

Nobody was wounded, but Tim wondered if anyone would find out what had actually happened. He hoped Matt would get over his embarrassment and his bruised ego enough to let Ryan come for a visit at the Katydid soon.

The office phone rang, bringing him from his reflections. "Katydid Farm, Tim speaking."

"Tim? It's me, Ryan Earl Collins. I'm at school, and I got sick. I called home for Daddy, but nobody answered. Can you come get me? I feel really bad." The boy's voice was whiny, which wasn't like Ryan at all.

"I don't think I can pick you up without permission, Ryan. I can try to find your dad, though. Hang tight. Someone will be there to pick you up soon." Tim hoped the boy believed him.

After ending the call, Tim dialed the Circle C—the name of Matt's ranch. The phone rang forever, and when it wasn't answered, a more aggressive plan was needed.

Tim forwarded the office phone to go directly to voice-mail before rushing to the driveway, hopping into the little, rusty-red pickup Tim used for running errands. It was big enough to haul most things needed at the ranch, but small enough to be easy on gas.

Going to the house to talk to Aunt Katie was an option, but it would waste time for someone to pick up Ryan. Tim headed straight to the Circle C and stopped in front of the barn, hearing the radio blaring from the hallway.

There wasn't an office in the barn of the Circle C like they had at Katydid, just an old phone in the hallway. With the radio playing so loudly and all the cowboys out of the barn, nobody would have heard the phone. Tim walked to the back sliding doors and took in the sight of a few hands who were busy installing cattle panels for an impromptu pen in the upper pasture.

Since Matt was nowhere nearby, Tim decided to go to the School Superintendent's Office where Jerilyn worked. He wondered why Ryan hadn't called his grandma in the first place, but that was a question for another time. There was a sick little boy currently in need of care. He got back into the truck and drove to the school complex, parking in the visitor parking area.

Tim walked into the office to see Jeri behind the front desk, so he rang the bell to get her attention. She glanced up with an irritated expression that quickly changed to a smile.

"May I—Well, hello Tim. What can I do for you?" Jeri walked to the reception desk between them.

"Ryan called the farm. He's sick, and he couldn't get his dad on the phone. I went to the ranch and saw everyone working on fences and pens, but I didn't see Matt, so I thought I'd stop by here to let you know. Not sure why he didn't call you straightaway."

Jeri shook her head, concern evident. "Matt's not happy with me because I made Marty leave him in jail for the night. He was behavin' like an ass, and he needed to have some time to think things over and decide how he should have better handled that situation with that bastard, Lanny Whitehead.

"When he got out of jail, he told me that I wasn't welcome at his house, and he won't be comin' over to ours. He said I shouldn't bring over suppers anymore, and I haven't seen my grandson in nearly a month. I'm just as stubborn as Matthew, so if my baby boy is sick, I'm beggin' ya to go take care of him. I'll call over to the school and give my approval for you to pick up Ryan. Are you gonna take him home or over to Katie's?" Jeri asked.

Tim was a little surprised by her confession about the state of her relationship with her son, but at the heart of the matter was a sick little boy sitting in the office of his school. "Well, when I'm sick, I want to be at home, so I'd like to take him to the Circle C. Unfortunately, I don't have a key to the house. I can take him home with me, but I'm worried about..." He trailed off as he thought about Matt being upset with him for butting into his and Ryan's life.

Jeri Collins produced a key and smiled at the young man. "Take mine. You're right; Ryan needs to be home if he's sick. There's chicken broth in the freezer. Just take it out and put the container in hot water to thaw. I always keep it on hand in case somebody's having tummy troubles.

"I won't come over to the Circle C unless you need me. I believe, Tim, you're destined to be a big part of our lives. Ryan needs someone who will give him undivided attention right now, so if you don't object, please pick him up. I'll deal with Matthew," she told him with an expression that led him to believe she was done with her son's bad behavior.

Tim most certainly would have avoided the situation if he wasn't so worried about Ryan, so he left the office with a note from Jeri Collins and drove to the grade school. When he walked into the office, he could see the admin assistant on the phone. Tim pulled out his license and the note Jeri had given him, placing them on the reception desk.

After the assistant hung up the phone, she smiled at him. "You must be Tim Moran. I'm Bonnie Eads. Jeri told me to expect you. Ryan's in the nurse's office. Let me make a copy of your license, and I'll show you where you can get him. His teacher, Miss Blankenship, said he threw up, and Nurse Tyler said he's running a fever. Sounds like a twenty-four-hour bug, I'd guess. It's been making the rounds," the assistant added.

She seemed nice but she wasn't a damn doctor, so Tim nodded in agreement and followed her down the hall to the nurse's office. When they walked in, he saw little Ryan Collins sitting in a green plastic chair with his backpack on the floor next to him. His eyes were half-closed, and he looked utterly miserable.

Tim walked over and knelt to the boy's level. "Hi, buddy. How are ya?" The boy glanced up at Tim with a sad smile.

"I wanna lay on the couch," Ryan whispered.

Tim picked up Ryan and his backpack before heading back to the office. After Ms. Eads handed back his license, he took Ryan out to the pickup and belted him in. "We'll be home in a few minutes," he assured the sick little boy.

Poor Ryan looked so pathetic. Tim fought tears and anger built inside him at Matthew for not being there to get the boy when he called. It was horrible to imagine the boy didn't have anyone he could rely on.

As the pair made their way through town to SR-131, Tim glanced over to see Ryan was asleep. He continued to the Circle C, and when he drove up the road to the house, he noticed nobody was around, yet again. As he stopped the truck, Ryan's eyes sprung open and he leaned forward, throwing up on the floor.

Thankfully, the floor could be hosed out, but the sick little boy staring at him with things he didn't want to consider on his shirt made Tim hurry around the truck. He opened the door and unbuckled the seat belt, picking Ryan up as an unfortunate sound came from the boy that wasn't coming from the top end. When Ryan started crying, Tim knew there was more going on than a bug.

"Aw, sweetheart, don't worry. We'll get you cleaned up and settled into your bed. I'll take care of you," Tim told him.

The little guy was sobbing so hard, Tim was afraid he was going to throw up again, so he hurried inside the house with the aid of the key Jeri had given him.

He took Ryan down the hall to the bathroom and carefully helped him out of his clothes as Tim continued to speak quietly to him. "Don't worry. After we get you cleaned up, I'll wash your clothes, and this remains between us, okay? When did you start feeling bad?" Tim asked as he stripped off Ryan's little white briefs. They'd definitely need to soak, so he tossed them into the bathroom sink and continued to help the boy get settled under the warm spray of the shower to get cleaned up.

Tim took off his shirt so he didn't get soaked, and after he pulled down the portable showerhead and sprayed off Ryan's backside, Tim handed him a washrag with soap on it so he could wash. He just didn't feel right about doing it himself because he wasn't Ryan's father, but since his father was nowhere to be found, Tim was forced to improvise.

After Ryan was cleaned up and his teeth were brushed, Tim helped him into one of his dad's T-shirts and his little boy briefs before he put him in his bed on a large towel, just in case. "How's that?" he asked the boy.

"Feels nice. I'm sleepy. Can I sleep for a little bit before Daddy gets back?" Ryan asked.

"You can in a second. Let me see if your dad has something in the medicine cabinet for tummy troubles. I'll be right back."

He went to the hall bathroom, not finding anything of help in the medicine cabinet or the vanity, so he bucked up his courage and went to the bathroom in Matt's master bedroom. Luckily, he found some pink stuff he remembered taking when he was a kid and had *issues,* so he turned it to the back to check the dosage.

Tim poured the thick pink liquid into the little cup, sniffing it to remember the smell. He hurried back to Ryan's room with the medicine and a glass of water.

"Here we go. Let's see if this helps. I used to love this stuff when I was little." Yeah, he was lying, but if the kid took the meds, he'd chance a black mark on his immortal soul.

Ryan took the little cup and sniffed it, wrinkling his nose a little before he reached up and pinched it closed as he drank down the thick, pink liquid. He took a sip of the water before he placed the glass on the side table.

"Okay, get some rest. I'll be in the family room so just holler if you need me," Tim told him before he kissed the boy's forehead, not detecting a fever as Bonnie Eads had mentioned earlier.

Ryan was important to him, and he truly wanted the boy to be well. Seeing him sick made Tim's heart hurt.

After Ryan was tucked in, Tim went into the kitchen, rummaging through the freezer to find the broth Jeri mentioned. He found a large glass bowl in the cabinet and filled it with hot water. Once he was satisfied it was hot, he floated the container of broth in it and checked the clock to see it was about two in the afternoon.

Tim stared out the deck doors to see the cowboys still in the field. As he thought about it, he got pissed all over again, contemplating how the hell Matt would ever get a call from school if something was wrong with Ryan? *Doesn't he have a cell? Doesn't he give a shit about his kid at all?*

At 3:10 that afternoon, Tim glanced up from the magazine he was reading to see the bus drive by the house at the same time as the back door opened and closed. The whistling that followed only served to piss him off even more. There was a sick little boy in a bedroom down the hall, and Matt was happy go lucky? *Fuck that noise.*

Tim moved to the kitchen hallway where Matt was pulling out a beer from a twelve pack before he closed the door and opened the freezer, retrieving a glass dish. "Hmmm. Lasagna? Yeah," Matt said to himself as he placed the dish on the counter and started toward the front door.

"Unless you can eat the whole thing, I'd save it." Tim quietly stepped into the kitchen.

The bull rider jumped, which startled Tim. Matt wheeled around, his face filled with anger. "What the fuck are you doin' in my house?" Hostile, but it was nothing compared to how Tim felt about him at that moment.

"Your mother gave me a key to get in. Your son called me at the farm to pick him up from school because he's sick. If you think I'm making it up, you can go see the puke on the floor of my truck or go look at the dirty underpants in the bathroom sink that I haven't had the chance to toss in the washer. He has the flu, I'm guessing. He called the house and the barn, but nobody was here to answer, so he called me.

"You weren't reachable, Mr. Collins. If you can't take care of the boy, I'm pretty sure my Aunt Katie would help me take care of him. I hate to judge people by their circumstance, but it seems like you suck at multitasking." Tim didn't hold back, keeping all his righteous indignation firmly in place.

Matt laughed, seemingly without humor. "What the fuck do you know about raisin' a kid? You... You won't ever have a family of your own, now will ya, *fag*?"

Tim held back the litany of names he had in his arsenal for the type of men who pointed the finger at him because of his orientation. *Well, it's not the first time I've been called that. It's only a word.*" He chose to ignore the ugly slur because no good came of arguing with an ignorant jerk like Matt Collins.

Tim took a deep breath because as much as he wanted to beat the shit out of the bull rider, he quickly determined he'd likely end up on the bad end of that stick. It seemed prudent to try another approach.

"I'm curious, Matt. What are you running from so hard? You're making your life so damn difficult, and from the outside, you have a beautiful life. You have a son who worships the ground where you walk. Your parents love you and only want to help you raise your precious little boy, offering everything they have to help you with Ryan. You have friends in town who are always willing to pitch in for any reason. Whatever happened with Lanny Whitehead is your business, but don't let your night in jail make you lose sight of the bigger picture—the well-being of your son."

Tim stopped talking to give Matt a chance, but the man just stared at him, not acknowledging anything he'd said.

After a calming breath, Tim continued. "You can call me all the names you want if it makes you feel better. I'd never hit on you because you're not my type at all, but as a friend of your family, I'll do anything I can to help with your son. That little boy is amazing, and he deserves to be put first. I just want to help you make that happen, just like everyone else." Tim spoke with as much sincerity as he could muster, given the current situation and the man's harsh attitude.

Matt sunk into a kitchen chair, exhaling a held breath as he took off the NFL team cap he was wearing and hung it on the back of another kitchen chair. "I owe you an apology, Tim. That shit with Lanny just... He dropped the charges against me, and I dropped the ones against him. He was tryin' to get me to leave Ryan with Mom and Dad, just like Bertie wanted me to do. Lanny believed the two of us could go back to ridin' bulls and things would be like they used to, but that ship sailed a long time ago, really."

Tim couldn't tell if Matt was bullshitting him, but he seemed sincere. Or Tim was the most gullible person on the fucking earth.

Matt sniffed before he spoke again. "I'm sorry nobody was around to answer the phone when Ryan called. I never thought about that bein' a problem 'til now. I'm tryin' to get used to bein' a single dad, but it ain't easy. Sometimes, I'm lost."

That was a sorry fucking excuse if Tim had ever heard one. It was clearly not the time for Matt to host his own private pity party. Tim hauled up his balls and decided to be brutally honest with the large man.

"Well, the time for you to be lost is long gone, Matthew. You have a son in first grade because your wife was so fucked up she couldn't see to it the boy got to school every day, so he has a late start. However, it's still workable.

"Ryan was sick at school today and had no way to get in touch with you. That's inexcusable. First and foremost, you should be reachable for that little boy at all hours of the day and night. My father decided, because of the fact I'm gay, it was enough reason to shoot my mother and himself," Tim admitted, though his mouth was running away with his common sense because he was so pissed.

He couldn't stop yet. "I can't ever get them back, Matt. You're the dad, for fuck's sake. That little boy should be your first thought when you wake up in the morning, even more than your cattle. If you don't want him, give him to me."

Yes, he was provoking the big man without regard for the potential consequences. Matt could literally beat Tim to death without breaking a sweat. Surprisingly, he merely bent over to rest his elbows on his knees and his head in his hands, eyes closed.

When tears rolled down Matt's cheeks, Tim was stunned and immediately sorry for his harsh words, but before he could apologize, Matt spoke quietly. "I'm fucking it all up, Timmy, because I just don't know how to be a good dad. I've tried, but I honestly don't know what to do for Ryan. Hell, before Bertie took him away, I was barely there for him. I did my own thing and left it to her to take care of him. Now, I see how wrong it was, but I don't know how to be the kind of dad I had growin' up. I love Ryan so much, but I don't think about things like the fact he can't get me on the phone if he's sick. Why didn't he call Mom?" Matt asked.

Tim took a deep breath and decided to plow forward. He'd stepped into it up to his knees, anyway.

"He didn't call Jeri because *she's* not his dad, and he knows you're not speaking to her at the moment because she pushed Marty to leave you in jail overnight. But, at the end of the day, he's *your* responsibility, not your mom's. You... You're a selfish bastard!" Tim snapped at the man because it was the truth.

Matt looked up at him and the look on the bull rider's face completely deflated Tim's ire. The big man dropped to his knees in front of Tim and took his hand. "You have every right to say those things, Timmy. I've been so screwed up since I got Ryan back, and then when I met you, I got thrown for a loop."

The tears flowed down Matt's face, and it took Tim completely by surprise.

"When Lanny showed up here, well, he wanted me to leave my family because he wants me for himself. We fooled around a little back in the day, but we both said it was just outta desperation and fear of gettin' the clap or somethin' worse, so we stayed away from the buckle bunnies. Bertie and I didn't have sex very often after she had Ryan. In reality, I just didn't care about bein' with her 'cause she just didn't do anything for me.

"Lanny showed up here without callin', and he thought things could go back to the way they used to be, but I knew better. I wanted to talk to him alone, which is why I called Miss Katie to see if Ryan could stay with y'all. I needed to explain to Lanny things weren't the same, but I hoped we could still be friends. Unfortunately, that's not Lanny's way.

"He doesn't like to lose... ever. When I turned down his offer of sex, he got mad. He likes it rough but this time, I wasn't gonna let him hurt me like he has in the past. I told him I had feelin's for someone else, and he threatened to kill me if I didn't stay with him. He pulled a gun from his bag and made me sit in the living room while he pointed that thing at me all night long, giving me all the reasons why we were right for each other and how he wasn't gonna let me get away from him again."

Tim's mouth dropped open, and he couldn't close it. Matt's words brought back too many memories he'd rather not think about regarding his own parents.

Matt wiped his eyes, but he kept talking. "When I heard Danny's truck comin' up the road, I knew I couldn't take the chance Lanny might try to hurt him, so I charged Lanny. We wrestled for the gun, and it went off. That's when Danny called the cops. We took the fight outside and when the sheriff showed up, we were both arrested. Lanny has gun charges pending against him, but he skipped out on his bail. I doubt they'll ever find him."

Tim wasn't sure how to feel about the news, but he was pissed at that Lanny guy, the stupid fucker. "Do you know where he went?"

"Look, Tim. I know I'm a mess, but I don't know how to sort this shit out. I know I can't do it by myself. I've been tryin' and makin' no progress at all, so I know *now* I need someone to help me figure out what the hell to do." The tears continued to slide down Matt's handsome face.

Suddenly, there were god-awful sounds down the hall, so Tim hurried toward Ryan's room, seeing the boy dart into the bathroom. Hearing that sweet little boy losing the small amount of water Tim had been able to get him to drink was horrible.

Tim walked in behind the boy and knelt. "Try to breathe slower." He gently stroked Ryan's back, wishing the little guy could feel better.

After Ryan dry-heaved a few more times, he turned to Tim with tears on his sweet face. "Am I gonna die?"

Tim's chest nearly caved in at the boy's shaky words. Considering how fucked up things were at the moment, Tim couldn't form words fast enough to dissuade the boy from those feelings.

Fucking Matt should have been a normal, loving father. The man had great parents, but there was something missing from his upbringing. Tim was starting to think maybe Matt had been spoiled when he was younger and never had to bear responsibility for anything.

Jeri and Marty loved him and had proven they'd do anything for him, so Tim guessed he'd never learned when one had children, sacrifices came with the territory. He'd seen it with his own mother, so he knew it was something parents did for their children.

The other thing was Matt's closeted status. He had a loving family Tim was guessing would learn to accept his orientation if he'd give them the chance. Why he'd chosen to stay in the closet was a bit of a mystery, but Tim wondered if it had anything to do with his profession. That was something he'd have to investigate, though he was pretty sure gay cowboys weren't accepted much in professional bull riding circles.

Tim considered his own situation. When he stomped out of that closet, it eventually cost his mother her life. She'd made the ultimate sacrifice for him, and he'd never forget it.

Ryan Collins had a lot of things to worry about for such a little boy. Tim didn't believe it was fair for him to have all of that on his shoulders. Then and there, Tim decided to step up to the plate for the boy. Fuck, someone had to do it.

"No, sweetheart, you're not going to die. It just feels like it right now, but you're gonna get this behind you in a day or two. Let's rinse your mouth and then how about I get you a little juice and some medicine?" Tim asked the boy.

"Will it help?" Ryan asked, looking as pathetic as anything.

Before Tim could answer, Matt walked into the bathroom, his gorgeous hair slicked back. He'd changed into a pair of sweats and a T-shirt, and he looked damn nervous. "You okay, little man?"

"I called you," Ryan whispered as he washed his face after brushing his teeth. Tim noticed Matt's face turned red, and in his mind, the man *should* be fucking embarrassed. He hadn't been available to his son when he was needed. It was time for a change.

"I'm sorry. We were busy fixin' fence," Matt answered as if it was an acceptable excuse. It wasn't in Tim's mind.

"Your dad's gonna get a cell phone tomorrow because you should always be able to call when you need him." Tim's tone brooked no room for argument. Someone needed to take over the shitshow Matt was currently running because he'd proven he had no clue what to do when it came to raising a child.

"I am?" The cowboy appeared to be completely surprised.

Tim arched an eyebrow. "Grow up, Matthew. Your time to be... Yes, you're getting a cell phone tomorrow. If I have to go to Roanoke myself to pick it up so you can be here to take care of him, I will. If Ryan's sick, you should be the first call."

Tim picked up Ryan and carried him to the living room, pulling a throw from the back of the couch to cover him. Matt was nowhere to be seen.

"Do you think your tummy is able to hold something to eat?" As Tim touched the boy's forehead to check for a fever, Matt stormed into the living room and flopped onto the couch next to his son, his expression not a happy one.

"I'm sure hungry, Tim, but I don't wanna puke again," Ryan answered.

Tim chuckled at the boy's response, heading to the kitchen to pour a little broth into a coffee cup. He put the liquid in the microwave for thirty seconds to warm it.

When he removed the cup, he found the liquid to be tepid, which was likely best for Ryan's hypersensitive stomach. Tim grabbed a spoon and headed back to the living room.

"How about you try a couple of spoons of broth? Your gramma made it." Ryan snuggled in Matt's arms, clearly worried about trying to eat for fear of losing it again.

Finally, Ryan answered. "Okay, I'll try a little bit."

Tim nodded as he sat down on the couch next to where Matt was holding his son, the man's face finally showing the concern Tim believed worthy of the situation. Tim held the spoon up to the boy's mouth, waiting to see if it was going to settle. When it did, he got about a third of it into Ryan before the boy began to fall asleep.

"Go put him to bed. I'd suggest you put a towel under him in case... Well, earlier wasn't good. It'll save the mattress." Tim stood and took the cup into the kitchen to clean up the dishes. Once he had the dishwasher loaded, Tim walked back into the living room to see Matt hadn't moved.

"Wait, you're not gonna leave, are ya? I can't... I don't know how to take care of a sick kid," Matt whined, his face mimicking that of a child not getting their way.

Tim chuckled. "How'd you... Who took care of Ryan after he was born?"

"Well, Bertie did it while I was on the circuit, but she had help. Momma came over a lot, as did a couple of Bertie's friends from high school. Bertie's momma didn't approve of our marriage, so she didn't come around. She moved to Denver after Bertie left me.

"Mona divorced Bertie's dad a long time ago, and I only met the Colonel one time when I was in El Paso for a rodeo. He seemed like a decent guy, but he didn't care much for the women in his family." Matt seemed cautious to admit anything about his ex-wife.

Tim shook his head. "So, you didn't...? Never mind. Right now, you have a little boy who has the flu. He's been vomiting, and he has diarrhea. I put his dirty clothes in the washer, so when they finish, put them in the dryer. Maybe your ex-wife was a worthless bitch, but you have the boy now. He's your responsibility, cowboy. He thinks you hung the moon and the stars, so start trying to live up to all that adoration." Tim walked toward the hallway to let himself out the front door.

He still had to clean the puke out of the truck, which he wasn't looking forward to, but a man has to do... a lot of dirty jobs.

Chapter Eight

"You can sit here and feel sorry for yourself, or you can come with us to the Circle C. Matt's having a party there because there aren't many places for Ryan to trick-or-treat out near the ranch." Aunt Katie seemed on a mission that early afternoon as Tim sat at the kitchen table with his laptop working on the books for the Katydid.

He hadn't seen Ryan since he'd picked him up from school when he was sick, which was also the last time he'd seen the boy's father. As a result, Tim had been sulking, and Aunt Katie seemed to know it after he begged her to keep tabs on Ryan through Jeri. Now that Matt had apologized to his mother, she was helping out with Ryan again. For Tim, it was a huge relief.

Of course, Aunt Katie could sometimes have a heart of stone with no sympathy for people she thought were behaving like fools, but Tim pushed his agenda yet again. "You know I'm in love with Matt Collins, and he doesn't even know I'm alive. Why would you want me to go to this party to torture myself by being around him when it will be hard for me?" Tim couldn't help but whine at her. It wasn't his finest hour, to be sure.

Instead of snapping back at him, Katie moved forward to hug him. "Timothy, I love you so very much. You were a gift from God for me and Joshua just when we needed you, so don't make me mad. Matthew Collins needs to figure out some very important things in his life, but he needs help doin' it. Seems to me, you're good at remindin' him of his responsibilities, so you should be there to support him when he's tryin' to do the right thing for his son. It'll give him some positive reinforcement." Tim knew his eyes grew wide as she spoke.

"Aunt Katie, he only wanted me to help him out because he didn't know how to take care of a sick kid. Matt Collins has a lot of issues, and I'm not going to become another one of them." He was trying to make a point, and he felt as if, for once, she was listening.

There was a knock on the front door and since Aunt Katie's hands were covered in pie dough, Tim walked down the hall to answer. When he opened the door to see Ryan Collins standing there with his hat in his hands—literally—he grinned. "Hey, bud. How are you feeling? What can I do for you?" Tim asked as he sunk to his knees, so he was at the same level as his little friend.

Ryan smiled at him nervously for a second, then he walked closer and touched Tim's shoulder as he began to speak. "I'm doin' a lot better, Tim. I was kinda hopin' maybe you'd come help me pick out a Halloween costume for the party. Daddy said it could be my pick, but I want you to come tell me what you like.

"You and my dad should be friends, Tim. I like both of you, and I think you'll like each other. Can ya not be mad at him right now and come with us?" The boy's eyes showed sincerity, which touched Tim's heart.

Before Tim could answer, Aunt Katie walked over to where they were assembled and bent over to hug Ryan. "Of course, he will. Maybe you wanna come over and help me bake some cookies as we get closer to the holidays?"

Why couldn't the floor open and swallow him whole after what Ryan said? Matt and he had nothing in common to make them friends, save that exceptional little boy talking to his aunt. Was there any way Tim could keep his crush under control if he spent time with Matt and Ryan? Was he that strong?

Ryan blushed a little, which was cute. "I'd like that a lot, but maybe you and Gramma Jeri could do it together 'cause she asked me if I'd help her, too. I guess I could figure out time to help both of ya, but I gotta help my dad pick out Christmas ornaments and a tree, and then we gotta get gifts." As Ryan listed off all his upcoming engagements, Tim wanted to laugh. Each short finger stuck up to emphasize his busy holiday schedule.

Tim smirked. "I think you'll have plenty of time for all of that, but right now, it's time to shop for a costume. How'd you get here?" Tim glanced at the driveway, not seeing a vehicle.

"Daddy's at the barn with Mr. Josh. They had some business to talk about. So, will you come, please?" Tim didn't have it in him to turn Ryan down, especially in the quasi-begging way the boy had presented his case.

Finally, Tim gave in. "Sure. Just give me a minute to put on a decent shirt and shoes," Tim told the boy as he looked down at the holey T-shirt he was wearing. He'd been power washing the vinyl fence around the yard because Aunt Katie wanted it cleaned up before they started putting up

Christmas lights on Thanksgiving weekend. It had been a warm October, and the weather was slated to be warm through November. The climate in Texas was different than what Tim experienced in Pittsburgh growing up.

Ryan nodded and followed Katie into the kitchen as Tim hurried to his room to change his shirt. He then noticed he was wearing old, dirty jeans, so he decided to change the rest of his clothes. As he was removing the T-shirt, he caught a whiff of himself and knew he didn't need to be quite so ripe, so a shower was definitely in order.

Once he'd grabbed a change of clothes and headed to the bathroom down the hall to shower, he glanced into the medicine cabinet mirror, noticing he'd forgotten to shave that morning before he started working. He had a decision to make—a little scruff, or a clean-shaven face? *Why do you even give a shit?*

After surveying the situation, Tim decided to clean up his jawline just a little, leaving the scruff in some sort of shape which might eventually become a goatee. He didn't hold out a lot of hope it would be a great one, but it was getting closer to winter, and maybe a little facial hair would keep him warmer when he worked in the barn? It was an idea, anyway.

He quickly showered before changing into clean jeans, a brown-and-white-checked, western shirt, and the new boots he'd bought when he first arrived at the farm. He combed his hair, noting he might need a haircut, but he felt like he looked good. Why did he think it mattered? *That's a loaded question.*

Tim walked into the kitchen to find Ryan with a glass of lemonade and a piece of the apple pie Aunt Katie had made earlier that day. "How's that pie? I asked for a slice for breakfast, but she said no," he told Ryan as he gave Aunt Katie a smile.

Ryan pulled a sly smile as he kneeled in the kitchen chair. "Maybe she likes me better than you, Timmy."

Aunt Katie's lilting laugh was a joy to hear, but at that moment, Tim didn't appreciate it. "He's got ya there, Timothy. Now, while Ryan finishes his pie, go down to the barn, and find Matthew. The two of you need to talk before y'all go shoppin'," she instructed in her sweetest voice.

Tim knew better than to argue with her, so he merely nodded. He left the house and headed to the barn where he saw Matt's King-Cab F-250 sitting out front. When he walked into the building, Matt was talking with Uncle Josh and Hank Sachs. Ethan, Hank's son, was standing there as well, and they were talking about Josie, the little jenny tied to a ring in the barn alley while Hank trimmed up her mane with electric clippers.

"I'm tellin' ya, Mr. Collins, she's as gentle as anything. She's low to the ground so he wouldn't get hurt if he fell off, but she's had trainin' somewhere along the way," Ethan told Matt.

"For a starter ride, you think she'd be good?" Matt asked the young man.

"I wish to heck I'd have had a ride like her to start. I was ridin' some rangy old nag who spooked at the least little sound.' Ethan chuckled at his own comment.

"Hey, that *rangy old nag* was my horse, and she only spooked 'cause you thought you needed to wear *spurs* all the damn time. I never had to spur that mare one time when I rode her," Hank scolded, but he failed to hide his smirk.

They were all laughing when Tim made his presence known. He stood next to Matt and smiled at everyone. "Ryan's finishing his pie, and then he's ready to go." Tim turned to stare at the handsome cowboy. When the man grinned and winked at him, Tim's heart sped up.

"Okay. Josh, give me a price on that jenny. I'd like to keep her here until closer to Christmas. I need to get the boys to fix up a stall for her, and that'll take a little time. I'll pay ya board." Matt seemed set in his decision, and Tim knew Ryan would be over the moon.

Uncle Josh laughed. "She's fine here, son. We'll keep her for free. I sure wouldn't mind breedin' her some time. A lot of people love to ride mules, and I bet she'd throw a good foal if you're interested."

Matt chuckled and glanced at Tim. "I'll keep it in mind, Josh. Come on, Tim, we better go. We got an excited little boy who's dyin' to dress like a Ninja Turtle. I hope to goodness Walmart has somethin' left."

Uncle Josh winked at Tim, which was odd, but Matt turned to him and grinned, setting Tim's world right. This thing he had for the cowboy—it was going to be the death of him for sure.

The two men collected Ryan from Aunt Katie and after Tim settled him into the booster in the back seat of the big pickup, he climbed into the front passenger seat next to Matt, not sure what to talk about.

"Buckle your seatbelt, please. I don't plan to have an accident, but I wanna make sure *you're* safe." Matt's comment pushed Tim off balance. For a moment, he couldn't speak, so he nodded and buckled up.

Matt started the truck and glanced at him, a grin lighting up the cowboy's face and making Tim light-headed. "I think you should get yourself a costume, Timmy." The comment ended with a low chuckle from Matt, making

Tim roll his eyes as the three of them headed down the driveway, Walmart bound.

"This is so cool," Ryan enthused when he came into the living room dressed as his favorite Ninja Turtle, Raphael. He walked over to Tim to take his hand and lead him around the room to greet the guests.

All the hands from the Circle C and Katydid were there with their families. The kids and many of the adults were dressed in costumes, and there was a Raphael-shaped piñata tied to a tree in the backyard, chock full of candy.

There were coolers with drinks of all kinds, and a table set up on the patio with snacks. Everyone brought candy bags for the kids, and Tim was pretty sure they hadn't missed *not* going trick-or-treating around town at all.

Aunt Katie and Miss Jeri put out a spread for the party, and everyone was having a ball. Tim was dressed as a carrot, which was the only costume in the adult section that he'd even consider wearing. There were orange tights, which he wore with trepidation, but at least the foam carrot shirt covered his junk. The worst part was a green beanie hat with long stalks of greenery attached. He knew when Ryan talked him into dressing up, he'd never be able to deny the kid anything again.

Aunt Katie was dressed as Annie Oakley and Uncle Josh was dressed as Buffalo Bill. They looked so cute together that Tim had to take a picture with his phone. Jeri and Marty were dressed as a couple from a reality television show.

The camo gear and fake beard on Marty were lost on Tim, but everyone at the party seemed to recognize the costumes, so he laughed along with the crowd before he took a picture of the couple.

Tim walked to a cooler and grabbed a bottle of beer, laughter ringing through the evening air behind him. He popped the cap on the bottle and turned to see a green ball walking into the room. For a minute, he was confused, but when Matt Collins removed his cowboy hat and stepped from behind the couch, Tim was shocked. The man was wearing green tights covered by a green ball for a costume, which was set off by the well-worn cowboy boots. It seemed to be uncharacteristic behavior for the man, according to the stunned expressions on everyone's faces.

The big cowboy walked over to Tim and smiled, extending his hand. "Hi, Carrot. I'm your pea."

Before Tim could comment, Josh walked up and grinned as he twirled the fake, handlebar mustache glued above his lip. "Ah, peas and carrots. I suspected somethin' of the sort." Without waiting for a response, he walked away leaving Tim to look at Matt Collins and wonder what the hell that was about.

Three hours later, Pea and Carrot were saying goodbye to the guests, making certain the kids had the trick-or-treat goody bags filled with homemade cookies and candy prepared by Miss Jeri earlier in the day. Ryan was still making his ninja moves as Aunt Katie recorded him on the new video camera she'd turned up with, much to Tim's surprise. He didn't even think they had a camera, much less a video camera.

Glancing at Matt—who looked so cute dressed as a pea—Tim wasn't sure what to think about the night. Matt was leaning against the wall, talking to Uncle Josh without a thought to the fact he was wearing green tights and cowboy boots. Tim couldn't resist taking a quick picture before walking to where they stood.

"How about we change into normal clothes so we can help clean up?" Tim could see Miss Jeri and Aunt Katie running around like crazy, and he knew there were still people hanging around to make it a quick job.

Uncle Josh reached up and ripped off the mustache, releasing a short yelp. "*Damn!* That hurt. I'm not lettin' Katie talk me into that crap again. Go change. I'll start cleanin' up that cooler on the deck." Josh grabbed his empty bottle and headed out to the deck where Marty was standing in his street clothes, puffing on a cigar.

Matt took Tim's hand, which surprised the younger man. When the cowboy led Tim back to the master bedroom where his clothes were folded and waiting on the bed, Tim couldn't hide the surprise on his face. He'd left his clothes in Ryan's bedroom when he'd changed.

"How'd my clothes—"

"I brought them in here earlier. We need to talk, okay? You can change first." Matt pointed to the bathroom.

Tim gathered his clothes, closing the bathroom door before turning to gaze into the mirror. His eyebrows were up near his hairline and didn't seem as if they'd ever come down. The night had been one surprise after another.

"How'd you let that kid talk you into dressing like a damn carrot? What the hell were you thinking?" Tim asked himself the question out loud as he pulled off the Velcro straps that held the costume together.

Once it was off, Tim slipped out of the tights, glad the *boys* had a little more room to move around. He quickly dressed in the long-sleeved, western shirt and jeans from earlier in the day before he walked out, socks in hand. His boots were still in the hallway tray.

"So, how much is left—" Tim stopped talking when he saw he was alone as he entered the kitchen. He glanced toward the back deck to see nobody there either. The great room was empty, and Tim suddenly felt he was in a science-fiction movie where he was the last man on earth.

Since he was alone, he started picking up orange cups and matching paper plates to carry into the kitchen. He found a trash can under the sink and took it with him to continue the cleanup.

Where had Ryan disappeared to? It was only nine, and Tim doubted the boy would be ready to settle down for the night, given the amount of candy he'd covertly consumed all evening.

Tim wasn't sure where everyone had gone, but he decided to make quick work of the mess before he went out to the little truck he'd...*fuck! He* remembered he'd ridden to the ranch with Matt and Ryan to help decorate after the trip to Walmart. As he looked out onto the driveway, he saw the cars and trucks were gone as well.

When Matt returned to the kitchen, he was dressed in a pair of worn jeans and a faded, teal T-shirt that happened to highlight his dark hair and bright blue eyes. For a moment, Tim was stuck in place. *Matt Collins is so fucking handsome...* He was snapped from his gawking when the man spoke.

"Um, Ryan went home with Momma and Daddy. I had a conversation with Momma last night, and I'm happy to say she was very supportive of me. Actually, Momma didn't seem too surprised, but that's a worry for another day.

"I talked to Josh this afternoon, and I asked him if he'd loan you out for a bit. You can still work for him from here because I have Wi-Fi—well, the guy told me I have it. I have a new computer I don't know how to work yet, but I hoped you could help me figure it out. I'd like to have you spend time here, helpin' me set up an operation like you did for Josh. He says it's helped him, and I'm sure you can see I need all the help I can get."

Matt seemed a little apprehensive to ask, but based on Tim's severe ass-chewing fit when the man hadn't been available to pick up his own son from school, it was really no surprise.

"Matt, I don't—"

"Please, Tim, give me a shot. I know I've been runnin' ya in circles, but I've finally got myself figured out. I'm a gay man in a business not exactly acceptin' of my orientation, but if I provide first-class stock, it shouldn't matter to the buyer who I choose to snuggle up with when I watch TV.

"I'm not gonna hide anymore. I just can't do it and be the man I need to be. I'd appreciate it if you'd help me out here with things I need regardin' the business, but more importantly, would you consider havin' dinner with me and Ryan? I mean, you and me *are* peas and carrots." Matt's face lit up at his own joke as he took Tim's hand.

Tim was completely stumped, but when Matt pulled him close and kissed him softly, Tim couldn't believe it was real. Against his better judgment, Tim was sucked back into Matt Collins' orbit.

The cowboy was amazing, but he wasn't without flaws. Tim knew it, but he was still diving in, headfirst. If Matt wanted to date him? Well, Tim couldn't find it inside himself to turn the man down.

Tim giggled and stared at the cowboy. "Peas and carrots, huh? Well, when you put it like that, *Forrest*, how can I say no? Dinner with you and Ryan sounds great. Let me know when and where. In the meantime, I need to get back to Katydid. Do I gotta walk?" Tim gave Matt a shy smile.

Matt grinned and leaned forward to nip Tim's neck. "I'll take ya home. We can work this as slow as you wanna, hon, but eventually, I'm gonna live up to the idea of the man you could love. I wanna be the man you expect me to be." Matt seemed steadfast in his admission, which touched his heart.

Tim's face flushed, though he wasn't sure why. He wrapped his arms around Matt's shoulders before he pulled the man down for another soft kiss. He quickly became the aggressor, however, sweeping his tongue over Matt's lips, and when he opened his mouth to suck Tim's tongue inside, it was like going to heaven.

Their tongues continued to wrestle in the sweet kiss, and Tim felt Matt draw his body closer, his hands finding purchase on Tim's ass. He felt Matt's hard cock against his stomach, and he was sure Matt felt his against his thigh. Tim wasn't sure where they were at the jumping-off point in a possible relationship, so he chose not to take things further.

He might have wiggled against the bull rider just to feel the sensation, but that was as far as he was going to go with the man at that moment.

"Let me take you home, sweetheart. I don't want us to go too fast into this. I got too much ridin' on this, Tim. You can leave the carrot here." Matt pointed to the costume hanging over the back of the couch with a wide grin. Tim was having a hard time catching his breath from the kisses and the clothing-covered contact.

Of course, the taller man's comment was so out of left field, Tim couldn't help laughing at the offhanded way Matt had dissolved the tension—which was totally sexual.

"You sure? I wouldn't want to *peas* you off." It was Tim's turn to tease. Matt laughed as he took Tim's hand and kissed it before the two headed for the front door.

"You're a piss riot, ya know." Matt led Tim out to his big pickup and opened the door, helping him inside to drive Tim home.

When they turned into the driveway at the Katydid, Matt turned off the headlights as he took the fork toward the barn, stopping and turning off the truck. He tuned the radio to a station to play softly in the background, staring at Tim with a sexy grin.

"So, how... I mean, I'm not sure how this works. We have a lot of shit on the floor, here. I know what I want, but I'm not sure how to get there," Matt stated quietly with only soft acoustic guitar sounds and their own breathing in the truck.

Tim exhaled, biding his time to respond. He knew the two of them needed to discuss how they'd go from strangers to lovers—if that was the way it was going to go—but Tim wasn't exactly sure how to get there because he'd never been in a relationship.

He could also see Matt wasn't exactly sure how to walk the walk either. It became clear that if Tim wanted there to be a chance for the two of them, he'd have to take the bull by the horns—so to speak.

After a minute, Tim finally had the words together. "Okay. First, we don't have to tell anyone about us until we figure out ourselves. You said you told your mother you're gay, but nobody else has to know until you're ready, Matt. Certainly, Ryan doesn't have to know. We can hang out platonically for a while, get to know each other better, see how it feels as you get ready for your new reality. I guess it'll take some time to become comfortable in your skin since you've only just accepted that you're gay. I know it took *me* some time when I figured it out."

Thankfully, Matt nodded, so Tim continued. "Second, the situation with working for you and working for Uncle Josh won't be that hard for me. Of course, I'll need to spend time at your place to figure out how you do business before I can gear the software to meet your needs.

"I mean, in your situation, automation will be much more productive for you than it is for Uncle Josh because you function on a much larger scale. His business really just needed something simple and easily maintained, which I was able to create pretty quickly, though I made sure it was secure and easily upgraded should he decide to expand." Tim knew he was rambling, but it was important to hammer out the business—or was he stalling?

"Uh, for you, I need a more in-depth plan, and after I spend time there and observe you guys in action and peg your business style, I can figure out what's required to make things run smoothly. After that, I'll be better able to design a computer system geared toward the types of challenges you face, hopefully, making things easier on all of you." When Tim finally reached the end of his convoluted explanation, he released a nervous sigh.

It was as pitch dark as Tim had ever seen because of a new moon. When Matt's hand touched his on the middle console, Tim grabbed it and twined their fingers together.

Mat squeezed Tim's hand before he spoke. "That's doable, but I guess I'm wonderin' how we figure out *us,* 'because I want there to be an *us*, Tim. I think about ya all the time, and I know Ryan loves ya."

There was a prickle up his spine, and he couldn't help himself. "You're not just doing this because you need help with Ryan, are you?" Immediately, guilt swamped him for asking the question.

Fortunately, Matt snickered. "I can see why you'd think such a thing, but no. I'm gonna take care of my boy. I got that cell phone like you told me, so he'll always be able to get me if he needs me. Can I get your number?"

Tim reached into his pocket for his phone, handing it to the man without comment. He watched as Matt programmed his information and called himself. "I'm new to texting, but I'd like to text you if that's okay. I know you love my boy, Tim. He's easy to love, but I know you don't think I am. I'm hopin' to change your mind." Matt leaned forward and nuzzled Tim's ear.

Tim shoved his phone into his pocket and turned his head to capture Matt's lips, pushing his tongue between the cowboy's lips. They twirled their tongues together and when Matt cradled the left side of Tim's face, pulling him closer, the younger man fell into the most glorious spiral he'd ever imagined.

Matt was the epitome of Tim's dream man, and anyone would have been just as gobsmacked by the man as Tim was in that moment.

Matt pulled away and stared into Tim's eyes, laughing quietly. "You're just like I always imagined the man of my dreams would be."

Tim giggled because the line was unbelievable and a little cheesy coming out of the man's mouth. "So, you like blonds?"

Matt reached up to run his hand through Tim's blond locks. "On you, they're great. It's more the inside of you that has my head spinnin', though you have the most amazin' eyes." With that, Matt kissed him again.

Tim was so lost in the kiss he almost forgot he was trying to be strong and not throw himself at the man like the slut he clearly wanted to be. He pulled away and placed his hand on Matt's face, stroking the soft stubble of his jaw.

"I had fun tonight. Can Ryan come over here sometimes? It's still warm enough to go for a ride after school, you know. I'll pick him up if you'll notify the office and give them my information."

"Actually, um, I'm buyin' Josie as a Christmas gift for Ryan, but I was hopin' maybe you'd let me bring Chester over to the ranch sometimes so you could ride with him over there. I'm gonna buy a horse for myself, but Josh is lookin' for an American Saddlebred because they're bigger than the quarter horses he has on the Katydid. He says I need a bigger horse.

"Miss Katie offered to help me find tack for Ryan to grow with, and I'd like it if you'd work with him on ridin'. He can't stop talking about riding Betsy and Chester, and when I asked Josh about the gelding, he said it was a good horse to have around when it came time to move cattle. Of course, he reminded me when y'all moved my cattle while my ass was in jail for bein' stupid."

Tim couldn't help but laugh at Matt's honest admission of the situation, which brought a chuckle from the cowboy, too.

Matt continued. "Anyway, he told me Chester's your horse, so maybe you wouldn't mind ridin' with Ryan at my place?"

Tim had to give it to the man—he was a slick talker. That was a cowboy trait Aunt Katie had always said to watch out for. That was how Uncle Josh won her heart.

"So, you're trying to kidnap my horse so I have to come to your house to take a ride, and you talked to my uncle about me helping you set up a ranch management system so I couldn't use my work at the farm as an excuse to say no? Matthew Collins, you could have asked me to go to McDonald's for a burger, and I'd have said yes. No need for covert operations with me, but now I'm definitely going to keep my eye on you. You're a schemer, I think, and you're teaching that great little boy the same thing." Tim winked to soften the blow from his accusatory term.

Matt laughed along. "Well, I guess I'm not a good one 'cause you figured me out. I'm only askin' for a chance." The whisper in Matt's voice plucked a chord deep inside.

Only one thought came to mind. *Who am I to say no? After all, I'm in love with the man.*

Chapter Nine

Tim was sitting in the office at the Katydid, working on entering invoices into Uncle Josh's management system. He was a little behind because of the work he'd been doing at the Circle C when he had free time, especially since Terri, the part-time office manager Matt had working for him, was getting ready to go on maternity leave.

Matt hadn't been able to find anyone who was willing to take over the job temporarily, so Tim stepped in to help out as often as he could. He wasn't, however, willing to leave Aunt Katie and Uncle Josh in the lurch, either. They were the people who loved him the most, and he refused to let them down.

The office door opened, and that little straw cowboy hat Tim recognized was pushed up to reveal those beautiful blue eyes the boy shared with the man who had Tim wrapped around his finger. Matt was planning to come over to fix a shoe on Pally, one of the farm's working horses, so he wasn't surprised to find Ryan in the office.

His mind wandered back to the first date with the handsome bull rider and his son. It was at Tio's, a little Mexican place in town the previous weekend, and it had been on a loop through Tim's mind for two weeks.

They'd let Ryan pick the place for the date, and they'd all had a great time. There had been plenty of conversation about the inner workings at the ranch and stories about Ryan making new friends at school, including a girl named Gracie who wouldn't leave the boy alone.

In return, Tim had told them about growing up in Pittsburgh. He'd given them a few stories from his childhood before his father had turned all the hatred in his soul toward Tim. He'd been pretty sure Matt could tell he was glossing over some things, but the man had been kind enough not to mention it or push for more. Tim had appreciated the man's kindness greatly.

Later that night when the Collins' men dropped Tim off at the farm, Matt had walked him up to the front door. The house had been dark, and Ryan had fallen asleep in the back seat of the truck, so Matt had kissed Tim good night—very, very well.

Tim believed the man had to use some sort of lip treatment because he'd never kissed lips so soft in his life and being held in the man's arms was like nothing Tim had ever imagined. When Matt had finally released his hold, Tim had floated into the house and dreamed about the tall brunet all night.

"What can I do for you, Mr. Collins?" Tim noticed Ryan had grown a bit taller than the last time he'd seen him in the office at the farm.

It was a Saturday in early November. Tim was still trying to create the perfect ranch management system for the Circle C Ranch. It wasn't an easy operation to understand at first blush because Matt needed to be able to track so many components related to his breeding operation, and then the follow-up information about who bought the bulls and steers and what they did with them. Keeping such detailed records was important to his business model.

A rodeo company Matt knew from his bull riding days had contacted him about acquiring bulls. As he told Tim, for the Circle C to be considered as a stock provider, the ranch had to be able to show proof of animal health and fitness and the progress of the bloodlines.

Matt had breeding cows, but he purchased the semen of prize bulls for insemination to ensure top-notch stock. He'd established a remarkable breeding history in a damn short time, and the fact the bull rider had primitively tracked everything in a notebook and was able to keep it all straight definitely impressed Tim.

"I was hopin' you'd take me for a ride, but it's awful busy out there." Ryan hitched his thumb over his shoulder, pointing to the hallway of the barn.

Tim got up to see Uncle Josh had people in to inspect the barn, as well as observing Matt while he replaced Pally's left front shoe. Two of the boarders had moved from the area and taken their horses, so there were open stalls for new boarders.

Not surprisingly, the reputation of the farm was fantastic and had traveled primarily by word of mouth, so there was a waiting list for new boarders. Tim knew Uncle Josh was sizing up the potential boarders to see if they would fit in with the way he ran things at the Katydid. He would leave Uncle Josh alone to do it. Besides, he had a little boy who wanted to go for a horseback ride, and Josie still had her own personal stall in the barn.

"How about we try something new today? You've seen that jenny in the barn, right? Josie?" She was an adorable little roan donkey, and Ryan had helped Tim feed her a time or two. He'd pet the small animal, and she, in turn, would nuzzle his head, bringing a happy giggle from the boy. Tim was glad she was so damn gentle.

"Yeah. She's a cuddler." Ryan had a happy grin on his face when speaking of the donkey.

"How about we saddle her and Chester, and you and I take a ride down to the back of the pasture to ride the fences? You've done it a time or two, right?" The two of them had gone, riding double on Chester. It would be the first time they'd done it with Ryan on the jenny.

The boy's excited giggle made Tim's heart soar. "You think we can get away with it?" Ryan started out of the office to the hallway, holding the door open for Tim.

"You and me? We're partners in crime. Let's get to it." Tim's mood lifted considerably just being around the boy.

After Chester was saddled, Tim went to the tack room and picked up the kid saddle Uncle Josh had on hand. It had been Shane's, and he knew Uncle Josh must have thought a lot of Ryan to bring it out from its place of honor in the office.

Josh had asked Ethan to clean it up and put it in the tack room for Ryan to use when he came over to the farm. It seemed like the perfect opportunity to try it out.

Tim knew Matt was having a saddle made for the boy for Christmas to fit Josie, though it wasn't quite ready. He also knew Uncle Josh loved to see Ryan sitting on the old one while Tim led the boy around the pasture. It likely reminded Josh of leading Shane atop his horse when he was a boy. Tim was glad the memories were happy.

Once Josie was settled after being tacked up, Tim helped Ryan get into the saddle and stood next to them. "I'm gonna lead her for a bit to see if she's gonna act up. If she doesn't, I'll take off the lead, okay?" Tim handed over the reins as he snapped the red lead rope to the halter.

Matt had brought Ryan over to the farm a few times for Uncle Josh to give him riding lessons, with Ethan Sachs there to offer advice. They'd been the ones to introduce the little cowboy to the jenny while Tim was working at the Circle C, and Tim wished he'd been there to see it in person.

"I rode her before, Tim. She likes me." Ryan settled his cowboy hat forward, obviously taking his newfound status as a 'cowboy' very seriously. Tim hid the smirk.

"I'm sure that's right, but for my *own* piece of mind, could I lead her for a bit?" The very last thing he wanted was for that little boy to get hurt. He was becoming more important to Tim every day, just like the boy's father.

The two adult men were progressing slowly in their romantic pursuit, with only a few kisses exchanged and some grinding together in the hallway of Matt's house one afternoon after Tim had fixed him lunch before Matt headed back to the barn. There was a carpenter building new stalls in the barn, and Matt believed he needed to be there to supervise.

"Come with me down to the barn," Matt whispered as he kissed from Tim's neck to his shoulder, holding the blond tightly in his strong arms. Tim felt Matt's hard cock against his stomach, and he tried not to concentrate on it because, without much effort, he was sure he'd make a mess in his jeans right there. He certainly didn't want to embarrass himself just as the bus stopped at the end of the drive to deliver Ryan.

"Matt, you know I can't. Ryan's due home any minute, and I've got a conference call scheduled with Dean Campbell at the MFA to establish a direct-order system for the ranch." Tim tilted his head so the taller man could continue to kiss and suck on his neck.

"Damn. Okay, but we're gonna take Ryan over to Momma's on Saturday night and we're gonna go out, just the two

of us, okay?" Matt sounded—and felt—very firm with his plans.

Tim was breathless at the man's attention, but he was able to respond. "I'd love it. Pick a place, and I'm there." He whispered as he moved Matt back to his lips. Tim sucked the man's bottom lip into his mouth and moaned when Matt's tongue stroked his top lip, too.

"Timmy." Tim had zoned out, which wasn't really a surprise to him as he thought about the bull rider. He turned to see Ryan with his arms crossed in frustration as he led the boy around the upper pasture.

"Oh, sorry. Here, you keep walking her around while I get Chester. We'll get on the move in a few minutes. You need anything?"

"Nope. Just come on. I think Josie wants to go, but she's bored bein' here in this little pasture." Tim almost laughed at the little boy's comment, but it was probably true.

Tim nodded as he unclipped the lead rope before heading for the barn. Once inside, he walked Chester out of the stall he'd come to occupy. Since Uncle Josh gave the horse to Tim, he'd been elevated to inside stock. The old gelding certainly didn't hate it.

As Tim was hoisting the saddle up onto the horse's back, a young guy strolled into the barn, looking around. "You board here?"

The visitor was decked out in full cowboy gear, from a beat-up black felt hat to a pair of well-worn roping boots. He walked from stall to stall looking over the top of the gates at the horses inside. Tim stopped saddling Chester to walk over and meet the guy.

"I work here. Can I help you?" Tim carried a lead rope with him in the event things got tenuous, but he wasn't going to start any trouble without a reason. He would, however, defend himself and the farm against anyone who intended harm.

"I'm lookin' for a job. I heard the buzz around town that maybe Mr. Simmons needed a seasoned hand. I'm just up from Kentucky. Name's Mickey, uh, Michael Warren, but I go by Mickey. I worked at the Bar K for Jerry Kessler. He sent me in this direction."

The guy was damn good-looking. He was about six-foot tall with a slender, muscular build. Tim guessed he was about twenty-five, and he had a swagger about him that hinted he was no stranger to horses.

"How long have you been at the Bar, K and why'd you leave?" A little information up front would help Tim run a background check on the new cowboy before there was any thought of a job offer.

The other guys at the farm were solid, and Tim knew from Uncle Josh that nomadic cowboys could be trouble, so he was determined he'd vet any new hands before the offer of a job was extended.

Uncle Josh's operation wasn't large, but Tim knew his uncle was considering adding another barn to the property to expand his business, and if the guy was a decent hand, Tim was sure Uncle Josh wouldn't want the cowboy to get away.

Stevie and Carl only worked on Saturdays because they had school during the week. With Tim helping at the Circle C, there was enough work at Katydid for another full-time hand.

"I worked at the Bar K for three years before Mr. Kessler sold out. The new owner, well, he had some issues with me, personally, and I didn't want to stick around to see how it turned out. The bigoted types were never the kind of people I wanted to spend much time with, anyway." Clearly, Mickey was a no-nonsense kind of guy which Tim could respect.

Tim nodded, not sure where to go next with his questioning. Just as he was about to tell the man to let him find Uncle Josh, Ryan Collins wandered inside on Josie. "Timmy? We're gettin' bored again." The boy had a cross look on his face, reminding Tim of the older Collins' man when he was displeased.

"Sorry, Ryan. I'll be with you in a minute. Do you know where Uncle Josh is?" The little cowboy had been riding the upper pasture, and if Josh was around, Ryan probably would have seen him outside.

"I saw him goin' into the house with Daddy. You want me to ride up and get him?" Ryan was observing Mickey Warren with a squinted eye. Tim wanted to laugh at the little guy for giving the stink eye to the stranger, but he held it.

Mickey slowly ambled over to the boy and smiled. "Hello, cowboy. Name's Mickey. I like your donkey. She's a beaut." Mickey stroked the small animal on her neck to put her at ease, and the grin didn't fade from his face.

Of course, Ryan Collins was far worldlier than his age. "What can we do for ya?" Ryan pushed his cowboy hat to the back of his head to get a good look at the newcomer. He was the perfect picture of irritation, and Tim, once again, had to hold the laugh so he didn't upset the young boy.

"Well, sir, I'm lookin' for a job. Are you on the hirin' committee?" Mickey smiled.

Ryan looked at the two of them before he crossed his hands over the saddle horn, letting the reins rest on Josie's neck without him holding them. To the jenny's credit, she didn't move a muscle. "No, but I'll get the *boss*," Ryan stated as he turned Josie out of the barn and headed up the gravel drive leading from the barn to the house.

"He your little brother or nephew?" Mickey walked over to Chester. He picked up the right front hoof and looked at it, gently placing it back on the floor as he brushed up the horse's leg to his shoulder.

It appeared the man knew his way around horseflesh, so that was another "pro" for him in Tim's opinion. "He's a friend of the family. Anyway, what brings you to Virginia? You got any family here?" Tim asked, getting back to the interview-style questioning he was intent to undertake.

"Got no family to speak of, as a matter of fact. Mr. Kessler told me about Mr. Simmons and what a good man he believed him to be, so I looked up the website for Katydid Farm at the library. It's a small operation, which is nice, but it's got a good reputation for prime horseflesh. It's my first pick of places in the area.

"I figure if I can get a job here, the boss might let me camp for a few days till I get myself a place to sleep." Mickey's explanation surprised Tim a little.

"It's damn near Thanksgiving, and we've been lucky with the weather, but I'd imagine it won't be so warm much longer." It was late fall in southern Virginia, and he didn't know many people who wanted to camp there.

"I've got a truck and a sleepin' bag. I just need a place to park, and I'm not particular," Mickey stated as he continued to inspect Chester's feet. "Good shoes." He put down the rear left leg of the gelding and patted it on the ass.

"Thanks. I appreciate someone who admires my handiwork." Tim turned to see Matt walking into the barn with Josie following closely behind. Ryan was on her back and had a grin on his face like the cat that ate the canary. Tim *really* wanted to laugh.

"You Mr. Simmons?" Mickey asked the bull rider.

Matt stopped next to Tim and smirked without looking at Mickey. "I thought you and Ryan were gonna ride?"

"We are, but Mickey came in as I was saddling Chester. He's looking for a job. I thought Ryan was going to get Uncle Josh to come down to meet with him." Tim cocked his eyebrow at Matt.

"Oh, Josh said he'll be ready to meet him in a few minutes, but I thought I'd see if everything was okay. You gonna be ready for tonight? I'm droppin' Ryan at Momma's at six. I'll pick you up at six-thirty, okay?" Matt said it loud enough for Mickey to hear... clearly.

Tim felt the flush of his face, and then, without warning, Matt placed his right hand on Tim's cheek, turning the younger man's head. "I don't deserve someone as handsome as you, but I'm not gonna push my luck by questionin' anything. Now, you two go ahead and ride for a while. Josh will be here directly, but I'll wait with the cowboy. I need to run home and meet Doc Grant for a bit to inseminate a dozen head of cows, but I'll be back to get Ryan at five, okay?" Matt spoke quietly, stepping into Tim's personal space.

"Okay. I'll make sure he's fine and have Aunt Katie feed him a snack before you pick him up. Make sure you leave Doc's invoice on the desk so I can pay it on Monday. Terri has her sonogram, so I agreed to work for her. Make sure the vet leaves me a list of the semen he used so I can update the database, and this time, make sure you know which cows get which semen. No guesswork." Tim's tone was scolding as he stared into those blue eyes that filled his dreams, but Matt only grinned.

"Got ya. Anything else, babe? You're gonna stay the night, right?" Matt's request was quiet, meant for Tim's ears only. Tim hadn't anticipated Matt would want him to stay that night, but then the bull rider had gone so far as to make sure Ryan was staying at his parents' place, so it should have been expected.

Tim's face and neck flushed again as he smiled at Matt, nodding in complete agreement. When Chester pawed at the floor, it snapped Tim out of the fog of love Matthew Collins often put him in when he was anywhere around.

Mickey, with a tender smile on his face, walked over to Tim and Matt and put his arms on both of their shoulders. "I knew there was somethin' special about this place. I've got a boyfriend back in Kentucky, and I told him if I found a place for both of us, I'd come get him. He's goin' to community college and worked at the Bar K part-time. Unfortunately, when Mr. Kessler sold out, Mr. Leslie didn't like queers, so we were both fired. I do, however, think I'm gonna like it here."

Much to Tim's surprise, Matt laughed and stuck out his hand as he pushed Mickey's arm from Tim's shoulder, wrapping his own around Tim's neck to draw him closer. "Matthew Collins. The boy is mine... well, this boy, too, I hope." He turned to Tim and grinned. Of course, Tim was irritated at the possessive show, but he smiled in return. He was a lovesick fool to be sure.

Matt and Mickey shook hands. "Nice to meet ya, Matt. You do the shoes on this gelding? Nice job. He has a cleft on his..."

Mickey discussed Chester's hooves with Matt as Tim turned to see Ryan smiling at him from the doorway. The little shit actually winked before he turned Josie out of the barn.

Tim knew he'd have to watch the kid. He had the potential to be dangerous—which only captured Tim's heart more.

Matt finished saddling Chester as he and Mickey talked about horses. It sounded more like a job interview than Tim believed he'd be able to give.

Once Chester was ready, Matt turned toward Tim. "Go ahead and take Ryan for a ride. He's been chompin' at the bit since he found out we were comin' over. I'll take Mickey up to the house to talk to Josh and Katie. I'll see ya later." Matt placed a gentle kiss on Tim's needy lips, surprising him, but then again, Matt Collins surprised him all the time.

As Tim climbed up on Chester, Mickey waved before he followed Matt out of the barn. "Nice to meet ya, Tim. Hopefully, I'll get to see ya again." Without waiting for a response, Mickey and Matt went in the direction of the house.

Tim hoped Mickey impressed Uncle Josh because he liked the guy. The tall, slim cowboy seemed decent, and it sounded like the pair might have things in common. At the end of the day, it appeared to him Mickey was another guy for Aunt Katie to mother. Tim had the feeling she'd welcome Michael Warren with open arms.

Chapter Ten

"Aunt Katie, do I look okay?" Tim felt like an idiot asking her for wardrobe advice, but he'd tried on everything—literally—in his closet. Nothing seemed right, and he was a nervous wreck for more reasons than his mind could process.

Earlier at breakfast, Tim had sat down with Aunt Katie and Uncle Josh to explain to them that he and Matt were going on a date. Neither of them had been surprised, and it seemed like Aunt Katie had planned it herself, telling him she knew he and Matthew "would have a wonderful, special friendship and be great co-parents to Ryan." Tim had insisted she shouldn't get ahead of herself, though the beauty of the idea made him a little wishful.

"Give me that shirt, Timothy. I need to teach you how to iron if you're gonna be takin' care of Ryan and Matt. There will come times when all y'all will need to be pressed and polished. I might not be around forever, you know."

Tim wanted to laugh at the comment because Aunt Katie always reminded her family of her impending demise. They all knew she was too stubborn to go anywhere before she had everyone on the straight and narrow.

After his cranberry-colored shirt was ironed, Aunt Katie proceeded to give Tim a lecture regarding saving a little "something for the honeymoon," or so it sounded. Again, he wanted to laugh at her, but he loved her so much and as he listened to her, the advice was sound. If he gave everything away on the first date, why would the man make a repeat trip to Tim Town?

When they finished dinner, the two men went back to the Circle C. Tim was a little uneasy regarding how far to go with the blue-eyed god, but he wanted more than just a kiss goodnight on the front porch steps. Especially since they weren't Tim's steps!

Apparently, Matt picked up on it. "I know I told you this relationship would go at your pace, but please, can I at least see ya nekkid? It's been drivin' me crazy."

Matt whispered those words in Tim's ear as he pulled Tim onto his lap while the two of them sat on Matt's couch with a couple of beers. The two had been kissing, neglecting whatever the hell was on television, and Tim was so worked up, he was afraid he'd come in his jeans.

They stumbled to Matt's bedroom, stripping each other the whole way up the stairs and down the hallway. By the time they were on the bed they were naked, but Matt didn't pressure Tim into anything more than taking both of their cocks in his hand and jacking them together. He reached into the bedside table and grabbed lotion, slicking up his hand before he grasped the pair of them again.

"Oh, fuck." It felt so good to have Matt's hands on him.

The act was familiar, so Tim didn't freak out. Kenny and he had gotten that far before the shit with the soccer team messed up their friendship.

Tim, however, wanted a hell of a lot more with Matt. Maybe not that night, but in the very, very near future.

"You have a great cock, Tim. I'm so fuckin' close to losin' my shit. You?" Matt continued to work them both while they kissed, licked, and sucked each other's upper torsos.

"*Too close, too fast!*" Tim erupted between them, embarrassed for a second until Matt's cock went off, making him sigh in relief. He didn't want to be a Johnny-come-too-soon, but with Matt coming right after him, he was more confident in his sexual endurance.

"I think we both got worked up too quick. I've been half-hard this whole night. I usually have a lot more staying... Well, I don't come that fast. Maybe it's just because I'm with you? I wanna be with you so much, I think I've lost the ability to hold back." Matt kissed the tip of Tim's nose. Tim giggled, not caring how it sounded.

"Maybe it's something to work toward for the both of us?" Matt asked as he climbed out of bed and walked toward the bathroom.

He returned a moment later with a washcloth and a towel, gently cleaning Tim's chest and abs before returning to the bathroom. When he slipped into bed with Tim, Matt wrapped his arms around the blond and held him tightly as Tim fell into a deep sleep. It was wonderful.

"Mmm. You smell good." Tim opened his eyes to see the handsome face of Matthew Collins in front of him. The cowboy had his hand on Tim's bare ass, pulling him closer where a hard cock poked his stomach.

"I seriously doubt I smell good." Tim was a little groggy, and he was sure his breath was horrible. He'd worked up a sweat when the two were grinding against each other the previous night, and he thought they both probably needed a shower.

Matt laughed quietly in the early morning calm. "I can have my own opinion, Timmy. To *me,* you smell incredible, but I've been enjoyin' that scent for a while now. So, what do you like for breakfast? I have coffee, of course, and I can offer toast, bagels, or cereal. As I'm sure Ryan told ya, I'm not much good with anything more complicated."

Tim pulled away so he could see the handsome face and bedroom eyes of the bull rider he'd grown to love more than anything... except for the man's son. "How do you like *your* eggs, Mr. Collins? I mean, you have eggs, right?"

"I'm pretty sure Momma put eggs in the fridge. You ain't gotta cook me breakfast, Timmy. I'm tryin' to be a good host."

Tim chuckled as he hopped up and took his naked ass to the bathroom, grabbing his boxers on the way.

After modifying his morning routine—washing his face with hot water instead of the face wash he usually used; swirling mouthwash instead of brushing his teeth because he'd forgotten to bring the overnight bag he'd packed; and spraying on a little of Matt's Axe to help mellow out the musk he'd smelled from under his pits instead of taking a shower—Tim returned to the bedroom to find Matt with his eyes closed. "You asleep?"

"Nope. Just tryin' not to make a mess in the bed by concentratin' on anything but your hot ass headin' toward the bathroom." Matt hopped up and took *his* very attractive, naked ass to the bathroom.

Tim pulled on jeans and an undershirt, contemplating what had happened the night before as a few revelations occurred to him. They were at the beginning of a physical relationship, and Tim was very excited about it.

He was grateful to Matt for not rushing things between them. It was Tim's first *official* relationship, and he wanted it to be more than just booty calls like he'd heard about from other guys.

From what Tim had observed since he started spending more time with Matt, the bull rider had the potential to step up and be a decent guy who was capable of commitment. Matt had been making hefty strides regarding the responsibilities resting on his broad shoulders, especially those involving Ryan.

Tim had seen a huge change in Matt since they'd begun spending time together, and subsequently, Ryan seemed more confident in his father as well. Tim had high hopes for all of them.

He could hear Matt in the bathroom brushing his teeth, so he plodded to the kitchen to make breakfast. In short order, he had sausages frying in a skillet with eggs on the counter to come to room temperature.

Tim found the toaster and some whole wheat bread in the cabinet, which surprised him. French toast was one possibility, but he didn't know if Matt liked it.

As he stood in the kitchen considering his options, muscular arms surrounded his waist as a kiss landed on the side of his neck. "What's got ya thinkin' so hard, babe?" Matt's lips against his ear were soft and enticing.

Tim didn't hesitate to sink into the large, tight body behind him, melting in the process. It felt incredible to be in Matt's muscular arms.

A kiss to Tim's neck and a little bite brought him back from fantasy land. "I was trying to decide if you'd like French toast or just maybe eggs and toast." Forming the words wasn't exactly easy.

"Can you do that thing they do at the diner where they cut out the center of the bread and crack an egg in it? It's one of my favorites." Matt continued to hold Tim and suck on his neck.

Tim pulled away for a second to turn in the cowboy's arms. "Over easy or over hard?"

Matt pushed his crotch forward and smiled. "Depends on what you're askin', baby. Always hard, but I like my eggs runny, unless they're scrambled. I like cheese in those."

Tim couldn't hold the laugh, and when he pinched Matt's nipple, the cowboy pulled away and grabbed Tim's hand. "Why'd ya do that?"

"Just checking out your tits. I wouldn't hate to give them a tongue bath, but now I've got to fix these eggs." Tim added a teasing whine to his voice.

Matt laughed. "Make anything ya want, Timmy. I wanna hear more about this tongue bath, and I have a suggestion for other places besides my tits, though I happen to have very sensitive nipples." Matt seemed to be proud of his nipples, which made Tim laugh.

At Matt's request, Tim made the man hens-in-a-nest, and when they finished eating, the couple went back to Matt's bathroom to shower. Tim licked, nibbled, and bit Matt's nipples under the gentle spray of the rain-style showerhead before he dropped to his knees to suck Matt's impressive cock into his mouth... another place he wanted to give a tongue bath.

After choking for a second, Tim remembered to breathe through his nose as he attempted to deep throat Matt's generous length. He took a second to remember how he'd done it with Kenny back in college, which had brought forth positive results.

Tim felt like a pro at it, and Matt didn't hesitate to agree... "*fuck, yes,*" "*oh, god... baby, yes,*" and Tim's favorite "*yessssss!*"

The bull rider emptied a substantial load into Tim's mouth. After swallowing it, Tim was pulled up and Matt kissed him silly, swirling his tongue around Tim's mouth enough to clean up any little swimmers he hadn't swallowed. Tim was pretty sure there weren't many left.

Much to Tim's surprise, Matt acquainted himself with Tim's cock, in the shower, on his knees with a soapy finger circling the blond's entrance. Tim nearly lost his mind.

After Matt achieved his goal of draining the life out of Tim, the pair exited the shower, drying off and dressing to go to the Collins' place to pick up Ryan. Tim, however, was worried. "You *did* tell your parents you're gay, right?"

Matt turned and grinned, taking Tim's hand and kissing it. "I told Momma. Dad... Well, she's gotta get him used to changes. Eventually, he gets there. I have no doubt there'll be no difference with this. I'm not worried, Timmy."

No worries? Was he fucking crazy?

Martin Collins was a great guy, according to Uncle Josh. Josh had told Tim he respected Marty and based on what Tim had witnessed in the time he'd been back at the Katy-did, he had every reason to believe Mr. Collins was, indeed, a great guy. However, Tim had no idea how the man might react to having a gay son.

Would Martin think Tim corrupted Matthew and hate him for it? That would never make for a good relationship between Tim and Matt's family, he was certain.

"Sweetheart, stop it. Dad's gonna be fine, I promise. It might take a little time, but he'll get there, or my momma will beat him to death with a rolling pin." Matt offered a tender smile. Tim wasn't as confident.

When they pulled up the driveway of Matt's parents' place, Tim was suddenly conscious of the fact he was doing a walk-of-shame in his *date* clothes. The shirt was wrinkled from where it had been tossed onto the floor the previous night when Matt undressed him.

Tim wasn't coherent enough to pick it up and hang it up at that point, and he was pretty sure Matt's parents would figure it out and be upset by his disheveled appearance. "Maybe I should wait in the truck?"

Matt hopped out and walked around the front of the truck to the passenger door. He pulled it open and un-buckled Tim's seatbelt, swinging the man's legs around to address him, face-to-face.

"*Now*, you know my momma loves ya, and Ryan would be pissed at me if he knew you were waitin' in the truck. Come inside, Timmy. The sooner we get this out in the open, the sooner they get used to it."

Matt pulled Tim out of the truck and took his hand, leading him to the front of the house. They walked up to the porch, and as Matt reached for the doorknob, he stopped and turned to Tim, leaning down to gently brush their lips together in a reassuring kiss.

Matt pulled back and winked, which made Tim smile. "You're as cute as a speckled pup." The bull rider was trying to put Tim at ease, and it made him laugh.

"And you're full of..."

Tim was ready to tease as the front door opened to reveal Ryan with a look of annoyance on his face. "It's 'bout time. I got things to do, ya know."

Matt swept Ryan into his arm and carried him like a football as he walked in through the door, his cowboy boots clunking on the hardwood floor. He turned to see if Tim was following him, motioning for the man to come inside.

Tim followed the two of them into the kitchen where Marty and Jerilyn Collins were having coffee. "Hey, boys. You want some coffee and a sweet roll? I made 'em this mornin'," Miss Jeri offered.

Tim heard Ryan groan, but he was following Matt's lead. "Well, Tim made breakfast, but I could have a roll."

He turned to Tim and smiled. "You want a sweet roll?" Tim wanted to fall through the floor at that very moment.

He saw Marty look at him with a curious expression. "How's that computer thingy goin'?" Marty asked.

Tim breathed a sigh of relief. On that subject, he could speak until he was blue in the face.

"It's good. I've got a program written to track the semen imported to the ranch and cows bred with it so we can trace the bloodlines. It's set to track sales of various breeds and the cost of feed to get the feeders Matt sells ready to go to market so he has an idea of how much he needs to get in order to claim a profit, plus it lets him know how much he needs on hand to feed the herd on any given day. When I finish it, it'll automatically notify the feed store when to come refill the grain silo. It also tracks the expenses for tax purposes, and then..." Ryan climbed into his lap and clamped his lips closed.

"We need to get home so I can do my homework. This stuff is borin'. Just eat, please." Tim laughed because as he glanced up, he could see the glazed look on the faces of Marty, Jeri, and even Matt.

"Sorry. Let's just say things are going well." Without further comment, he cut into a tasty-looking caramel roll.

"What was so important for Ryan to stay last night? He was up in arms about somebody named Mickey at the Katydid," Marty said.

Matt laughed. "He's a new hand Josh and Katie hired. He seems to know his way around horses, and I believe Josh knows a good hand when he sees one. I think he'll be a good addition to the farm."

"He likes Timmy," Ryan chimed in with a furrowed brow. Jeri laughed as she walked over to the table and refreshed the coffee.

"He does *not*. He was just asking questions, young man," Tim scolded. Ryan laughed as he leaned forward and kissed Tim's cheek. Hugging the boy's shoulders, Tim smiled because the kiss was appreciated.

Marty cleared his throat. "So, Matthew, your mother says you have something to talk to me about, but she won't say what it is. You care to enlighten me, son?"

Tim looked at Ryan, hoping the boy could offer cover to get away from the kitchen before all hell broke loose. "You have your stuff together? Should I help you?" Ryan hopped down with a big nod.

As Tim was about to rise from his chair and excuse himself, Matt grabbed his hand and pulled him back into the seat, turning to him with that damn smile. "You ain't goin' anywhere, Timmy."

Oh, Tim begged to differ with him, but suddenly Jeri was out of her chair, taking Ryan by the hand to lead him down the hallway. Tim looked at Matt, hoping he could see the pleading look on his face to not make him sit there when the bull rider came out to his very macho, very *hetero* father.

"Dad, let me start by sayin' I love ya, and I respect ya. You and Momma have been my support system all my life, and I can't tell ya how much I appreciate it. I know you love me, and you've accepted the decisions I've made in the past for my life without question because I know y'all only want me to be happy." He turned to Tim and smiled, which made the younger man want to slide under the table and seep into the kitchen tile.

Tim was praying his name wouldn't come up, but... "Dad, I'm in love with Timmy, and we're gonna try to make a life together, I hope," Matt blurted out quickly and nervously.

Tim prayed a UFO would show up in Virginia and start firing at the front yard to distract Matt's father because as he looked at Marty Collins, he was sure the man thought

Tim had corrupted his only son. He was certain the older man hated him.

Matt continued, "If I thought it was possible to have someone snap their fingers to turn me straight, I'd have welcomed it because it would have been so much easier to live that life, Dad. Unfortunately, that hasn't been the case. I've accepted the fact I'm a gay man in a business where my sexuality isn't understood, but I can't change myself. I'm the same guy I was when I walked in here and sat down, and I'm not gonna hide how much I love Tim, either. If people stop buyin' my stock, then it's a price I have to pay, but I ain't gonna live a lie anymore."

After hearing Matt's speech, Tim decided to man up and be supportive because the man he loved sounded so determined, and he was proud of the statement the cowboy had made.

Tim cleared his throat and looked at Marty Collins, hoping he was hiding the fear which engulfed him from head to toe. "Mr. Collins, sir, I love Matt and Ryan, and I only want the best for them. I know it's not anything you're used to, but I pray you'll remain open-minded and give us a chance to show you we're no different than any other couple."

When Matt turned the chair to gaze into his eyes, Tim felt like he'd once again gone to heaven. "I do, Matt. I love you so much, but I didn't want to scare you by telling you too soon. I've loved you for a while but I thought you were straight, so I didn't say anything. You and Ryan? You two are everything to me," Tim told Matt quietly, feeling like they were the only people on the whole planet.

Unfortunately, as Matt was leaning in to kiss him, they heard a throat clear and both pulled away. Surprisingly, Marty Collins had a big smile on his face. "I'm glad that shit's all sorted out. It'll make Christmas easier, and Matt, son, don't give up your day job and take up actin' anytime soon. You ain't good at it. When are you gonna explain things to Ryan?"

Tim was speechless, and when he looked at Matt, he could tell for a minute he was as well. Suddenly, the cowboy laughed, and when his father joined him, Tim was a little lost. They weren't beating on each other, though, so he couldn't help but be happy.

Jeri walked down the hallway with Ryan and a backpack. She smiled when she saw there was no bloodshed and the two of them were laughing. She walked over to Tim and kissed his cheek before she whispered, "Welcome to the family, Tim. I'm so happy I have you to look out for my boys. They need you more than Matthew knows."

Tim could only nod because it felt really good to be a member of the family... another family. Hell, he was giddy at the prospect of being a member of *two* families. He barely had one for so many years, it was such a great thing to hear he had another. He smiled throughout the rest of the visit. The acceptance of Matt's parents left Tim riding a high, for lack of a better word. It was amazing.

Chapter Eleven

"So, how long you been with Matt?" Tim was helping Mickey clean stalls at the Katydid. He was coming to like Mickey, thrilled that Uncle Josh had hired the cowboy after he spoke to Mr. Kessler in Kentucky and received a glowing recommendation.

In the spirit of being overly cautious, Tim had run a background check on the nomadic cowboy too, but he'd asked the guy's permission first, so he didn't feel like he was being underhanded about it. Mickey had agreed with an easy, lopsided grin, saying he understood how careful ranchers had to be in this day and age.

Not surprisingly, Aunt Katie had insisted Mickey take the bedroom next to Tim's because she felt bad for him not having a family of his own. Tim wanted to laugh when she explained herself. He'd known the guy wouldn't be *camping* in that beat-up truck as Mickey had suggested when he'd first arrived at the farm.

"Not too long. I came home when I finished college, and that's when I met Matt." Tim stepped out of a stall and dumped the dirty sawdust into the wagon parked in the barn hallway.

Uncle Josh was predictable in the way he trained hands at the Katydid. Everyone started at the bottom—cleaning horse shit from the barn—all the while learning how to calculate the amount of straw and sawdust needed for the bedding, along with hay and feed for the horses boarded there.

It wasn't easy work, but it was easily learned. Tim still helped out when he could in the morning before he went to the Circle C to continue the work he was doing there. His life was coasting along, and for the most part, he supposed it was pretty damn good. Well, on certain days, it was *really* damn good.

"So, you must make a lot of money between the two jobs." Tim gave Mickey a quick explanation of the work he did at the Circle C for Matt along with his job for Uncle Josh. Of course, he laughed at the absurdity of Mickey's statement regarding his net worth. In the words of his mother, Tim didn't have a pot to piss in, nor a window to throw it out.

Tim surmised the young cowboy was inquisitive and trying to learn the dynamics at the Katydid. He wasn't malicious with his inquiries, but Tim sensed there was something else behind his questions that day.

"Here, I work for room and board. At the Circle C, I haven't exactly figured out any kind of salary because Matt's my boyfriend." Tim's explanation made him sound like a sucker but explaining his financial situation to Mickey—especially when Tim hadn't figured it out himself—wasn't exactly on his agenda that day.

Mickey seemed to consider Tim's comments for a moment before he spoke. "Well, he sure has a sweet deal, if you ask me. I mean, you're workin' your ass off to fix him up with a first-rate operation, and he doesn't pay you anything? On top of that, he gets to fuck ya too? Damn, that's a nice setup... or so it sounds from Matt's place at the table."

At Mickey's comment, Tim felt even more as though he needed to defend himself. Mickey's assessment of the situation somewhat chapped his ass.

"It's not like that, Mickey. Matt and I are in a relationship, and I'm trying to help him reach the level of success he deserves. Hell, he earned it before I came along, but now that I'm in his life, I'm gonna do everything I can to help him make the most of his operation because I have a stake in the game, okay? It's really none of your business. When are you bringing *your* boyfriend up?"

Guilt swamped Tim as he shifted the subject matter to Mickey's life. It didn't seem right to discuss something with a stranger that he was yet to discuss with Matt.

When Mickey slammed the pitchfork into the wooden wall of the stall where Josie resided, Tim jumped as if he'd been shot at. It sent the jenny into a startled fit at the shock of the sound.

"What the fuck, man?"

Mickey picked up the pitchfork, propping it against the wall before he turned to Tim. "I called him last night... The night before... The night before that... And the night before *that*. He's not answering, so I guess he couldn't wait for me to find a place for us. I'm sorry I'm a prick. I loved Jackie so much, but I guess I was the only one in love."

Tim understood the man's behavior. He was doubting his partner, and that had to be a damn hard pill to swallow. Tim started to answer, but Mickey held up his finger.

"Make sure it's not that way for you, Tim. It happens too fast in a relationship—one minute they love ya, and the next, they're gone without a fucking word." Mickey quietly pushed the wheelbarrow out the back door of the barn to the manure spreader, loading it to spread later that afternoon.

Tim started spreading new bedding around the stall so they could bring Ruby inside. He felt bad for Mickey because it was a shit place to be, losing someone you loved because they lost faith in you too quickly.

Fortunately, Tim didn't have the frame of reference to understand the man's position, and he prayed to God he never would. He could, however, empathize with Mickey's obvious pain.

Tim hoped Mickey would find a new guy to be happy with in the near future. Nobody should walk through life alone.

On the Tuesday before Thanksgiving, things were bustling around the Katydid. It had been unseasonably warm in southern Virginia, but as everyone knew, the weather could turn on a dime.

The inhabitants of the farm needed to be ready to provide a warm place for the horses, especially the mares who were set to foal in the spring, at a moment's notice. Everyone pitched in to ensure they were ready for the unpredictability that could suddenly occur.

Tim had been scrubbing the oiled canvas stable blankets they used on the horses in preparation for when the weather turned. He was wet and felt disgusting from the sweat he'd worked up, so after he had them spread on the fence that enclosed the round pen outside so they could dry, he walked up to the house and straight to his room.

Grabbing his cell from the dresser, Tim called Matt, who answered on the second ring. "Hey, whiz kid. You done with chores?"

Tim exhaled a troubled breath. "You love me?"

The need to get reassurance from the bull rider that he felt the same way was coursing through Tim for reasons he couldn't pinpoint. He guessed it was because he'd been watching Mickey moping around the farm for the last few weeks after he told Tim about his breakup, and Tim guessed seeing how heartbroken the cowboy appeared to be had taken a toll on his confidence in his own relationship with Matt.

Mickey had been so certain of Jackie's love when he first arrived at the farm, it was hard to watch the poor guy fall apart when it ended. It didn't help that Tim had been so busy at the Katydid and wasn't spending as much time with Matt and Ryan.

Matt had more help at his ranch than Uncle Josh did at the farm, so Tim had been working more from the Katydid as was needed. He missed seeing Matt during the day as he'd become accustomed when he worked at the Circle C.

Matt hummed in response and Tim grinned. He'd learned the big bull rider made the noise when he was trying to figure out the right thing to say because, as Tim came to know, Matt was as much a newbie at a romantic relationship as him, regardless of the fact Matt had been married to that '*wretched woman*,' as Tim called her in his head.

"Hell yeah, I do. Why don't you pack your shit, Timmy? Move here with Ryan and me. I know you love your aunt and uncle, but we need you here with us because you're a part of *our* family, too. I love you more than I've ever loved anyone other than my son," Matt whispered over the phone.

Tim took a breath and exhaled as a sense of relief encompassed him. It was everything he needed to hear. "I'll be over after I get cleaned up, and we'll talk about it, okay? I don't want Ryan to think I'm... I don't know how we explain *us* to him, Matt. I wanna be with you so much, but I don't want to traumatize the boy. He's so damn great." The lump in Tim's throat proved to him he was all in with Matt, and Ryan was a fantastic addition.

When Matt laughed, it caught Tim by surprise. "Aw, now darlin', the boy ain't stupid. Just come over. We'll all talk about it, and I'm pretty sure he'll explain it to *us*."

An hour later, Tim drove up the driveway of the Circle C and parked next to Matt's large truck. He hopped out of his red work truck, walking to the front of the house and ringing the bell. When Ryan opened the door, he greeted Tim with a bright smile on his cute face.

It reminded Tim that he wanted to ask Miss Jeri to show him pictures of Matt when he was a little boy. "You got a key, don'tcha? You're movin' in, or so Daddy told me. Why the heck would ya ring the bell?"

Tim picked Ryan up and tossed the boy over his shoulder as they headed into the house, both laughing. "*SHHH!*" Tim turned to see Matt on the phone in the living room, so the two of them stopped talking.

He carried Ryan into the kitchen, placing the boy on the counter. "Can I have a soda? Daddy said there's beer in there." Tim glanced into the living room, seeing the big cowboy nod as he headed down the hallway toward the bedroom.

Tim retrieved two beers before he picked up a can of root beer to open for Ryan. He poured it into a glass, contemplating the fact the young boy seemed completely unaffected by the prospect of Tim moving in. He sat down on a stool at the counter next to the little cowboy, watching as Matt returned and paced around the family room uttering only "*uh-huhs.*"

When the bull rider looked at Tim, the exasperation was evident. Tim took a deep breath because he really had no idea what was to come, but in his heart, he knew he'd be there for Matt, regardless of the circumstances. He loved the man, after all.

"Who's he talking to?"

Ryan responded between sips of his soda. "Somebody named Janelle Rowland. I can't figure out what the hell they're talkin' 'bout." Tim hid the smirk at the boy's slip.

"Now, let's watch the language. Your grandma would have a cow if she heard it." Matt walked down the hallway toward his office again, slamming the door. Trying to avert the boy's attention, Tim asked, "You eat anything?"

Ryan was enthusiastic with his response. "Daddy pulled out some hamburgers Gramma Jeri put in the freezer. I know how to start the grill."

Tim hauled Ryan off the counter to follow him outside to the deck, beer bottle and glass of soda in hand. He noticed a new gas grill in the corner, so he followed Ryan over to it where the little boy pointed to the handle that turned on the gas.

After they had the grill settled to heat up so they could cook the burgers, Tim turned to Ryan. "So, you want me to move in? Why?"

Ryan studied him for a few moments before he answered. The boy sat down in one of the chairs set around a black iron and glass table, smiling at Tim. "You make my daddy happy, Timmy. He talks about you all the time when you're not around, and if you lived here, maybe he'd talk about other stuff."

"Like what stuff?" Tim was trying like hell to hold the laugh at the boy's comment, and his curiosity got the best of him. He was fascinated with the way the boy's mind worked.

"Like when Josie can come live here." Tim loved the sly look on Ryan's face.

The boy's father often had the same damn look on his face when he'd shove his hand down the back of Tim's jeans as the couple was making out somewhere. The two Collins men were always scheming, as Tim was learning.

"Now, why would Josie want to come live here?"

Ryan giggled a little. "'Cause I'll love her like my daddy loves you. He told me you make his heart happy, so I figure since Josie makes my heart happy, she should come live here, too."

Tim had to give it to the boy—he had a pretty good command of making an argument for his cause, but knowing the little jenny was a Christmas gift, Tim felt the need to deflate the expectations a little to compound the upcoming surprise.

"Well, I don't think Uncle Josh is ready for Josie to leave the Katydid quite yet. He likes having her around. Maybe in the spring, we can borrow her for a little while? I'll take you over to the farm to ride anytime you want, okay?"

Before Ryan could respond, Matt came out onto the deck with a frustrated look on his face. "I started the grill." Tim watched Matt drain his beer.

Matt took a deep breath and exhaled. He stood with his eyes closed for a minute, finally opening them to gaze at Tim with a tender smile.

"Thanks, babe." He turned to Ryan and walked over to the table, picking up the boy and placing him in his lap.

"That lady I was talkin' to was a lawyer. Your Nana Mona wants you to come live with her. Your mom moved to Canada with some guy named Vic. You ever meet him?"

Tim didn't like the direction the conversation was heading because it sounded like maybe the grandmother was going to fight Matt for custody. If that happened, would having Tim in their lives be detrimental to any legal action the woman might bring?

Tim was well aware of that shit from a friend of his late mother's back in New Jersey. Custody issues were a brutal mess. Nobody came out a winner.

Tim saw the expression on Ryan's face, and it wasn't happiness. "He's mean. When he stayed at the 'partment, they locked the door to Momma's room, and I had to be quiet and not make any noise. I couldn't even watch cartoons. Nana doesn't like havin' kids around, Momma told me, so we couldn't go to her house. I don't wanna see her, Daddy." The little cowboy laid his head against Matt's chest, crocodile tears gliding down his cheeks, which broke Tim's heart.

Tim stared out into the yard, knowing there was only one right thing to do. "Okay, so let's table any discussion of me moving in for the time being, and let's get some dinner going. I'll search around and find a lawyer—the best one I can because I won't let anyone take you away from your daddy. I have some friends from college who were the kids of lawyers, so I'll start looking there." Tim's appetite diminished at the mere thought of Ryan being taken away from a father who loved him. That was unacceptable in Tim's mind.

Matt kissed the top of Ryan's head and looked at Tim with that lopsided grin. "Timmy, I've got a lawyer outta Richmond. He represented me during the divorce, and he knows all the ins and outs of the situation. I'll call him tomorrow. Now, we ain't gonna let Mona stop you from movin' in with us, are we little man?"

Ryan appeared resigned. "Nope. You belong here, just like Josie."

Tim started laughing at Ryan's relentlessness, feeling the tension leave his body. The boy was certainly entertaining, especially when he was on a mission. "Nice try, kiddo. Let's get the burgers for your dad to grill while you and I make something else to go with 'em."

Tim finished his beer and rose from his seat. Ryan kissed Matt's cheek and hopped down, grabbing his soda cup to follow Tim inside.

Tim quickly returned with the burgers after he set Ryan to tearing lettuce for a salad. When Tim walked out to the deck, Matt was scrubbing the grill with a wire brush, totally lost in thought.

"You okay?" Tim whispered as he walked up behind Matt after putting the plate of burgers on the nearby table.

Tim wrapped his arms around the bull rider's waist and held him tightly, just absorbing the feel of Matt's muscular body. Holding the man felt so good, Tim hated the thoughts racing through his mind. He truly didn't want to give up the Collins' men, but he would if it was going to cause a problem with the custody of Matt's son. Tim loved Ryan too much to see him jerked away from the father he only just got back.

Matt's large hand clasped over his own, resting on the cowboy's hard abs. "I had a thought about how to diffuse the Mona situation. I really don't think she wants Ryan because she loves him, but I can't say that in front of him. That's his grandma. My gut tells me this is money."

Matt closed the lid on the grill and turned in Tim's arms, resting his forearms on Tim's shoulders and leaning forward to kiss Tim's forehead, nose, and finally, lips. It was like the breath of life had been breathed into Tim.

Pulling Matt closer, Tim tightened his grip on the man to enjoy the closeness while he could. Letting both of them go would kill Tim, but it wasn't really about him. It was about the little cowboy in the kitchen making a salad. It was all about Ryan Earl Collins and the father who loved him.

Chapter Twelve

"Where's our book?" It was later that night as Tim sat on the side of Ryan's bed.

Since he'd started spending more time at the Circle C, Tim and Ryan had gotten into the habit of the boy reading to Tim before bed. Ryan had little problem with reading multisyllabic words because he'd sound them out, much to Tim's surprise, but sometimes he had to explain the meanings because they were reading mystery chapter books for adolescents.

Ryan had an incredible imagination when it came to the stories the pair read, and they made a habit of only reading one chapter on school nights so they could talk about them a little before it was time for Ryan to go to sleep. For Tim, it was wonderful. It was like they had their own private book club.

"Can we just talk tonight? I have some questions I don't wanna ask Daddy, but I know *you'll* tell me the truth, Timmy. We're friends, right?" Ryan's face was so sincere, how could Tim say no. They were friends and more, in Tim's mind.

"You and Daddy kiss like Gramma and Papa, right? Is it okay for boys to kiss boys?"

Damn! I never saw that coming. The two men had thought they were being discreet, but apparently, they were only fooling themselves because they sure weren't fooling Ryan!

Tim squeezed Ryan's leg as he stood from the bed to step into the hallway. "*Matthew!*"

Tim waited a second before hearing the squeak of the desk chair which meant Matt was coming to Ryan's room from his office. Tim stepped back inside and sat in his usual spot. "When did you see your dad and me kiss?"

"I see'd it the night we went to Mexican. I woke up when we was at the Katydid and you two were on the front porch smoochy-smoochy. When I asked Papa 'bout it, he laughed and said to ask Daddy. Then, I saw ya smoochin' and huggin' in the barn a bunch a times. I wasn't sneakin' around... honest." Ryan fidgeted with his hands, looking very nervous.

Tim smiled and placed his hands atop Ryans' hoping to reassure him it was fine that he had questions. "You didn't do anything wrong, Ryan. We should have paid better attention to who was around. So, um, you know how you have friends at school? Tommy Morrow?"

Ryan nodded in agreement, so Tim continued. "Well, your dad and I are friends, but we're *special* friends who like to hug and kiss sometimes. Um, there are men and women who are special friends, and there are women and women who are special friends, and there are men and men who are special friends. My Aunt Katie and Uncle Josh were special friends a long time ago, and they decided they loved each other enough to get married and be together for the rest of their lives." Tim was sure he was making a horrible mess of the whole thing.

Matt's soft footfalls alerted Tim to his presence before the man's large hand landed on Tim's shoulder as Matt sat behind him. "What's the topic of discussion tonight?" Matt rested his other hand on Ryan's blanket-covered leg.

"We're talking about *special* friends. You know, like you and me. Ryan asked about us kissing. Apparently, we're not as crafty as we thought." Tim glanced over his shoulder with a raised eyebrow, smirking at the surprise on Matt's face at having been caught.

After a second, Matt leaned forward and kissed Tim's cheek, pulling away with a huge grin before turning to his son. "Does it bother you that Tim and I are special friends?"

The boy sat up and leaned forward to whisper. "Does that mean you're fags?" Tim felt his stomach drop to his feet at the mention of the word.

Matt's body tensed at hearing the ugly word, one Tim had heard too many times in his life. Matt started to move away, but Tim grabbed the hand that was resting on his shoulder and held it to keep Matt where he sat.

"Ryan, where'd you hear that word?" Tim approached the matter gently, knowing the boy had no idea how disgusting and painful the term was.

Based on Ryan's expression, he'd figured out quickly the word wasn't a term of endearment. Tim was pretty sure Ryan had no idea why...*exactly*. "It's a bad word, isn't it?" the sweet boy whispered.

Tim squeezed Matt's hand again and turned to him. "We can let it go and wait it out if you're not sure about us.

If you are, then we owe him the explanation. Why don't you get us some water and think about it?"

With all the shit Matt was facing regarding a custody fight with Mona, it was his right to keep Ryan in the dark about his sexuality. The boy had turned seven in the summer, and Matt had said he thought Ryan was still too young to explain the facts of life to him.

That was why Tim had tried to offer a vague explanation regarding the kissing. He wasn't sure, but Tim thought maybe it was better to give Ryan more information than it was to try to shield him from the truth.

Matt cleared his throat and reached for Ryan's busy hands to still them again. "It's not a cuss word, bud. It's a mean word ugly people use to talk about stuff they don't understand. See, I love Timmy like Papa Marty loves Gramma Jeri. When I see him come into the house, or the office, or even the barn, it makes my heart happy like we talked about before, which is why I kiss him. I want him to live here with us, and if he ever agrees, he'll sleep in my room with me, not in the guest room where Gramma sleeps when she stays over sometimes."

Ryan lay back down, though Tim could tell he was still listening. Thankfully, Matt continued.

"Love is different for everybody. Sometimes, boys love boys or girls love girls, but that don't make it wrong, okay?

It just makes it different, which isn't a bad thing. Not everybody agrees it's okay, which is why people use words like fag or faggot. It's not nice to use those words because you could hurt someone's feelings if you say them, and I know you'd never do that on purpose."

Tim believed the explanation was eloquent, and in that moment, he couldn't have loved the bull rider more. His heart was ready to explode with all the love inside it for Matthew Collins.

"You mean like when Brian James said Momma was a slut that time?"

Tim was stunned by Ryan's comment, but when he looked at Matt, the man winked. "Exactly. Brian James heard that from his Uncle Keith because your momma used to date him when she was in high school before we met. It was a mean thing for Brian to say, but I guess when Keith and your momma broke up, Keith might have been mad and called your momma names. You know how mean kids can be when they're mad? Well, adults can be even worse." Matt patted the boy's leg and gave it a little squeeze.

When Ryan yawned, Tim leaned forward to kiss his forehead. "I'm gonna go clean up the dinner dishes. You and Daddy snuggle a little while. I'll see *you* on Thursday, bud."

The Collins and Simmons families were planning to have Thanksgiving dinner together at the Katydid. Aunt Katie had insisted she should host since Katydid had a bigger kitchen and dining room, so she and Jeri had agreed to cook together and invite all the ranch and farm hands who had nowhere else to go. Tim volunteered to help, and he was looking forward to learning from the masters.

"I love you, Timmy."

A lump formed in Tim's throat at the boy's words, but he swallowed it down, not wanting to embarrass either of them.

He gave the boy a broad grin. "I love you, too, kiddo. We're partners in crime, remember? We'll go for a ride at the farm on Thursday afternoon while the turkey's cooking." Ryan returned Tim's smile and nodded before Tim left the room.

After he finished loading the dishwasher, the fridge door opened behind him. "Beer?"

Tim closed the dishwasher and turned to look at his man before he dried his hands. Matt's very attractive ass was sticking out as he bent over to grab the bottles.

"Naw, babe. I need to get home. Was he okay?" Tim tilted his head toward the hallway where Ryan's room was located.

Matt chuckled as he took a seat in a kitchen chair, putting the beer on the table as he reached for Tim. He pulled him closer and lifted him onto the table in front of him. "He asked if we were gonna get married like Mom and Dad, and he asked if we could get a dog when you lived here because he thought you'd like company in the office when you're workin'. He's a conniver, I'll tell ya."

Tim couldn't hold the giggle when he put his hands over Matt's larger ones resting on his thighs. Matt moved his chair closer to Tim, his eyes not leaving Tim's face. "He's a very intelligent little man, Matt. He's like seven going on twenty-seven."

Matt laughed as well before he pulled Tim to straddle his lap, surprising the younger man. "Now, that's better. So, you're movin' in when? I really want you and Chester to be settled before Christmas so when we bring Josie over, she'll have familiar comp'ny. Josh has that new Appaloosa stallion, Chief. He's that small, gaited horse. I think that'd be a cute foal if we bred Josie to him."

Chief was a six-year-old stallion Uncle Josh took as a trade for a mare, Pegasus, that one of the boarders had given him. They couldn't afford the board because the husband lost his job, so they gave Josh the mare in lieu of payment.

Uncle Josh had found the little stud horse on the internet and liked his lines, so he negotiated a trade with the seller in West Virginia. The smaller horse had plenty of get-up-and-go, as Uncle Josh had told him when he bought the stallion home.

When Josh and Katie went to pick up the horse, they stayed an extra day to go to the casino and horse races in Charlestown. They had a good time and suggested Matt and Tim might want to try it sometime.

"Yeah, well, maybe we let Ryan have his time to ride her before you get her knocked up with a family." Tim was teasing, which brought a fantastic laugh from Matt before he brushed his lips over Tim's, reminding him why he was ass-over-appetite in love with Matthew Collins.

Tim wrapped his arms around Matt's neck and threaded his fingers in the man's dark, silky hair. Matt's hands were resting on Tim's ass, kneading his cheeks like they were sourdough. It felt good, and once again, Tim wanted to throw himself at the bull rider and take him to bed, but then the other shit crept in regarding Matt's mother-in-law and her desire to upset a happy family.

He pulled away and stared into those stunningly beautiful, blue eyes of Matt's. "I love you, Matthew, but I think, maybe, we should slow things down until you deal with the issue of Mona. You can't give her any reason to challenge your custody of Ryan. I'm afraid, with the political climate here in Virginia, a relationship between the two of us would be like a gift from the gods for her case if she got the right judge."

Tim whispered the words because saying them in a regular voice made it too real. Feeling the bull rider's arms around him was like a dream Tim didn't want to wake from.

Matt smirked and pulled Tim closer, rubbing their hard cocks together through their clothes. "I'm not gonna let that crazy bitch come between us, Timmy. I'll handle her, you got my word on that. I won't push you into stayin' tonight, but I want you here this weekend, please? I thought maybe we could take a ride up to DC and show Ryan the sights. It's supposed to be a nice weekend, and I got us a room at a little hotel in Arlington, not far from the Metro. What do you think? We can go up on Saturday morning and spend the night. You game?"

How could Tim say no to such a wonderful invitation? "Sounds perfect." He leaned forward and kissed Matt again as the man wrapped his arms around Tim tightly. The embrace was orgasm inducing.

Tim was certain of the decision as if a neon light were hanging over Matt's head. "Take me to bed and make love to me."

Tim knew it was a big deal to both of them because it meant a commitment Tim had been hesitant to give... but he couldn't deny how much he loved Matt, and he was more than ready to show him.

Giving himself to Matt Collins seemed to be the perfect way to show the universe how happy he was that the man had come into his life... even if it was only that one time.

If Tim believed in all the negative signs flashing in front of him, it was as though the fates were conspiring against them on a daily basis—the latest being Mona's interest in gaining custody of Ryan. *Things have been going too smoothly. It was bound to happen that everything would catch up and eventually implode."* Tim cringed at the thought.

In his opinion, giving Matt his virginity seemed like a fitting send-off. He doubted he'd love again, but while he had the man's love, he was going to embrace it.

Chapter Thirteen

Tim was sitting in the office at Katydid Farm the next morning, squirming a little when Mickey Warren walked in with the tally sheet from the white board in the barn, giving the count for hay and grain to go into the inventory system.

He gave Tim a smirk and sniffed around the office, then he moved closer to Tim, sniffing like crazy. "What the fuck are you doing?" Tim's face heated up, embarrassed for no reason at all.

With the most serious look Tim had ever seen, Mickey leaned over the desk and held his hand under Tim's chin, forcing him to look into the cowboy's eyes. "Aww, I'm right. You smell different cause you're not a virgin anymore."

Tim was mortified and slapped the hand away. The only question: How the fuck could Mickey tell? It had only happened the night before...

Tim pulled away and looked into Matt's eyes, certain of his decision. "Take me to bed and make love to me."

"Are you sure, Timmy? I can wait, I swear. I don't—I won't rush you." Matt whispered against his collarbone where his tongue was getting acquainted with Tim's body after he pulled off the younger man's T-shirt. All the while, Tim was losing his fucking mind.

"God, yessss!" Tim hissed his consent, doubling as commentary on how wonderful Matt's mouth felt on his skin.

Matt stood and pulled Tim up his body, bracing his hands under the younger man's ass as the bull rider carried him down the hallway and up the stairs to the bedroom. It wasn't the first time Tim had been in that room, but it was the first time the two had planned to make love. They'd fingered and sucked each other, but they had yet to take the biggest step forward, physically.

Tim was nervous, but as Matt held him in his arms before he put him on the bed, Tim knew he was in good hands... literally and figuratively... especially when the man took off Tim's jeans and briefs.

Feeling Matt's touch on his naked skin was unbelievable. The man's tongue explored every inch of Tim's chest, nipping and sucking his nipples to hard peaks while further down his body, the cowboy's fingers found their way to his entrance. A large, calloused finger circled the sensitive skin, and he gasped for a second until that large finger breached the ring of muscle.

The bull rider seemed set on loosening him up so his body could accommodate that hefty cock. Tim was a little worried about the size because he'd had it in his mouth more than once, but in his heart, he knew if he asked Matt to stop, he would in an instant.

Tim truly wanted to feel the man inside him. To test the waters, Tim shoved four fingers up his own ass while jacking off after he measured Matt's cock while sucking him. It might be uncomfortable at first, but Tim knew his body would stretch to accept the girth, and he was hungry for it.

"Please, Matty, now. I need to feel you inside me, baby." Tim was breathless as he reached for a condom. He opened it with his teeth and pushed Matt onto his back.

They'd been kissing as if the world might end, so when Tim put the condom in his mouth, he saw Matt look at him like he'd lost his mind. Tim had seen the move in a porn video, and he was trying to be sexy. He was pretty sure he wasn't making the grade, but he was definitely giving it his all.

When he bent forward and pushed the condom over Matt's cock with his mouth, unrolling it with his lips, Tim glanced up through his lashes at Matt, seeing welcome surprise.

He was smugly satisfied. It was another notch to help build his confidence, and he was also relieved. He wanted to be the man to satisfy Matthew Collins in bed, so he'd need all of the confidence he could muster.

After Matt was encased in latex, Tim lubed him up and moved up the man's body, such that his thick cock was lined up with Tim's tingling channel. He took a deep breath and held Matt's dick where he needed him, slowly beginning the process of losing his virginity. It would be a moment that stuck with Tim for the rest of his fucking life.

"Oh, fuck, that feels so good, baby. You're grippin' me so fuckin' tight." Tim slowly sank onto Matt's hard cock after easing off and inching his way down the ample member again.

There was a bit of a burn, but it wasn't exactly uncomfortable in the beginning. When Matt wrapped a slick hand around Tim's protruding dick as it rested on the bull rider's tight abs, Tim was fucking lost to the sensation.

Tim had never figured he'd enjoy a little pain with his pleasure. It was like he was floating above himself with all the sensations Matt was bringing forth in his body and mind.

They got into a good rhythm of moving together as Matt jacked him, but when Tim's body was nearly pushed over the edge, he stopped Matt's hand and moved it above the man's head as he leaned forward and kissed him softly. "You okay?"

"Oh, baby, I'm so far beyond okay I can barely breathe. Can I flip us now? I love you bein' on top of me but I wanna feel your legs wrapped around my waist. I love the feel of your body on me, but I want to be closer." Matt's whispered response brought gooseflesh to Tim's skin.

After Tim was on his back with Matt seated deep inside him, the bull rider made slow work of showing Tim how good he could make him feel. Tim had only imagined it would be so life-altering, but as the sensation of Matt inside him elevated his soul out of his body, Tim knew for certain he'd be changed.

He dozed with his head resting on Matt's right bicep after a soul-shattering orgasm, and Tim knew the way he'd viewed love and commitment would never be the same. He'd heard one never forgot their firsts... first kiss... first lover... first relationship. He was sure it was true, but he prayed Matthew Collins would not only be his first, but also his last and his everyone in between. Clearly, he fell in love like a penguin... forever.

SNAP! SNAP!

As the beautiful fog cleared, Tim glanced up to see Mickey with a huge, shit-eating grin on his face. "Ah, relivin' the magic, I suspect. Well, good on you. I hope he was gentle." The cowboy's words were actually touching.

Before Tim could ask how the hell Mickey knew he'd been a virgin and that he and Matt had had sex the night before, the office door opened. Hank walked in with a petite blonde woman behind him. She looked at Mickey and shot him a sexy smile, which he returned with a wink and a smirk.

"Tim, this is Rhonda Turnberry. She's here to see you." Hank moved aside for the woman to step forward and extend her hand to Tim. Hank glanced down at the woman's ass before giving an approving nod.

Tim did everything he could to hold the laugh because he'd met Patsy Sachs, Hank's wife. If she got wind of that gesture, she'd have Hank's nuts in a vise in two seconds, flat.

"Ronni, please."

Tim rose to shake her hand, not sure at all what she was doing at the farm or what she wanted with him. She was dressed in a tan pantsuit with an ivory silk blouse under the jacket, so she definitely wasn't there about boarding or buying a horse.

"Timothy Moran. How can I help you?"

Mickey tipped his cowboy hat as he walked toward the door of the office, Hank on his trail. They closed the door and left him with the woman...alone.

"Do you mind?" She pointed to the old, rickety oak chair in front of the desk.

"I'm sorry. Please make yourself at home." Tim extended his hand for her to take a seat. Once she was settled, she placed a briefcase on her lap, opening it and pulling out a stack of papers.

"You're a hard guy to track down, Mr. Moran." The woman gave Tim a smile that was non-threatening. She didn't seem to be combative, so he wasn't overly concerned about the visit.

"I wasn't aware anyone was looking for me."

"I work for Clauson Associates in Philadelphia. Your paternal grandmother, Joanne Moran, was a client of ours.

We've been managing your trust since her death. You turned twenty-three on May 3, correct?" The woman already knew the answer.

If it had anything to do with his grandmother, Tim was pretty sure it was bad news. "I did. What's this about? She didn't like my father, and she liked me even less. I can't imagine she'd leave me anything more than a chunk of coal." Just then, his phone chimed with a text from Matt.

The young woman, who he was guessing was about thirty-years-old, smiled at him and studied the papers in front of her for a moment. She looked up, staring into Tim's hazel eyes.

"Your grandmother wasn't the easiest client we've had, to be sure. Richard Clauson was her lead attorney and managed all her business ventures until she died. Along the way, they became personal friends, but he moaned about dealing with her every time she came into the office."

Tim chuckled. No doubt the man complained. The woman was a pain in the ass.

The woman continued. "Richard knew what happened with your father, and he worked very hard to keep Joanne's name out of the press during the inquest because your grandmother was a woman of means. She was extremely disappointed by the choices your father made, including his marriage to your mother, but you are her blood relative and she respected familial ties more than family relationships. These papers are a list of her assets; the investments made on behalf of the trust over the years; and an accounting of the expenses associated with the administration of the estate, including the fees our firm has collected acting as trustee."

Tim wasn't sure why the woman was sitting in front of him with a notebook while saying the words *blood relative.* "I'm sorry. I'm completely confused. Did you say a trust?"

"Yes, Mr. Moran. She insisted a trust be established to manage the inheritance until your thirtieth birthday. When you enrolled at Penn State after your mother's death, she revised the trust documents so the proceeds could be turned over to you on your twenty-third birthday. We lost track of you after graduation, unfortunately." Tim was more confused with every word.

The first thing that popped into his head came out of his mouth. "Look, I don't have a lot of money. I work here for my uncle and aunt, part-time. I work at another ranch in the area part-time as well. If there are fees associated with this mess, just keep whatever there is left by the old woman. I don't have the time nor the inclination..."

The young woman turned the folder to face him and pointed to a line at the bottom of the page, stopping Tim's ramblings dead in their tracks. He flipped through the pages, trying to understand what the hell he was seeing.

There were a lot of properties listed around Pittsburgh and Philadelphia, including the house where he and his mother, Sherry, had lived when they resided in New Jersey before his father hunted them down. "What are these? Houses?" His confusion was evident in his voice.

The young attorney cleared her throat. "Your grandparents were pioneers in the house-flipping business in Pennsylvania. They bought up deteriorating properties around Pittsburgh and Philadelphia, including ten multi-family dwellings, and they remodeled them, earning more in rental fees than the houses had been worth prior to the purchase.

"The only good thing your grandmother did after your grandfather died was to freeze the rents in those apartment buildings. She made certain that as the tenants aged, they were still able to afford their residences so as not to have them displaced."

"Imagine that. I didn't think she did anything nice for anyone." Tim had a hard time believing what he was hearing.

"She held all the properties and banked the rents since they were free and clear of mortgages. When your parents split up, she bought the house your mother rented and lowered the rent to a sustainable level in order for the two of you to have a roof over your heads."

Tim remembered his mother questioning the management company about the notice that the rent had been cut in half. She'd even dragged him to a church in the neighborhood one night so they could thank God for the blessing. He wondered what Sherry would have said if she'd known it was thanks to Joanne.

"As far as we've been able to ascertain, your mother never knew your grandmother owned the property. After the murder and your relocation, Joanne had the house boarded up, but she held the property. She wanted you to do with the house as you saw fit, but she recommended tearing it down and building some sort of a community garden or a park in dedication to your mother." The idea brought tears to Tim's eyes.

None of it made sense to Tim because none of it sounded like the grandmother he vaguely remembered. Somewhere in the paperwork, there had to be a clerical error. The lawyer was obviously looking for someone else, though the facts she'd recited, chapter and verse, fit the history he remembered of his family.

"Look, Ms. Turnberry, I'm not sure if someone put you up to this to pull a prank on me, or if you've confused me with someone else, but Joanne Moran disowned me when she found out I'm gay. I'm sure if you dig a little deeper into the records, there's paperwork filed somewhere stating she revoked this trust and changed her will, or whatever you call it. It's probably on file with another attorney somewhere because she wanted nothing to do with me, which is why I didn't go to the funeral." Tim tried very hard not to become upset. Joanne Moran wasn't worth it.

The attorney smiled again. "Look, Mr. Moran, I dealt with Joanne one time as a second-year associate. She was horribly nasty, but she was clear in her wishes. You are the sole heir to her estate. The only expenses charged against it were her funeral, our fees, and the continued maintenance and insurance of the properties in her portfolio.

"Her personal home in Philadelphia was left to the Episcopal church where she was a member. They're using it as a space for an after-school and youth program for neighborhood children. She established a trust to fund the program from the sale of her personal effects. The church named it "Moran House" in honor of Joanne.

"Anyway, the bottom line is you own approximately twelve, single-family, and ten, multi-family properties in Philly, Pittsburgh, and Trenton. The trust is currently valued at $5.5 million dollars. The annual tax burden is..." She leaned over the desk and pointed to lines on the documents. Unfortunately, Tim didn't hear a word of her analysis. It was all too much to take in.

Later that afternoon, Tim was in the office of Matt Collin's home at the Circle C, working on updating the ranch's website with new information regarding recent sales of stock. The links on the various websites he'd constructed to correspond with the ranch site would update at midnight, so he was rushing to finish the project.

In all honesty, Tim was trying to block out the crap from earlier in the day which was weighing heavily on his mind. That was when he'd decided to change the scenery and had driven out to the ranch.

He'd called Jeri and told her he'd pick up Ryan at school, but she insisted the boy would be happier riding the bus. Matt was in Richmond meeting with his lawyer about the Mona situation, so Tim was at the ranch, alone, waiting for Ryan.

The shit Ronni Turnberry had told him kept spinning around his brain, making it difficult to really do anything of substance. Updating the website was the task he'd chosen because it was simple, and it would take his mind off the fact he'd suddenly become a multimillionaire.

Hell's bells, Tim didn't even know how to budget the small amount of money he had left from his mom's life insurance policy that had paid for the expenses his scholarship didn't cover. He surely had no handle on what to do with millions.

Ronni and he had parted with him asking her to continue to manage the trust exactly as it had been handled since Joanne's death to give Tim time and space to figure out what the hell to do about all of it.

After she'd left that afternoon, he'd vacated the barn office without talking to his aunt or uncle. He needed to wrap his head around everything because he had decisions to make.

Chapter Fourteen

"Tim!"

Tim hurried to the hallway in time to see Ryan drop his backpack and take off his fleece jacket. He tossed his baseball cap on the bench by the front door and sat down to remove his sneakers.

"How was school?" Tim picked up the boy's jacket, going through the pockets to pull out the crap little boys kept on them all the time. Keys to nothing, spare change, a small, plastic dinosaur, a green rock, and some sort of animal tooth were placed on the bench. Tim chuckled at the collection. The kid was something else.

"I'm gonna wash your jacket so it's ready for after the break. It's supposed to warm up tomorrow and the weekend, so you won't need it." What Ryan didn't know was that they were planning to take him to DC for the weekend because neither of the men wanted to answer a million questions. He had a dressier jacket Tim was going to insist he wear.

Tim was looking forward to the time away. Hopefully, it would help him get a little perspective he was sorely lacking on the latest bombshell dropped on him earlier that day. Inheriting a fortune was definitely an unexpected surprise... and a possible burden.

"Good. It smells funny," Ryan told him, so like a moron, Tim held the jacket to his nose, wincing because the odor was gag-worthy.

"What the hell *is* that?" Tim fought to keep his coffee down. He hadn't eaten all day because his stomach was in knots due to the earlier revelations. The smell permeating Ryan's jacket, which was a cross between a rotting animal carcass and a cesspool, was enough to put him off food for the *rest* of the day.

"My hook and cubbie are next to Rocky Whipple. He hung his coat on top of mine today because one of the other boys took his, and his jacket smells. See, he don't getta take a bath or shower cause they don't got hot water or 'lectricity sometimes. He said his momma's been too sick to boil water for him to wash so he just washes up a little at school. His momma's got a disease." Ryan explained the situation with a scrunched-up nose.

He smelled his little polo shirt and stuck out his tongue. "My shirt stinks, too."

Tim leaned forward, sniffing the boy, wondering what a sucker he'd turned out to be when the scent of Ryan turned his stomach. "Okay, God. Let's get you a shower and some clean clothes because your dad should be home pretty soon. He had to go to Richmond, but he thought he'd be home before dinner. You have anything we need to worry about for school?" Tim ushered the boy upstairs.

Tim wasn't racing to "officially" move in because of the Mona situation, but he spent a lot of time at the ranch with Matt and Ryan. He'd brought clothes with him for the next day because he wanted to get to the Katydid early and ready for work on the Thanksgiving feast.

Aunt Katie insisted on doing the turkey herself, so he wasn't expected to show up until ten, but he wanted to get there early to watch how she performed the magic. He'd tasted the bird over the years, and he wanted to know the secrets to keeping the bird so damn succulent.

Tim wanted to be able to put satisfying, nutritious meals on the table for Matt and Ryan, and he was certain Aunt Katie and Jeri Collins would give him all the help he needed with that mission.

Tim turned on the shower in Ryan's bathroom and walked to the boy's bedroom where he was stripping off down to his little boy briefs. They were light blue with navy trim. He looked so cute, but Tim knew better than to say anything. Boys at that age were always self-conscious...or Tim remembered being so.

"School work?" Tim put the backpack next to Ryan's desk.

"Nope. I just gotta write in my journal over the vacation. Are we goin' shoppin' on Black Friday?"

Tim chuckled, amazed at the things the boy could come up with without any encouragement at all. "Where'd you hear about Black Friday?" He picked up Ryan's clothes and followed him to the bathroom to check the shower water, so the little cowboy didn't scald himself.

"Miss Blankenship 'splained it to us today in class. Her momma's comin' to Holloway for Thanksgivin' and they always go to Roanoke for Black Friday. It's a tradition. I'm s'posed to write about traditions in our family for Thanksgivin', but I don't 'member any because I was little when me and Momma moved away. Last year, we went to a church where they were havin' a dinner for a lot of people we didn't know. Momma said it would be nice to meet new people, but we didn't talk to nobody, really."

Tim was pretty sure Ryan was referring to a shelter, and his heart pounded in his chest. To think that Ryan was having Thanksgiving at a shelter when his father and grandparents would have loved to host him was nearly too much.

"I did getta talk to Santa, and he gave me a candy cane. I told him I wanted to see my daddy for Christmas, and he said he'd try. I didn't get to see him at Christmas, but I gotta see him pretty soon after." Ryan climbed into the shower, pulling the curtain closed. He tossed his little briefs out from behind it and Tim saw the boy's hand reach for the body wash.

"Don't use that on your hair. Use the shampoo." Tim left the room, wiping away a stray tear. He went to the laundry room to put Ryan's jacket into the washer, and as he was walking into the kitchen, Matt's big truck stopped on the driveway.

Walking to the kitchen window, Tim watched the bull rider drive down to the barn and hop out. Danny, the foreman, walked out at the same time, and the two stopped to speak. Tim could see him smiling as Matt explained something, pointing to the little farm truck of Uncle Josh's parked on the driveway by the house. Heaven only knew what they were saying.

Matt shook Danny's hand and waved toward the barn where Tim saw the two part-time hands, Stevie and Carl, walking out as they waved back. They all went their separate ways, and Tim went to the back door to meet Matt, listening to ensure the shower was still running.

When the handsome man walked up on the deck, Tim walked out to greet him in stocking feet. "How was Richmond?" He placed a soft kiss on Matt's cheek.

Matt wrapped his arms around the younger man and held him tightly, taking off his cowboy hat to hook on the deck post. "I missed ya. I shoulda taken ya with me." Matt nuzzled Tim's neck affectionately.

Tim was reminded how tall the man really was when Matt had to bend over to slick his velvet tongue across Tim's neck, caressing the spot that drove him crazy. It nearly paralyzed Tim because he had a hard time imagining Matt was his lover, but the fact remained...he was. Nevertheless, if Tim had gone with him to Richmond, he'd have missed out on Ronni's visit. He wasn't sure if it was a blessing or a curse; his mind was split, fifty-fifty, on the matter.

"What did your lawyer say?" Tim gently stroked the man's dark, wavy hair, enamored by its softness. He noticed Matt had gotten it cut on the way to meet with his lawyer, and he wished he'd have thought to take Ryan for a haircut the previous weekend. The boy's hair had a little curl to it, so it wasn't totally unruly.

Matt kissed him silly, as he was known to do without much provocation. Their tongues tangled together, and Tim could taste cinnamon from the gum the bull rider liked to chew when he was nervous.

Tim laughed at the man's chomping when he was trying to teach Matt how to use the new software programs that Tim had written to assist with ranch business. The more frustrated Matthew became, the faster he'd chew. Tim thought it was cute.

Matt finally gave Tim a little breathing room and guided him toward the screen door, stopping to take off his dress boots before he went into the house. Matt wasn't a fan of mopping the floors, as Tim had come to learn.

"My lawyer's name is Jonathon Wells in case he calls here. I told him 'bout the call from the lady lawyer, and he took down all the stuff I could tell him about Janelle Rowland and Mona Stanford. Based on what we were able to find out, I'm gonna need to cancel our trip to DC. I gotta go to El Paso on Friday mornin' with him." Matt looked concerned.

"What the hell is in El Paso?" Tim couldn't for the life of him figure out why Matt had to go to El Paso, but if he did, then he did. Tim just wanted to know his lover wasn't going to get himself into trouble.

Before the bull rider could answer, Ryan came running into the room in sweatpants, a long sleeve T-shirt, and thick socks. He hurled himself at Matt, who scooped him up and kissed his temple. "How was school, little man?"

The two of them chatted while Tim went to clean up the bathroom mess, which wasn't as messy as he thought it would be. Ryan had even stretched out his damp towel over the side of the bathtub to dry before it went into the laundry basket. Regarding them living together, things were heading in the right direction.

Matt built a fire in the fireplace and the three of them roasted hot dogs using the tree switches cut from a white ash in the back yard. After the impromptu campout dinner, they made a pillow fort/bed on the living room floor and listened to music instead of watching television.

Tim read two chapters out loud in the mystery book he and Ryan had been reading together, and the three of them discussed it while they had ice cream with chocolate cookie sprinkles. They all settled down on the floor, insisting it wasn't bedtime, as they watched Ryan trying to hide his yawns.

Ryan turned to his side to look at his father. "Can we go to the mall in Roanoke on Black Friday? I have money I saved from doin' chores at Gramma's house and my 'lowance. I wanna buy somethin', and I need to see Santa." Ryan was very serious.

Matt moved Ryan to sit on his stomach and motioned his head for Tim to move closer to them. Once the three were settled, Matt looked at his son and smoothed back his curly hair. "You need a haircut, little man. Tell me, what do you need to buy? Do you have your letter for Santa ready so soon?"

The boy shook his head. "I wanna go to a store where they sell warm coats, and I don't need a letter to Santa 'cause I don't want nothin' this year. I got what I wanted last year. This is for somebody who don't get to go see Santa, Daddy."

Tim remembered the earlier discussion. "Is this about Rocky Whipple?" He took Ryan's hand and held it. Matt turned to look at him with a cocked eyebrow, so Tim knew he needed to explain.

"Ryan has a classmate, Rocky Whipple. It sounds as though his mother's ill, and the family is having a hard time with finances. I don't know them, but I don't know too many people in town. Do you know them?" Tim glanced at Ryan to see his eyes were drooping a little, so he pointed toward the boy.

Matt nodded and pulled Ryan down to his chest to spread out. "I know Cindy Whipple from Bertie. They were in the same class in school. Seems Cindy moved up to Northern Virginia to go to hair dressin' school and ended up in the family way. She moved back after the boy was born and from what I've heard, she's had a hard time 'cause her folks wouldn't help her out. Rocky's biracial and her parents don't approve, apparently.

"Cindy's stuck around here since she don't know any-where else to be, kinda like me. I can check on her to see if there's somethin' I can do." Matt glanced down, smiling at Tim when he pointed to the sleeping boy. They situated him between them, tucking him in tightly.

"We don't have to sleep on the floor, do we?" Matt started to get up.

Tim pulled him back down. "Actually, babe, we do. Ryan needs traditions to record in his journal for school, so we're going to make some. We're sleeping in the fort tonight. Tomorrow, I'll take him over to Aunt Katie's to help with Thanksgiving dinner while you and the boys do whatever you've got planned here.

"On Friday, we'll take you to the airport and then go to the mall to shop. Those can be some new traditions, though I hope you don't always have to go to El Paso on the Friday after Thanksgiving." Tim allowed himself to be drawn into the blue eyes which seemed to be able to see into his soul.

"I'm gonna go change then. I'll be right back, okay?" Matt quietly rose from the cozy pillow and blanket fort they'd made with couch cushions, bed pillows, and some homemade quilts. The fire was burning low, but it was just enough light to spread a glow throughout the little house.

After Matt left them, Tim snuggled up closer to Ryan and studied him. He was the most remarkable little person Tim believed he'd ever met, though he hadn't met many. The boy had a heart of gold, and Tim wanted to make sure nobody, and he meant *nobody*, tainted it. He knew he wouldn't be able to keep the boy from the evils of the world forever, but he'd watch over Ryan Collins and keep him from the dregs of society as long as possible.

Chapter Fifteen

Tim woke with a jolt. The house phone was ringing, but it was still dark outside. He prayed it wasn't bad news that made the phone blast off at that hour.

He hurried out of the fort to grab the handset on the end table by the couch. "Circle C." He was surprised to be coherent enough to remember it was Matt's home and not the Katydid.

"Who's this?" The female voice was slurring a little, and it pissed off Tim. Drunk dialing wasn't welcomed at... four o'clock in the morning. *Fucking hell!*

"Someone who was sleeping soundly before you called. How about you go sleep it off?" He hung up the phone and turned off the ringer in the living room in case the idiot called back.

Tim returned to the comfy, inviting spot they'd created on the floor of the family room and snuggled between Matt, who had moved behind him at some point, and Ryan, who was burrowed into the blankets in front of Tim like a little bug.

The boy looked so damn cute, and as Tim settled into his spot, both of the Collins' men moved toward him. He pulled Ryan into his arms as Matt did the same for Tim, and the smell of the two of them consumed him.

Ryan had that soft, clean, little-boy smell, which put a smile on Tim's face. His Matt smelled of spice and man. It was very comforting.

The next time he woke, Ryan was sitting next to him, slowly poking Tim's forehead. "Why on earth would you do that?" Matt wasn't behind him.

"Cause Gramma Jeri's already called and said you should call her before we go to Miss Katie's so we can stop at the store if they need stuff. I liked sleepin' here with you and Daddy. He made coffee 'fore he went to the barn. He said we should come down and tell him what time to be at Miss Katie's house 'fore we leave." Ryan grinned, obviously proud of his delivery of the information.

Tim noticed the boy was dressed in jeans and a cowboy shirt, though his snaps weren't lined up quite right and the sleeves appeared to be a little short. "We need to get you some new clothes, Ryan. You're growing like a weed."

Tim hopped up, adjusting his sweats to hide the inevitable morning wood. Thankfully, Ryan was too busy putting the cushions back on the couch to notice.

"I'll be right back." Tim hurried down the hallway to shower before they went to help with the Thanksgiving meal at the Katydid.

It took a while for the hard-on to go away because Tim couldn't resist thinking about Matt's body pressed against his as they slept. Of course, those lascivious thoughts didn't help settle things between his legs. As tempting as it was to fantasize about Matt taking him again, Tim knew there was a little boy waiting for him to finish up so they could go to the farm.

After Tim was dressed in a nice pair of jeans and Matt's sweatshirt since he'd forgotten to bring a dress shirt with him when he packed at the farm, he called Jeri to see if they needed anything from the store.

Luckily, they didn't, so Ryan and Tim bundled up against the early morning chill and walked down to the barn with two egg, bacon, and cheese sandwiches. The two of them had eaten at the house, but Tim knew Matt hadn't eaten anything. He wanted to make sure the man had something to tide him over until the big meal later in the day.

The cowboys were out in the pasture supplementing the leftover grass with feed pellets, but Matt was in the barn on his cell phone. Tim smiled to himself, remembering how hard it was to talk the bull rider into getting the damn thing in the first place. Was it sewed onto his head now?

Matt ended the call as he walked over to the duo, picking up Ryan and kissing his forehead before he leaned down and kissed Tim in the same spot. "How are my guys this mornin'? I liked that sleepin' on the floor together thing, but I think we oughta get some thick pads before we do it again. Maybe we should plan it for Christmas Eve?"

Tim and Ryan nodded in agreement. It was a great idea.

Matt grinned. "I don't think we can do it on Christmas Eve. Santa needs a clear path to the tree, but Christmas night, we can sleep on the floor, make a fire, and camp again. I like that idea." Matt's bright smile had Tim's heart fluttering.

"Here's breakfast." Tim handed Matt the two wrapped sandwiches. "We're headed to Aunt Katie's, so keep your phone with you. I'll call when I have a handle on what time you all should come for dinner. I'm going to guess about four, but it's only a guess. I love you." Tim stood on tiptoes and kissed the bull rider's lips chastely.

Ryan giggled, which made the two men smile as they pulled away from each other. Matt leaned forward and pulled off the Redskins cap on Ryan's head, ruffling his curls before he kissed his head. "I love ya both, and I'll see y'all later."

Tim and Ryan left the barn, hurrying to the little red truck just as the sky began to weep. Tim buckled him into the booster that had become a fixture. "I'm glad we'll be inside today."

Tim squeezed Ryan's arm before he closed the truck door. The two headed down SR-131 toward Aunt Katie's house. The weather was turning out to be shitty just as it began to rain harder, just as the weatherman had predicted.

An hour later, Ryan was kneeling in a chair at the kitchen table with a pair of safety scissors, cutting out pumpkin shapes from the construction paper Jeri photo-copied for place cards. Tim and Josh had added four leaves to the dining room table, along with a card table in the family room for the kids.

Aunt Katie had DVDs to keep the little ones occupied, and both women seemed optimistic the kids would be fine away from the adults for the meal. Tim wasn't so sure, but it was his first Thanksgiving with a group of that size.

When he was in college, he usually ignored holidays in favor of schoolwork or a job. Tim didn't go to Holloway very often, much to his aunt and uncle's displeasure. Based on the phone calls he received before, during, and after a holiday, they wanted him close by.

"What'd that blonde want yesterday?" Aunt Katie asked as she and Jeri busied themselves with their pies.

Tim was chopping vegetables for the dressing, or so he was told. He noticed the women didn't have recipe cards, just orders for him and Ryan.

Tim was learning to follow their instructions because it saved an argument. He suspected it was the same reason Ryan was quietly cutting out shapes on the construction paper. The boy seemed to have learned quicker than Tim not to question the women.

"What blonde?" Tim's attempt to evade the question was futile, he knew, but he wasn't ready to announce his business with Ronni Turnberry. He suspected that he wasn't going to be able to snow his Aunt Katie with a bullshit excuse for very long.

"Don't play stupid, Timothy. The little blonde in the tan suit who had Hank Sachs nearly tripping over his tongue when she followed him down to the barn. I saw her pull up the drive as I was cleanin' the turkey." Oh, Aunt Katie wasn't holding back.

Tim glanced up from his task to see Ryan and Jeri were now staring at him too, so he decided to be honest. Sort of. "She stopped by to tell me I'm a millionaire."

Aunt Katie looked at him and scoffed. "You're so full of sh... birdseed. Fine, don't tell me. If Joshua thinks he's gonna hire some fancy interior decorator to come in and redesign my kitchen while he sends me to Florida to see my cousin, Freda, he's crazy.

"This kitchen doesn't get redone without my input, and I don't wanna go to Florida. You tell him that, Timothy. He's been threatenin' it for a couple of years, but now that you're here, I'm afraid he'll live up to his promise." Aunt Katie wiped her arm over her forehead to move the loose hair out of the way.

"Okay, Aunt Katie. I'll tell him."

Of course, Tim had another idea he wanted to follow up on. He simply had to figure out how to achieve his goal.

Tim stopped listening to their gossip session as he continued to make a list in his head. The way he figured it, he had a lot to do in a short amount of time.

If he was going to give Ronni any credence with her claims regarding the inheritance, he knew he wanted to use the money for good things. For folks who deserved them most.

His Christmas list was forming itself in his head without much effort as he continued chopping onions and wiping his eyes. It was gonna be a great year if Tim Moran had any say in the matter.

"Holy... that food was so damn good. Your aunt's an amazin' cook. Momma can hold her own, but Katie seems to add somethin' special to everything. Anyway, I need to put some shit in a suitcase, I guess."

Tim and Matt had tucked Ryan into his bed at the ranch. It had been a long day, but it had been historic. Everyone had a great time, and when Matt said he was grateful for Tim's love for him and his son, nobody at the table fluttered an eyelid. They were accepted, and Tim was beyond grateful.

"When will you be home?" Tim went about unpacking the duffel he'd brought from the farm, placing underwear into the drawer Matt had cleaned out for him.

"I'm prayin' for Saturday, but I'll need to let ya know once I get a handle on things. What're y'all gonna do while I'm gone?" Matt pulled out a few pairs of jeans and a couple of shirts. He started to shove them into a small suitcase before Tim grabbed them.

"I'll pack it, you just get the clothes you want." Matt kissed his lips and went about gathering his things.

Tim packed them into the bag, being mindful of the fact his man wouldn't iron anything, and he had no idea what Matt was going to do in El Paso anyway. It was a lesson in faith, really. Tim knew he had to trust the man he loved. So he did.

"I think Ryan and I might go to the mall in Roanoke. He wants to do some shopping, and he wants to see Santa, remember?"

Matt stopped what he was doing and sat down on the bed, taking Tim's hand between his. "I hate to ask, but can ya hold off on the Santa thing till I get back home? I really wanna be there with him 'cause this might be the last year he still believes in Santa, plus I need to hear his list. Maybe you can stall him?"

Tim wasn't sure if it was possible to try to stall the boy because he'd talked about it all day, but he knew he'd do what he could. "I'll try. When's his saddle gonna be done? I can pick it up while he's in school and leave it over at the farm. Any news from Uncle Josh about a horse for you?" Tim went back to packing Matt's things. After they finished, Tim and Matt went to bed...naked.

"I'm gonna miss you, Timmy." When the man pushed it inside Tim after a few minutes of direct stimulation, hard cock to hard cock, it felt so incredibly filling, Tim was unable to speak for a few minutes.

Matt seemed to know how to drive Tim crazy with the movement of his hips, and he knew how to graze his cock against Tim's prostate, lighting him up inside.

"I love you." Matt leaned forward to kiss Tim's lips after he hooked his hands over the smaller man's shoulders to anchor him.

It felt so good, Tim couldn't stay quiet. "Oh, fuck, Matty. That feels..." His body got away from him, and before he had a chance to say anything else, Tim shot off between them.

Tim felt the man's cock pulse inside him, and when he leaned forward to kiss Matt, the man's love swept over him. "Fuck, baby, I love bein' inside of ya. It feels better than anything I've ever felt." Matt wasn't usually so forthcoming when they were together, but that night, he was giving Tim all the love he needed.

Matt made love to him again later that night after the pair had slept for a couple of hours. He kissed Tim like they might never see each other again as his thick cock breached Tim's entrance and grazed his prostate, causing him to climax as it hit him like a freight train.

Tim craved the feeling of Matt's hard muscles under his fingers as he wrapped his arms around the bull rider's broad shoulders. The man held him gently and continued to shower Tim with kisses as the two moved against each other in the heavenly dance of lovemaking. It felt so wonderful, Tim sighed as Matt kissed his neck.

As they settled in for more sleep, Matt chuckled in Tim's ear. "I heard a rumor over at the Katydid about you carryin' on with a cute blonde gal. What's that about?"

Tim cleared his throat. "That's about something for Aunt Katie. It's a surprise."

Matt snuggled close to his body. It wasn't a total lie, or so Tim justified. He'd tell the man everything, eventually. It really *was* intended to be a surprise for Aunt Katie. Until Tim had it figured out, there was no use bogging Matt down with the details. He had enough on his plate.

Chapter Sixteen

"We need to be smart about how we tackle this list. How big is Rocky Whipple?" Tim asked Ryan as they stood in the boys' department of Macy's at Valley View Mall in Roanoke.

Ryan brought along a handwritten list, and while everything wasn't spelled perfectly, Tim could make out the intent. The boy was on a mission to buy gifts for the Whipple family, and Tim was going to let him.

While Ryan was busy getting dressed, Tim had called his new lawyer, Ronni Turnberry. It was sort of a test regarding his *alleged* windfall... he instructed her to make a draw on the trust as soon as she could make it happen. She asked how much and for his checking account information.

When Tim stopped at an ATM to get cash, after taking Matt to the airport for his trip to El Paso, Tim did a double take at his account balance. The woman hadn't lied. The cash Tim had requested was there, down to the penny.

He also gave the lawyer Cindy Whipple's name and asked if she could have someone check into the Whipple family's living arrangements and the current status of the mother's health. Ronni told him it was no problem to investigate both issues, promising him information by close of business on Monday.

Tim decided it was best to try to dissuade Ryan of buying most of the things on his extensive shopping list because Tim had a better idea of how to help the family. No way was he getting out of buying Rocky a new coat. It was a priority for Ryan, and Tim damn well wouldn't do anything to quell the boy's compassionate heart.

"He's bigger than me, Timmy. I think Gramma Jeri knows his momma 'cause of school. Can we call and ask her?"

Tim nodded and directed them over to a quiet corner of the store, retrieving his cell phone to call Miss Jeri. It rang twice before the woman answered. "Hello, Tim. How you doin', honey? How's the shoppin'?"

Jeri and he had talked the day before about Tim's and Ryan's plans to do a little shopping after dropping Matt off at the airport. She'd hugged Tim tightly when he told her it was just going to be Ryan and him so they could start some traditions. It seemed to make her happy, but she didn't explain it more than saying, "It's about time somebody did."

"It's going fine, but I have a question I forgot to ask. Do you know Cindy Whipple and her little boy, Rocky?" Jeri was silent for a moment, and Tim heard a heavy sigh.

"I know *of* her, son, but I never met her in person. Hear tell, Cindy has MS, but she was in remission. Now, it's come back and she's havin' a hard time of it. She doesn't want any help, though, or so some of the gossips are sayin'. Why?" Jeri's comment made it sound like she definitely had her ear to the grapevine, and Tim wanted to laugh.

Tim filled Jeri in on what Ryan had told him and what the two of them were trying to do regarding the winter coat for young Rocky. Tim would explain the rest of the story to her another time because the coat was of immediate importance. "If you're buyin' the boy a winter coat, I'd get a size twelve. If I remember correctly, Rocky's older and taller than Ryan, and Ryan wears an eight," Jeri offered.

Tim chuckled. "*Gramma,* you haven't been paying a lot of attention lately. I bought him some shirts and jeans, and they're size ten. He's getting Matt's height, I'm sure. So, should I get a size twelve or a fourteen coat? I don't want the kid to swim in it, but it might be good for it to be a little big so he can grow into it."

"*Crap!* Let me call Miss Blankenship, Ryan's teacher. She'd be the one to know. I'll call ya back." The line went dead.

Tim put the phone in his coat pocket and looked at the boy. "Gramma's gonna call back. In the meantime, let's go pay for your stuff. We'll get the coat, I promise, but we need to wait until we hear from Gramma Jeri."

He took Ryan's hand and the two walked to the cashier. Tim paid for the clothes while Ryan looked at the Christmas decorations. After the bag was in hand, Ryan turned to Tim. "We need to get a tree and stuff. I wish Daddy was here."

Tim quickly stooped down to stop the boy from getting upset right there in the store. "Now, don't worry. We have plenty of time to get everything before Christmas. We also have plenty of time to go visit Santa. Your dad wants to be with you when you tell him what you want."

"I don't want nothin' for me, Tim. It's for Rocky and his momma. They need a lot of stuff I think, and I wanna use my Christmas wish for them." Ryan had the most earnest look on his face that Tim's heart squeezed in his chest.

Tim considered his words for a minute before he had another idea. "Okay, how about you run it past me while we have lunch, and we'll make a plan for Santa another day when your dad can come with us? We have plenty of time to tell your wish to Santa before Christmas."

Thankfully, Ryan's tummy growled, so he acquiesced to the suggestion of lunch. Tim was grateful because he didn't know how to put Ryan off his plans anymore, but he knew how important it would be for Matt to see the kindness and generosity his son showed at such a young age. It would melt the heart of someone as cold as Tim's dead grandmother, Joanne Moran.

That evening, Ryan fell asleep in the back seat of Matt's F-250 as Tim drove them home. They had the coat for the Whipple boy wrapped in plain, brown paper, and were planning to leave it on the porch without a note to save the mother any embarrassment.

Ryan was excited about their covert plans, so Tim was surprised he'd fallen asleep, but it had been a big, productive day. Tim was equally giddy at the prospect of the other plans he'd set in motion that day. It was going to be a wonderful holiday season.

On Saturday, Tim and Ryan cleaned the house to prepare for the pending arrival of the Christmas tree along with laundering Ryan's new wardrobe. They called Matt that morning in El Paso, catching him just out of the shower, and Ryan explained the shopping trip to his dad before turning over the phone to Tim.

Matt seemed to be worried about the money spent on Ryan, but Tim quickly dismissed his concerns, telling Matt he loved him before they disconnected the call. Things were better discussed in person when Matt returned, Tim was sure.

Sunday morning found Tim standing in the hallway of a very large horse barn in Blacksburg, Virginia, looking at the most beautiful stallion he'd ever seen in person. He'd found the horse on the internet, and he was sure the huge animal was exactly what he wanted.

He'd explained it to Uncle Josh on Saturday night when he and Ryan stopped by the Katydid on their way home from Roanoke. Josh quickly volunteered to call the owner to set up a time for them to take a look at the beast the next day while Matt was still out of town.

The horse was an American Saddlebred. He was black, about sixteen-and-a-half hands tall, with a full black mane and tail. He had white socks on all four feet, and he was five years old. He was a gaited horse, which Uncle Josh said would give Matt a smooth ride, and from what Tim could tell, the stallion had a good temperament.

Uncle Josh and the seller, Stan Hanson, talked about registration, confirmation, sire and dam, stud services, and many other things Tim vaguely knew anything about, leaving the details to Uncle Josh while Tim took in the appearance and demeanor of the horse. "What's his name?" Tim asked Mr. Hanson when there was a lull in the two men's conversation.

Mr. Hanson was a tall man with large shoulders, arms, and a beer gut to match. He had a worn look about him as if he spent a lot of time outside without taking proper care to use sunscreen. Tim was grateful Aunt Katie dogged him and Uncle Josh about using sunscreen to stave off skin cancer. Tim was sure Mr. Hanson was a good candidate for the disease.

Mr. Hanson glanced between Tim and Uncle Josh. "His papers say Ebony Prince Charles. He's a Kentucky Saddler, as they call 'em. I bought him a year ago from an Englishman who used to own the farm up the road. His wife passed, and he wanted to go back to England, so he sold me the horse. I got all the papers, and he's broke to ride. I will say he's not for the timid. He's a V-8 model, but it's like sittin' in a rockin' chair with jet engines on it when he goes into his fast trot. I know he pulls a buggy, but I ain't got one. I seen him do it when Mr. Marsh lived here. You want me to saddle him up?"

Hells bells, Tim wouldn't know how to judge a good horse from a bad one, but he only wanted the best for Matt. He turned to Uncle Josh. "Will you ride? I don't think I could handle him, and I damn sure don't want to ruin him."

Uncle Josh turned to Mr. Hanson. "Can you give us a minute, Stan? I need to talk to Tim."

The man nodded as he went to a tack room to grab a saddle.

"Tim, son, that horse is gonna cost a few thousand dollars. You think Matt wants to spend that much on a *pleasure* horse? He won't be much good on a cattle ranch because he's a show horse and a high-dollar, stud horse. I'd be happy to use him to breed some of my mares, but maybe somethin' less highbrow would work for Matt to use around the ranch," Uncle Josh suggested.

"Don't worry about the cost of the horse, Uncle Josh. Matt deserves the best I can give him, okay? Please just ride the damn thing and help me get a fair price. I've got the money to pay for it, I promise."

Josh gave him a look as if he thought Tim had lost his fucking mind, but he did as his nephew requested without argument. It was a first.

As Tim observed the stallion's fluid gait in the large, indoor arena with Josh on his back, he determined it was like watching poetry in motion. The massive horse traveled fluidly... like an ocean liner coasting across a calm sea.

Tim could easily picture his bull rider, not on the back of a heaving beast of a bull, but on the back of the sleek stallion looking quite handsome.

The horse's owner quoted a price, and Uncle Josh laughed before he walked away. Mr. Hanson followed Josh out and the pair returned to the barn a few minutes later where the barrel-chested man quoted Tim the final, negotiated price. Uncle Josh looked at him with a cocked eyebrow as Tim pulled his checkbook from the back pocket of his jeans and proceeded to scribble out a check.

"After my check clears, would you please call me so we can arrange delivery. I assume the price includes hauling him to Holloway. Also, I need him to stay here for a few more weeks. He's a Christmas gift, you see." Tim noticed his uncle smirking.

Stan Hanson stared at the two of them before he threw up his hands. "Damn. Y'all drive a hard bargain, but if that's what you want, I'll do it. You got a saddle for him?"

Tim nodded, already having mapped out plans for a hand-made saddle for Matthew.

"I'm planning to order a custom job, but if you've got an old one that you'd sell me for now, I'll take it. Put it on the trailer when you drop off Charlie, and I'll give you the cash on delivery." Tim extended a hand to shake.

They had a deal which seemed to make both men happy. Tim ticked off one big thing from his Christmas list.

During the return trip to Holloway, Tim knew he needed to come clean with his uncle regarding the new developments in his life, especially since Farris March was scheduled to drop by the Katydid on Monday morning to do an assessment of the kitchen.

Tim had come to learn Ronni Turnberry had contacts everywhere and had been a gem at providing him assistance that weekend during her off-hours... though he was sure he was paying for her time. He honestly didn't care at that point.

"You heard about the blonde on Wednesday?" Tim knew damn well Josh would have heard all about it from Hank.

Josh was yet to inquire about the visit from Ronni Turnberry, but Tim needed more help from the man, so decided his uncle deserved to know the truth.

"I heard talk of a blonde. I figured she was a sales-man... woman... or somethin'. You need some advice about somethin'? I'll do everything I can to help ya." Josh touched Tim's shoulder as they drove home in Matt's truck.

Tim fought back the tears once again because Uncle Josh had shown more love and concern in that moment than Tim's own father had shown in his whole life. He reached up and used the sleeve of his hoodie to dry his eyes without looking at the older man.

"You hungry? What time is Aunt Katie expecting us home?" Tim tried to divert his uncle's attention until he could find a place to stop the damn truck.

Tim took the next exit, finding a little mom-and-pop diner at the first stop sign in the little town off the state road. It was still early for the church crowd, so they hustled inside to get a table and food before the place became crowded.

Once the two men had their drinks... sweet tea for Tim and coffee for Uncle Josh... the older man pushed back his Katydid Farm cap and looked Tim in the eye.

Tim hadn't given his uncle time to shave that morning because he was in a hell of a hurry to get on the road after he left Ryan with Aunt Katie at the house. Jeri was coming over and they were going to start baking Christmas cookies, or so Aunt Katie told him the night before when they stopped by on the way home from Roanoke.

Uncle Josh cleared his throat, giving Tim the distinct impression that his time was up. Tim owed the man an explanation regarding where he got the money to pay for such an expensive horse.

He was sure his mention of a custom saddle was another topic Uncle Josh would want to discuss, so only full disclosure would satisfy the man he'd come to regard as a father over the years.

Tim took a deep breath. "I know you only met Joanne Moran a time or two, and I'm pretty sure she was as cold and rude to you as she was to everyone she met, including her son, Harold.

"Anyway, seems the old gal was a nasty piece of work, but I was the only grandchild she had, and as much as she hated the fact that I was gay, she still left me her money. That blonde woman is my new lawyer, Ronni Turnberry. She's nice, and she's helped me out with a lot of stuff this weekend.

"I have the money for Charlie, Uncle Josh, and I want you to help me get Matt a custom-made saddle and all the gear that goes with it. I'm sure it won't be ready by Christmas, but my gift to you and Aunt Katie won't be either. This is gonna be the Christmas of things to come, I guess."

Uncle Josh was silent, though Tim could tell he was trying to process the information he'd just admitted. Maybe a little more?

"I own properties in Philly and the 'burgh. I also own our old house in Trenton, which I'm gonna have torn down, but I'm planning to build something for the community there when I get a minute to think about it. I wouldn't mind you and Aunt Katie giving me advice about things like that, you know.

"I haven't told Matt about all of this yet because I'm not sure how he'll take it, but I inherited about five million dollars. I've got the papers at home in my dresser, and I'd appreciate it if you'd look them over with me. It's still a shock for me too, but I plan to do good things with that money, Uncle Josh."

Tim was dying to talk about the money and what to do with it. Josh Simmons was the most influential man in his life, and seeing the astonished look on his uncle's face made him smile. Josh wouldn't steer him wrong, that much Tim knew.

They ordered a late breakfast because they'd left before Aunt Katie had a chance to feed them, and as the two men quietly chewed their food, Tim could see Uncle Josh chewing on what he'd told him.

As Josh buttered a biscuit, he looked up at Tim and laughed. "That old bitch always did like to cause a shit storm. Your momma had a world of hell with her, but if she left you that money, I guess I can't hate her anymore."

Josh stared at Tim until the two of them both started laughing. No truer words were ever spoken.

When they calmed down, Josh took a sip of coffee and stared at Tim. "Sure, I'll help all ya need, son, but don't go spendin' money on me and Katie. We're fine. We do okay with the operation at the farm, and we have some money tucked away from when Shane died. He left us a nice nest egg we can use when we get too ornery to run the farm anymore. Hell, I hate the idea of touchin' that money since I had to lose my boy to get it."

Tim felt the sting of tears at his uncle's comment, seeing the pain in Josh's eyes and hearing it in his voice.

"That'll all come to you when we're gone, you know."

No, Tim didn't know that, and he didn't know what to say, but he guessed the tears that fell without his permission were all Josh needed to know how he felt about it. Tim prayed that day never came.

His uncle slid off his glasses and grabbed a napkin to dry his eyes, handing one to Tim, as well. The two men sat, staring at each other for a few minutes before Josh nodded and picked up his fork to finish his breakfast. Conversation done.

Tim wasn't really surprised because he knew Uncle Josh was the type of man who settled things in his mind once, leaving no need for additional discussion on the matter. Josh Simmons was a man of few words, as everyone knew, but when he spoke, people listened.

When the designer showed up at the Katydid, Tim knew he'd face hell from Aunt Katie for wanting to give her the kitchen of her dreams. After everything Katie and Josh had given him, a thank-you gift for their love and support over the years was definitely in order. He'd probably have to guilt them into accepting it, but Tim felt up to the task.

Chapter Seventeen

Matthew Collins wasn't the type of man to brag about his successes, nor was he one to shy away from admitting his failures. Every situation he'd endured made him the man he'd become, and he was still trying to determine if he was happy or pissed about it as he waited for his flight from Roanoke to Oklahoma City, then on to his final destination of El Paso... Fort Bliss, to be precise.

Sitting at that half-assed airport gave him too much time to miss the two loves of his life, but he didn't want to dwell on the absences. He looked around, not seeing anyone who he felt compelled to engage in conversation, so he took the opportunity of being alone with time on his hands to do a little stocktaking. It was beyond time to do something of the sort, so as he sat in the gate area, he thought about things he might have changed if he'd had the chance and forethought.

Matt had knocked up Roberta Stanford, no argument, but upon further consideration over the years, Ryan ended up being an eleven-month pregnancy instead of nine. He and Bertie had a son, and from the moment Matt laid eyes on the boy after he was cleaned up, he was in love with the child, nearly busting his buttons with pride as he stared at the boy through the glass of the nursery window.

When Matt came home between events, he'd sit in his son's room and hold the boy, happy to see the little smile on his face and listen to the gurgling noises he made as Matt rocked him. He wished for those first two years back, but at the time he was too selfish and only thought about himself and his ranking on the circuit. It was something he'd grown ashamed of.

Of course, back then, he had Lanny Whitehead keeping him sexually satisfied, so he didn't miss Bertie at all when he was on the road. Matt reasoned their sexual relationship wasn't really a threat to his marriage because he wasn't cheating on Bertie with another woman, and he wasn't fucking anyone.

Matt was the one on the receiving end back then, though he wasn't exactly thrilled about the situation because Lanny was someone who liked things rough. After their encounters, Matt's ass hurt a lot worse from the treatment it received from Lanny than any bull he'd ever ridden.

He knew he was missing things at home when it came to Ryan, but he needed to make the money in order to give the boy a promising future, or so he told himself at the time.

During the off-season, he worked with Ed Marshall to learn the farrier trade, and he was with Ryan as much as possible, going so far as to take the boy with him for jobs a time or two when Bertie had other things to do.

Matt was surprised how easily he'd warmed up to shoeing horses and concentrated on learning everything Ed was willing to teach him. He thought he had a handle on the future, and he wasn't worried about the time when he couldn't ride bulls anymore. He breathed easier once he felt he had a backup plan.

As if the universe wanted to remind Matt the backup plan was a good idea, the point was driven home at a Professional Bull Riding event in St. Louis. He drew a bull that would be his last ride—Strawberry Fields, a brown and white spotted American Brahman bull that was in the running for PBR Bull of the Year.

Matt was bucked off at the three-second mark in spectacular fashion, getting a lot of height before he came down on his left arm, breaking his humerus in one quick *snap*. The titanium rod in his upper arm was a reminder that bull riding was a dangerous sport, and Matt was lucky not to have been killed by the eighteen-hundred-pound beast.

When he returned home and told Bertie he planned to quit riding bulls after that injury, she totally lost her mind. After she called him every name under the sun, she stormed out of the house and left him alone with his son. It didn't really hurt his feelings. He fed the boy as best he could with his arm in a cast, but the two of them played and laughed together. It turned out to be one of the best weekends of Matt's life up till that point.

Unfortunately, Bertie returned on Monday morning while Jeri was at his place to babysit Ryan since it was a cold and rainy day and Matt was scheduled to go out on a job with Ed Marshall. His mother had insisted it was no weather in which to take a baby, so she came over to spend time with her grandson, much to Matt's relief.

Bertie, being the master manipulator Matt had un-
derestimated her to be, conned Jerilyn into believing her
tantrum was over and she was ready to be home and take
care of her family while Matt learned the farrier trade.
She'd even gone so far as to tell Matt's mother how happy
she was that Matt was home from the road and how much
Bertie looked forward to the three of them starting over as
a family.

Jeri was thrilled to hear things were headed down a good
path that she went home with the belief her son and his
wife would talk things over when he got home from work,
and the couple would determine the compromises necessary to weather the storms of married life, just as every
other couple learned to do.

Unfortunately, Matt returned home from his day and
found the house empty. Bertie and his son were gone. He
had no idea what to do next, so he did nothing. He sat
in their white clapboard house and waited for Roberta to
come home and bring Ryan back to him.

When Bertie called the first time and asked him for
money, Matt didn't hesitate to wire it to her and hopped
into his truck to go find them near the Western Union
address she'd given him outside of Bristol, Virginia. By the
time he arrived, they were long gone.

He'd learned from the clerk at the store that the money had been received, but then was transferred to a store in Tulsa, Oklahoma. The clerk couldn't—or wouldn't—provide any additional information. It wasn't the first time it would happen during the time Bertie kept his son away from him.

His then wife kept the boy away from him for three years to punish him for not giving her the opportunity to prance around the PBR venues in too-tight jeans and a low-cut blouse. In Matt's mind, it wasn't right for the mother of his son to slink around like a whore, even if he didn't love her. Her desire to step out on him was what caused her to leave in the first place.

When she finally brought Ryan home to him, it was because Matt promised her a check for one-hundred-thousand dollars if she kept her word and left the boy in his care. It was the amount of his final year's winnings, but he wrote the check without question because he wanted Ryan home where he belonged. All the plans he had for the ranch would have to wait—his son was more important.

After he had Ryan at home, things settled for him, and they were working to get into a good routine. Everything was going along just fine until the day he walked into the Southern States with the boy to order large spools of hay twine and a new hay pick for the tractor, along with some fly spray for the upcoming summer.

When Matt first set eyes on Timothy Moran, his heart skipped a beat or two. He was the most handsome man Matt had ever seen, with blond hair and big, hazel eyes that seemed to glow when they cast their gaze on him.

It wasn't an easy road for the two of them, but they had finally arrived at the place Matt always wanted to be with the man who had filled many of his nights with wonderful dreams of what Matt wanted most...making a life, together. He wanted a stable life with Tim Moran and his son, and he wouldn't allow Bertie or her mother to fuck it up for him going forward.

"Please put your seat up," the flight attendant asked, drawing Matt from his memories as the plane landed. The emptiness in his heart from being away from his family would have to settle because he had something important to do.

Matt had to ensure his lush of a mother-in-law wouldn't succeed in taking away Ryan, nor would he allow Mona to cast doubt on his relationship with Timothy Moran as anything but a loving, nurturing environment to raise the boy. It hadn't been easy to hammer it out, but Tim was on the verge of moving in with them to start a life Matt had dreamed of for a long time.

"Sure, ma'am," he responded as he adjusted himself in the aisle seat of the small plane he'd taken for his connecting flight from Oklahoma City to El Paso.

Matt wasn't looking forward to his second meeting with Colonel Robert Stanford. As Matt remembered, the man was Army all the way, and Matt was the jackass who'd knocked up his daughter.

He knew the Colonel wasn't exactly fond of Mona or Bertie, but they were still his family. It remained to be seen what he'd think of Matt being gay and the dilemma he was facing with Mona's demand to have custody of Ryan.

When the plane touched down, the bull rider retrieved his cell phone, a relatively new thing for him, and checked it to see a text from his Timmy.

> **We're at the mall. It's like being in hell, really. Any ideas for your parents for Christmas? I miss you and you're not getting out of shopping, Matty. Be safe. Xoxo**

Matt grinned as he read it twice, happy his guys were safe and having a day out together because he really had no idea how big the threat might be for Ryan to be taken from them.

Mona had contacted Bertie, and the two of them had joined forces to take Ryan away. Matt and his attorney had concluded it was because of the amount of money they believed Matt was earning with the advances he'd implemented at the ranch.

Both women had lived in Holloway at one time or another, and Mona had friends in town she'd kept in touch with. Everyone in town knew the Circle C was becoming more successful every breeding season, so he wasn't surprised they'd come at him for money—yet again.

Matt wasn't poor. He'd hidden most of his PBR winnings with his parents before the couple married because he didn't entirely trust Bertie after they were suddenly faced with an unexpected pregnancy. After the divorce, he'd invested some of the money in the ranch to make it as successful as possible, but there was the money he'd given Bertie to bring Ryan back to him.

If he'd had any sense about him early on, he should have figured it out in the beginning. Bertie was only after money. Unfortunately, Matt had the tendency to be gullible back then and believed Bertie would keep her word. It was something that wouldn't happen again.

> **I'll think about the gifts. I miss you guys. Love you both. Matt**

He sent the text as the plane finally stopped at the gate. After he collected his bag from the overhead bin, he headed to the rental car desk. He'd reserved a small car because he only planned to stay for a couple of days, and he was pretty sure he could find a cheap motel.

Folding his six-foot-five frame into a Toyota Corolla wasn't easy, but the car was thirty bucks a day, so he took it. He put the address the Colonel had given him into the GPS, and he followed directions. When he pulled up to the gate at Fort Bliss, he rolled down the window to speak with the soldier on duty.

"How can I help you today, sir?" the young man asked with a fairly blank, all-business, expression.

"I'm here to see Colonel Stanford. He's expectin' me." Matt presented his driver's license as the Colonel had instructed.

The young man looked at it and reviewed a list, finally giving Matt a firm nod after another soldier leading a very intimidating German shepherd nodded once the dog finished sniffing around the car. "Sir, just follow this route." The young man presented a photocopied map and traced out the route with a yellow highlighter.

With a thanks to the soldier, Matt drove away. He wasn't sure what to expect at the Colonel's home, but he needed the man's help.

Matt was pretty sure he was on shaky ground when it came to retaining custody of Ryan if the Stanford women found out he was gay, so he was going to appeal to the Colonel's sense of honor. Based on the things Bertie had told him, he didn't believe the Colonel had a lot of love for his family.

The man had a grandson he'd never met as far as Matt knew, and he was very interested in giving Ryan another strong role model. Matt prayed things fell his way, but he knew he might be walking into another lawsuit if Robert Stanford was a homophobe. However, Matt was willing to take the chance for the sake of his son.

He parked the car on the street in front of the two-story, brick federalist-style house with a well-manicured lawn. The weather was warmer in Texas than in Holloway, and things were still somewhat green with some still-flowering bushes.

Matt straightened his shirt and the blue sports coat he'd pulled out of his bag, praying it wasn't too wrinkled. He double-checked the front of his white shirt to see he hadn't spilled coffee on it as he tried to beef up his courage to make the walk to the front door.

Swiping the tops of his boots on the back of each denim-covered leg to clean off any dust, Matt buttoned the jacket as he started up the paved driveway. A few kids were outside riding bikes and playing basketball, and for a moment, Matt wondered if he was doing Ryan an injustice by not living in a similar neighborhood.

His son was relatively secluded at the ranch, but maybe if Matt discussed things with Tim, they could invite friends of Ryan's out to ride horses or maybe to play sports. Matt could have a slab poured and make a sports court next to the house, and they had his parents' place, just up the hill, where kids could swim and have a good time. It was something to discuss when he returned home.

Once Matt arrived at the front door, he cleared his throat to collect his nerves and rang the bell, shoving his hands in the pockets of his jeans to hide the shaking. The door was opened by a boy of about twelve with a short haircut—as if he were a new recruit.

The boy's face resembled pictures Matt had seen of Bertie as a young girl before her parents divorced. "May I help ya, sir?" the boy asked him, snapping Matt out his reverie.

"Uh, yeah... yes. Is the Colonel... I mean, is Colonel Stanford here? I believe he's expectin' me. I'm Matthew Collins." Matt extended his hand to the boy who just stared at it.

"Pop!"

Out of nowhere, a beautiful woman with flaming red hair appeared in a skirt and blouse with a bright smile on her made-up face. She looked like a beauty queen.

She had the same coloring as the boy when the sun shined on her in the doorway. "Mr. Collins, please come in. Robert is on the phone with Command, but he'll be right with you."

She extended her hand to invite him in. "I'm DeAnne Stanford, and this is our son, Robby. I think Savannah's around here somewhere. Please, come in."

Obviously, the man had remarried and found the right woman for him and his Army lifestyle. DeAnne appeared to be the epitome of a career officer's wife. In that moment, Matt could see how Robert and Mona's marriage could have never survived.

Matt walked into the house, absentmindedly reaching for his cowboy hat. When he realized it wasn't there, he nervously ran his fingers through his hair. It was a nervous tick, he believed, but in the current situation, it was a calming habit.

The slender woman showed Matt into an elegant living room and offered him a seat on a sofa next to a grand fireplace. He admired the shiny, hardwood floors and the rug under the furniture, wondering if he should ask Tim about redecorating the small, ranch house. Bertie had picked out most of the furnishings, but after she left with Ryan, Matt hadn't cared enough to think about changing anything.

"Can I get you some tea or maybe a coffee, Mr. Collins?"

Matt cleared his throat again. "Um, maybe a glass of tea, ma'am. I'm sorry to interrupt your holiday." He wished the Colonel had mentioned he had a family, but their phone conversation lasted about three minutes, and it centered on Mona and her threats.

The lady laughed lightly. "Now, don't give that any thought. Robert's anxious to hear about Ryan. I understand the other two are causing you grief. We'd like to help you as much as possible." The woman's cheery tone was interrupted by the sound of running feet.

Just then, two girls came into the room with bright smiles on their faces. They were holding hands, and when they saw people in the living room, they stopped. "Sorry, Mom. Andy came over while you were doing home visits. We're going shopping for sales. Can we bring you anything?" The young woman asking the question had long red hair and looked like Mrs. Stanford.

The other girl—Andy, he presumed—was a surprise. She was tall and solid, built like a softball player. She had brown hair, which was cut very short on the sides, showing the many piercings in her ears and the one in her eyebrow. The top of her hair was streaked with purple swatches, and the girl was in jeans and an old western-style shirt like Tim wore sometimes. She was relatively flat chested, from what Matt could tell, and she was wearing a nice pair of Ariat boots.

"Savannah, this is Ryan's dad, Mr. Collins. Mr. Collins, this is our oldest, Savannah. Andrea is her girlfriend." Matt was surprised to see Mrs. Stanford's proud smile. Unfortunately, both girls frowned at him.

Matt quickly gathered himself and stood, feeling a reality he hadn't even allowed himself to contemplate. "It's a pleasure to meet ya both. Ryan's at home with my partner, Tim. He's gonna die when I tell him about your family." Matt felt it was best to put it out there immediately that he was gay and had a male partner. If the Colonel's own daughter was a lesbian, Matt thought he had a chance.

"Nice to meet you. Got any pictures? Daddy didn't know much about Ryan." Matt pulled out his phone and showed them some of the pictures he'd taken of Ryan on horseback. Helping Tim make breakfast. Feeding bucket calves at the barn. Posing by his drawing of Josie that won him an honorable mention in a school art show.

"Oh, he's so cute." Savannah handed the phone to her mother, who looked at the pictures with Robby looking over her shoulder. They both smiled politely, but Matt thought he noticed interest on Robby's face.

He glanced at Matt, "How old is Ryan?"

DeAnne turned to her son, a look of concern on her face. When the boy smiled, she turned back to Matt, mirroring the smile. They were both interested.

"He's seven now. His birthday was just after the Fourth of July. That donkey is his Christmas present, Josie. He's just learnin' to ride. My partner, Tim, has an aunt and uncle who own a horse farm, and they're hidin' Josie for us until Christmas."

DeAnne handed Matt the phone and turned to her daughter with a smile. "Girls, you should go shopping. I don't need anything right now, but maybe next weekend we can all go together. Robby, you and I are going to drop off the care packages at the base community center, so go change into a decent shirt."

She turned to look at Matt. "I'll be right back with your tea and some coffee for Robert. Please, make yourself at home, Matt."

With that, she was out of the room as heavy footsteps traversed the wooden staircase. Matt prayed his orientation wouldn't freak out the Colonel.

Matt hoped his assumption was spot on that the Colonel was far more accepting than he'd have guessed.

The things Bertie had said about her father gave Matt the impression the man was a hard ass, but if the man accepted a gay daughter, the chances he'd be fine with a gay man—or two gay men—raising his grandson.

When a shadow cast tall on the gleaming hardwood floor, Matt looked up and shuddered. He watched the man stroll into the living room in a pair of khaki slacks and a green, plaid shirt. Out of deference, Matt stood from his seat, nearly swallowing his tongue.

Robert Stanford was as large as Matt remembered from the rodeo in El Paso a handful of years prior. He had a stern look on his face, but he walked over to where Matt was standing to extend his hand. "Matthew. It's been a while." There was no emotion in the man's deep voice.

Matt suddenly had the urge to piss himself or run for the nearest exit, but he beat it down and drew himself up to his full height. He was a few inches taller than the Colonel when he didn't slump, which made him feel minutely better, but the man was an intimidating presence, to say the least.

"Sir, it's nice of you to take the time to meet with me. I hope it's not too much of an imposition."

Mrs. Stanford walked into the living room with a tray. A glass of ice with a small carafe of tea along with a small pot of coffee, cream, and sugar. It held sugar cookies shaped like turkeys with wild decorations on them, and there was some cut-up fruit. Matt imagined it was close to going to see the President.

The Colonel looked up and offered a smile Matt didn't expect to see. "Sweetheart, I gave Vanna my credit card. Will you please text to remind her we're not the Bush's? Last time she and Andy went shopping, I nearly had a panic attack when the bill came. How much do you two need?" The man took out his wallet, pulling out a wad of cash.

DeAnne Stanford kissed his cheek as she took all the money in his hand. "We're dropping off the care packages the kids put together on Wednesday. I'll bring you change. Love you, Rob."

She headed for the foyer but turned back to smile. "Get Matt to stay for dinner. I think the kids would like to hear more about Ryan." Without waiting for a response, Mrs. Stanford headed off.

Pounding footsteps came rushing down the stairs as Robby skidded into the living room. "Pop, after this thing with Mom, can I ask her to drop me at Pedro's house? His parents are havin' a party with their family from Juarez this weekend. He invited me. His mom makes the best tamales." The boy grinned.

The Colonel smiled and pulled his son into a hug. When they parted, the man reached into his front pocket and pulled out a twenty, handing it to the boy. "That's fine. Have Mom stop and buy some flowers for you to take to Mrs. Mendes. Also, text your sister and tell her to take herself and Andy out for dinner on me. I'm gonna take Matthew and your mother out to the steak house tonight. You got your key?"

The kid pulled it out of his pocket to show his father, and the Colonel kissed the top of the boy's head before Robby ran out of the house.

Colonel Stanford sat down and poured the drinks for the two of them. The Colonel started laughing as he doctored his coffee and reached for a cookie before he sank back into the seat of a nice leather chair.

"You look stunned, Matthew, which tells me you heard things about me from my daughter and her mother that led you to believe I was a hard-ass prick who ruled with an iron fist. I expected it from Mona, but Roberta knew better.

"When she was young, we were close. It was hard back then, what with us moving every few years, but I did my best to make them happy. Of course, in Mona's case, I don't think making her happy was a possibility. Anyway, that's all in the past so tell me what I can do for you. We only spoke briefly on the phone. Tell me what Mona's trying to pull this time." The man clearly knew his ex-wife.

For the first time since Matt had been dropped off at Roanoke-Blacksburg Airport... the smallest airport he'd ever seen... he exhaled a huge breath to release all the tension that had been building in his body since he decided to take the trip.

It didn't seem things were going to go as badly as he'd expected. He might have a chance with the father-in-law he'd never been able to get to know. He prayed it wasn't too much to hope for.

Chapter Eighteen

Matt stood under the spray of the shower that was adjacent to the basement guest room of the Colonel's home. Well, Rob's home, as he'd been asked to address the man.

The events from the night before were replaying through Matt's head, and he was having a hard time reconciling the prick he'd heard about from his ex-wife and her mother with the man he'd met and enjoyed getting to know. Even the short visit they'd had at the rodeo in El Paso hadn't done the Colonel justice.

Matt was angry with himself for believing the bullshit Bertie and Mona had told him about Rob Stanford. He learned none of it was true, and he was bothered by how harshly he'd judged the man, especially when he considered their conversation as they'd had dinner at the steak house.

"When I met Mona, she was a great girl. We went out when I was off duty, and we had a good time. I was due to transfer from Fort Carson in Colorado where I met her, and suddenly, I found out she was pregnant, or so I was told. Turned out, Bertie was the longest pregnancy in history. Mona carried that girl for thirteen months." DeAnne laughed over the top of her wine glass as Matt considered another thing Bertie had in common with her mother.

The group was dining at a steak place named Bogart's, and when Rob told DeAnne he was taking them out for dinner, she'd squealed before she ran upstairs to change. Matt had looked at his clothes, glancing up when Rob chuckled. "It's not that fancy, son."

Matt swallowed a gulp of his Shiner Bock, meeting the man's eyes. "So, um, the fact Bertie pretty much did the same thing to me—"

"Doesn't surprise me in the least. Those two... I can't begin to understand 'em. I tried to be a good influence on my daughter, but during Desert Storm, I was deployed, and that's when Mona sorta went off her rocker and really started drinking. She hid it from me, but long story short, when I got home, she demanded a divorce.

"I gave it to her without an argument. She moved to Virginia with Roberta because she was following a man, I believe. By then, neither of them wanted anything to do with me except for my money, so I paid my share. Tell me what they're tryin' to do to you."

Matt finished his beer just as their steaks arrived. Rob had ordered a bottle of wine with dinner, and the three ate as Matt explained his situation, including his lover, Tim, and his concern regarding the women trying to blackmail him for money in exchange for custody of his son.

At the end of the night, Rob asked Matt to allow him to think things through overnight, and Matt agreed they could talk in the morning. The Stanfords insisted he stay at their home in the guestroom, and since he hadn't booked a hotel and was a little too intoxicated to drive, he'd agreed.

His cell ringing on the bathroom vanity drew him from his thoughts, so he turned off the water and grabbed it, seeing it was a call from his man... Timothy H. Moran.

"Baby," he answered, hearing a giggle from the other end of the line. It was Ryan's voice for sure. "Hey, little man," Matt greeted as he cradled the phone between his shoulder and his ear, trying to dry off to get dressed. He heard movement upstairs, and he didn't want to be a bad guest, but he'd missed his son and his man, so he needed to speak with them.

"Hi, Daddy. We went shoppin' yesterday, and I got new clothes. Timmy said my stuff is gettin' too small 'cause I'm growin' like a weed. I got new jeans, underwear, socks..." The boy continued enumerating the purchases, which worried Matt because he hadn't thought to leave any money for Tim.

He needed to talk to his partner about the fact he'd done all of the work to automate the processes at the ranch and Matt hadn't offered him a penny. That needed to be rectified as soon as Matt returned home.

"Ryan. Ryan. Listen son, I'm glad you're growin', but I need to talk to Timmy. How much did all this business cost?"

The boy giggled, bringing a quick grin to Matt's face. "I don't know, Daddy. Tim wrote a check for it. Anyway, we got stuff to do today. Here's Timmy. When you comin' home? We don't like ya gone," Ryan said. Matt seconded the sentiment.

Jon Wells was going to meet with Colonel Stanford and Matt at the home on base that afternoon. Jon mentioned he had friends in El Paso he'd like to visit, so he'd taken an earlier flight than Matt's on Friday. They were set to fly back to Richmond together on Sunday morning.

"Tomorrow. I'll be home tomorrow sometime. Take care of Tim for me, little man. Love ya."

After some fumbling, Tim's happy voice came on the line. It made Matt's heart pound faster and his dick begin to grow. "Matty? How's it goin'?"

It hadn't been lost on Matt that he hadn't Tim why he was going to El Paso, but his partner was kind enough to give him time before he demanded an explanation regarding Matt's sudden departure. The trip was one Matt knew would cause the younger man to worry, and he didn't want it to be something hanging over their heads to dampen the enthusiasm building for the upcoming holidays. Once he had more information, Matt would be able to case Tim's concerns.

"Baby, I know this isn't an easy situation, but I swear to ya when I get home, you and me are gonna have a talk about everything. You didn't have to buy Ryan's clothes, sweetheart. I shoulda left ya money but I didn't think about it. I'll give ya cash tomorrow, and we need to talk about the work you've done at the Circle C. I need to pay ya for it." Matt hoped Tim could hear how much he appreciated everything he'd done.

Tim giggled, which Matt didn't get to hear often enough, but when he did it set his heart racing. "We definitely need to talk when you get home, cowboy. Now, Ryan and I need to go. We've got places to be. I love you, Matty." Tim's voice was soft and warm, which was what Matt needed to hear.

"I love you, too, babe. See ya tomorrow. I'll text ya when the plane gets in." Matt grinned as he ended the call.

Tim's truck was likely on its last leg, so he sent a text to Danny about getting a new farm truck. Danny had a cousin who owned the local Ford dealership in Richmond, so Matt explained what he wanted and asked Dan to get somebody to drive it to the airport the next day so he could drive it home. It would be Tim's truck because Matt intended to have the man living at the ranch as soon as they could get a handle on the things with Mona and Bertie.

He quickly dressed in jeans and a yellow button-down shirt, slipping on his Tony Lama dress boots before he made his way upstairs to see a lot of young people in the dining room eating a buffet breakfast.

When Matt walked in, Savannah stood and smiled at him. "Can I get ya coffee, Mr. Collins? We're gonna be outta here in a minute. We're doin' a community service project this afternoon, and Momma volunteered to feed us all." Savannah gestured to all the young people sitting at the dining room table.

A young kid with a Mohawk hopped up and cleared his spot, motioning for Matt to take a seat. "Thank ya. Coffee would be great, but I can get it myself."

A hand landed on Matt's shoulder, and he turned to see a tall boy with dark hair staring at him. "You used to ride bulls, right? I saw ya at the Coliseum when I was a kid. You won second, right?"

A cup of coffee was placed in front of him on one side with a plate of food appearing from the other. He looked up to see Andy, Savannah's girlfriend, with a friendly smile. "We take care of our own, Mr. Collins." She then winked before she walked away.

The boy next to him passed down butter, salt, and pepper as all talking ceased at the table. Matt glanced up to see at least ten teenagers staring at him, waiting for an answer. He took a sip of coffee and swallowed. "Uh, yeah. It seems like a long time ago as I sit here, but I used to ride buckin' bulls. I did okay, but it's awful hard on the body. Now, I own a cattle ranch in southern Virginia. I've sold a few bulls to rodeo stock companies." He wasn't sure what the teens were looking for from him.

A tiny girl with a short haircut and a piercing in her nose stood and smiled. "Do you find discrimination to be a problem when you're selling those bulls to..."

Another girl pulled her to sit back down. "Excuse Candace. I stopped her before she got off on a tirade about gay rights, which would turn into animal rights, then civil rights. We don't have all day, love." The taller girl grabbed both of their plates and left the dining room.

Matt was relieved. He didn't want to explain to a bunch of wide-eyed optimists who seemed to have found acceptance in El Paso that the rest of the world wasn't as accepting as the community they seemed to have formed at Fort Bliss. His customers didn't know his orientation because he didn't think it was their business. He hadn't started flying a rainbow flag at the end of the driveway, but he didn't fly an American one either. He wasn't about to hide his family, which included Tim, from anyone. He just needed things with Bertie settled.

DeAnne Stanford walked into the dining room in jeans and a T-shirt. Her hair was swept up in a ponytail, and as Matt took her in, he decided she could have passed for one of the kids. He noticed a little tattoo on her long, sleek neck. It was a grouping of three stars, one was large, and two were smaller. He wondered what they meant, but he wasn't about to ask.

"Kids, we need to get over to the field if we're gonna finish before we help set up chairs for the awards' ceremony this afternoon. Bring your dishes into the kitchen 'cause the Colonel doesn't like to have to clear the table." DeAnne giggled.

Matt started to get up and grab his plate when he heard a hearty laugh. "Sit down and eat, Matt. She likes to play me as the big, bad wolf, but my bark is worse than my bite. I'm ready for round two." Rob stood and filled a plate from the buffet.

The two men sat together and ate as they watched the teens clear the table before they all left behind DeAnne. Matt got up to refill his coffee, bringing the pot to the table from the hot plate to refill Rob's cup. "Where're they off to?"

"Care packages for our boys overseas. DeAnne's the head of the local Military Family Association here at Bliss. Those kids who were here are a mix of Army brats and locals, volunteering to do it this month. They've been going all around El Paso collecting supplies, and I'm damn proud of every one of 'em. Savannah is the type of girl who picks up strays as she stumbles through life, and they all find their way to our house at one point or another.

"Regardless of their views on our occupation of overseas theaters, those kids don't hold the soldiers responsible.

Oh, they corner me and voice their oppositions as often as possible, but that's a good thing. They're forming their own opinions on the state of our country, and if we don't question our leaders and elected officials, then we're not taking advantage of our rights as set forth by the Constitution.

"Anyway, I'm glad they're gone cause they're a noisy bunch. Do you mind helping with dishes? It's my turn to give back."

The two finished their coffee and headed to the disaster zone in the kitchen. Matt wished to hell he'd known the man when he was married to his daughter. Well, that wasn't right because nothing could have talked him out of his desire to divorce Bertie. He prayed Ryan had the opportunity to meet Rob. He knew his son would love his grandfather.

Chapter Nineteen

Matt found himself on a plane once again, but he was headed home so it wasn't all bad. Jon Wells was sitting next to him, having upgraded them to business class with frequent-flyer miles. "We need to discuss a few things, Matt, and in business class, you get more privacy and leg room. I won't charge ya for the fifteen thousand miles I used. I fly the friendly skies often enough I got plenty of miles to use, trust me."

Matt nodded and listened as the good-looking man outlined what he believed to be the best strategy to handle the women who were determined to make Matt's life miserable and maybe do away with them once and for all. It would be great if Matt and Tim could begin to make a life together. The plan sounded good until Jon mentioned getting everyone in the same room.

"Whaddya mean? Like, Bertie, her momma, Rob, DeAnne, Tim, and me? How in the hell would that work?" Matt wondered if Jon Wells' help was money well spent after all.

Jon took a sip of his drink before he turned to look at Matt. "We can do it in Richmond at our offices, okay? With Roberta living in Canada, the proceedings must be in the US, and since Ryan resides in Virginia, they gotta come play on our playground. Colonel and Mrs. Stanford sounded as if they'd be happy to come to Virginia to support you, Matt.

"Mona knows where you live. She called your house at four o'clock in the morning on Thursday. The call lasted forty-five seconds. Did she leave a message?" Jon was visibly upset about the call.

"No. We were sleepin' in a blanket fort in the family room that night because—well, it don't matter why. I didn't hear the phone ringin', but I was tired so I wouldn't be surprised if I slept through it. I can ask Tim. He didn't mention anything about it."

"That's great, Matt. Ask him what she said, okay? Meantime, let's say after the first of the year, we try to get a meeting set between all the parties involved. The Colonel didn't say he had any timing issues, did he?" Jon finished his drink and held up his finger for another.

"No, Rob didn't mention any. He said I should just give him a date to meet, and he'd do whatever we needed him to do to help us out. Look, before we disrupt everybody's lives and subject my son to more bullshit, can you just ask the women how much money it would take for them to go away? I'll give everything I have." Matt didn't want to put Tim or Ryan through anything that would cause them distress.

Jon sighed. "Matt, I know you don't want your personal life put on trial but offering them money—offering your ex-wife *more* money—will only cause her to come back to the well again. You've given her over a hundred-and-twenty-five-thousand dollars to date, and now her mother is in the picture? They won't be happy until they have everything you own. Is that what you really want?"

Matt considered the man's words for a second and exhaled. "All I really want is my son and my partner. The rest of it doesn't matter."

Matt swallowed the lump in his throat. The prospect of selling the ranch and cattle to pay off Bertie and Mona didn't scare him. He'd started out with not much more than his parents' love and support years' prior, and he hadn't lost it even after he told them he was gay. It was enough of a foundation to start again.

"Please put your seats in the upright and locked position. Secure the tray tables and any electronic devices as we make our approach. The temperature in Richmond is forty-eight degrees, and the sky is overcast. We might hit a little turbulence during landing, so please ensure your seat belts are fastened."

Matt looked at Jon and smiled. "Let me talk to Tim. I need to explain all of this to him, and we need to figure it out together. I'm still tryin' to get used to havin' a partner who loves me and is on my side. I'll call ya on Tuesday, okay?"

The attorney nodded, and Matt closed his eyes as the plane tilted left and right, dipping and rising. The landing was awful, but once they were on the ground, he clapped along with the other passengers who probably thought they were going to die before they reached the ground. It was great to be back home.

Matt found a guy holding a clipboard with his name on a sheet of paper waiting outside at arrivals. Matt followed him to a pickup truck to go to the dealership so he could finish the transaction.

Matt made a draw on the line of credit he had with a bank in Richmond and walked out with the keys an hour later, headed home to his boys. He couldn't wait to see them.

When he turned into the driveway of the ranch, nobody was around. He dropped his things inside the front door and drove over to the Katydid, finding his F-250 in the driveway, along with his mother's Expedition. He saw Josh riding a horse down by the barn, so he waved as he went to the back door off the kitchen and knocked. Ryan was in the kitchen with his grandmother and Katie Simmons, and the boy had flour on his face, which definitely deserved a smile from Matt.

Katie motioned him inside, so he opened the storm door and walked into the warm kitchen, seeing a bunch of cookies resting on some paper on the kitchen table. They'd been baking for a while.

Ryan ran over to him, and Matt didn't hesitate to whisk him up in his arms and hug him tightly. The boy was his heart and soul. If he lost him... Matt had to stop that train of thought.

"How are ya?" he asked with a smile.

"Oh, man, we've been so busy. We're makin' cookies, but we gotta put 'em in the freezer. I get three of each to take home for now, but the rest gotta wait for Christmas. Why'd you go to El Paso?" Ryan played with the back of Matt's brown hair. The boy always played with his father's hair when Matt held him. Matt assumed It was comforting to both of them.

Matt decided to wait until they were alone to try to explain it to his son, so he changed the subject. "Where's Tim?"

Jeri walked into the room and hugged her son. "Why *did* you go to El Paso, Matthew?"

"Momma, not now, okay?" He gave her a stern look to quell any additional questions she might have. All of it could wait.

"Tim's at the barn, in the office," Katie announced as she pulled a tray out of the oven and put it on top of the stove to cool.

Matt smiled at her and winked. He turned to his son and ruffled his short hair. "You finally got fleeced?"

The boy frowned, tugging at Matt's heart. "Tim said it was time. I liked it long cause it was warm, but he said I looked like a shaggy dog, so he took me when he got back from Blacksburg with Mr. Josh."

"Why'd they go to Blacksburg?" Tim hadn't mentioned anything about it to him when they'd spoken on Saturday.

Katie hurried over and took Ryan from his arms, putting him on the ground. "We have cookies to ice, young man."

She turned to Matt and ushered him toward the back door. "Josh went to look at a horse for one of the boarders. I think he bought the damn thing, but I'm not sure. Anyway, your man is at the barn, and he's very excited to see you." She ushered Matt out the back door.

Once he was outside, he heard the women laughing. He had no idea why, and he didn't care. His dick was pointing him toward the large horse barn where his lover was waiting, and he was in a hurry to get the fuck home.

"No, baby, not like that." Matt pulled Tim up his body until they were face-to-face. He wanted to make love, not get a blow job.

When Tim was securely on top of him, Matt didn't hesitate to seal his mouth to Tim's. Their tongues swirled, getting reacquainted after the short absence. Matt felt goosebumps on Tim's back as he continued to stroke his hands along the man's spine. Their hard cocks were nestled together with their balls touching. Matt was in heaven.

He pulled away gently and gazed into Tim's bright, hazel eyes, happy he'd left a bedside light on. "I missed ya, Timmy."

Tim reached out to the bedside table and opened the top drawer, pulling out a condom and a bottle of lube to place them on the bed next to where they were reclined. Tim moved to sit up on Matt's hips, strategically placing his ass on Matt's hard cock.

Matt gazed up at Tim and saw a coy smile. "You gonna tell me why you went to El Paso? I've got some things to tell you myself, but you go first."

Matt thought about it for a moment. "I wanna make love first, then we'll talk for a bit before we go to sleep. How 'bout that?"

Tim nodded and started to back his sleek body down Matt's bulkier frame before Matt caught him. "Na-ah. Move up." He was in a commanding mood, moving the man up to his chest so he could take his lover's cock into his mouth while he got Tim ready for him. He blindly reached for the lube because giving Tim pleasure as he achieved the goal of loosening him up was what he wanted.

After Tim moaned and groaned as Matt sucked his cock while he was lubing his entrance, Tim pulled out of Matt's mouth before he came. "I wanna come while you're inside me."

Once the condom was on, Tim sunk himself down slowly onto Matt's cock. After the bull rider was seated deep inside, the two languidly kissed and nibbled on each other. Matt sucked on Tim's nipples as he moved the man's body up and down his shaft to give him the love and pleasure that they'd both missed.

The gasping, moaning noises coming from the bedroom would have alarmed Matt if he wasn't the one making them as Tim moved on his cock, bringing them both to climax. He pulled his lover down to seal their mouths as Tim's release provided the lubricant between their writhing bodies.

They slowly pulled back to catch their breath while studying each other's faces. Matt held his lover to him and whispered, "God, I missed you."

Tim looked up and reached to sweep Matt's hair off his face. "I missed you, too, cowboy. I have a few things I need to tell you.... Well, it's actually, one big thing. I don't want this to change anything between us, Matty." Tim's voice was soft and trembly.

Matt held the condom as his fat cock slipped out of his lover's body. He settled it on his thigh so as not to disrupt the discussion it seemed Tim wanted to have as he relaxed on his side. "Okay, baby, tell me what's goin' on."

Tim sat up and reached forward, carefully removing the condom. "I'll be back."

Taking advantage of the absence to grab a tissue and wipe up the residue, Matt thought about how to explain his visit to El Paso. The things about Bertie, Mona, and the Colonel. He regretted not telling Tim about the trip sooner and the reason for it in the first place, but until he had a handle on things, he didn't want to worry the man he loved.

He rose from the bed because he needed to relieve himself, and as Matt approached the bathroom, he heard Tim talking. "You can do this. It won't matter. You've got to be honest."

Matt's heart sunk in his chest—Tim had met someone, and he'd either had an encounter with the guy or he wanted to.

The hallway bathroom across from Ryan's bedroom was empty, so Matt went there to piss. After, he grabbed a washcloth to clean himself before he turned off the light and walked back to the master bedroom. He crawled into the bed and pulled up the covers over his waist, waiting for Tim to return from his prolonged trip to the ensuite.

Tim walked into the bedroom, flipping off the light, and Matt could see the worry on his face. "You already cleaned up?" Tim gave him a fake smile.

Matt nodded and flipped back the covers, having turned off the bedside light. The full moon lit the bedroom so they could see each other. When the smaller man climbed in, Matt pulled him into his chest and looked into his gorgeous hazel eyes. "I love you, Timmy. You should know you can tell me anything."

He hoped to hell it was the opening to hear what had happened because he was really prepared to forgive anything the man told him. The two of them hadn't *formally* agreed they'd be exclusive before Matt took off for El Paso, so if Tim had gone out with someone else, Matt knew he didn't really have a leg to protest on because he hadn't taken the step to solidify the relationship.

His lover was entitled to go out with someone else. If Tim had gone out with another man but it wasn't serious, Matt would make certain to take the steps to make them exclusive, so it didn't happen again.

Tim cleared his throat and looked into Matt's eyes. "Okay. Now, uh, this shouldn't become a big deal between us, okay? I mean, we love each other, right?"

Matt nodded.

"So, um, if I was to tell you about something that happened to me… which I didn't expect at all… you'd withhold judgment until we could discuss it and how we think it might impact our relationship?" Tim's was clearly worried. Once again, Matt nodded, feeling his gut clench.

Finally, he couldn't take it any longer. "You're killin' me, baby. Please tell me what happened." He truly loved Timothy Moran with everything inside him. In his mind, there wasn't anything that would be a deal breaker. He just needed to hear the truth.

"The blonde woman you heard about coming to the Katydid is my new lawyer, Ronni Turnberry. She came by to explain to me about my grandmother, Joanne Moran, leaving me some money in a trust, along with a few properties. I don't want it to come between us, Matty. You mean more to me than the money, and I'll give it all away if it bothers you." The tone of Tim's voice told Matt the man meant every word he said.

Matt was a little confused. "Joanne Moran? I'm sorry, baby, but I don't know what you mean."

He listened to a short explanation of the hierarchy of Tim's family, so far as it included his grandmother, a mean bitch, as Tim described her. "Okay, so she left ya some money. That's not a bad thing, sweetheart. *Your* money is *your* money. Not a big deal."

Tim cleared his throat. "She left me five million dollars, Matty. I'm not sure..."

Matt sat up and looked at the gorgeous man in front of him. He pulled Tim into his body and laughed. "You're worried about how I'd take the money? I mean, I won't *take* the money, but good for you, baby. You're a rich man." Matt showered kisses over Tim's face, happy the secret wasn't nearly as bad as he'd speculated.

Tim pulled away and placed his hands on both sides of Matt's face, studying him carefully. "I know you won't take my money, but I don't want it to come between us. It won't change anything between us, alright? I love you and you love me, end of story. Now, I want to know why you went to El Paso."

Matt's gut clenched because it was definitely the wrong time to discuss the situation about Ryan. He knew for a fact Tim would try to give him money to hire attorneys and private investigators and whatever else was necessary, but he wasn't going to accept it. "You wore me out, baby. Let's talk about it in the mornin', okay?"

With that, the two of them settled into bed together. Tim nestled into his chest and fell asleep, but Matt knew he wouldn't sleep for a while. On one hand, he was happy for Tim because he believed the guy deserved the best after everything, especially with the shit hand he'd been dealt with losing his folks the way he did.

On the other hand, Matt's problems with Bertie and Mona would spur Tim to action and if necessary, Tim would give them all the money he'd just inherited to go away. It wasn't Tim's place to make the sacrifice.

Matt loved the blond, but he was a proud man, and he needed to be the one to take care of his family. He just couldn't let Tim bail him out.

He didn't want the money to come between them either. It was like walking a damn tightrope, and while Matt wasn't afraid of heights, he wasn't too good at walking a fine line when it came to his stubborn male ego.

Chapter Twenty

Tim rolled over to see the bed was empty, though it wasn't really a surprise. The weather had turned colder, so he knew Matt would want to check in with Danny regarding the herd. He heard the trucks out in the fields unloading the feed and round bales to feed the livestock located in the various pastures. Tim hopped up from the bed and gingerly walked to the bathroom, feeling a little tender *down there*.

The previous night, their lovemaking had been more than unbelievable... tender, slow, exciting, *climactic*... everything Tim loved about those times when he and Matt were alone in their own, beautiful bubble of love.

Things had been perfect up until he told Matthew about the surprising windfall he'd been given over the weekend. Since they hadn't really discussed it, Tim had no idea how the bull rider took the news, but he'd resolved to give it all away if it would cause problems in his relationship. In Matt and Ryan, Tim had everything he needed, and he didn't need money he'd never counted on receiving in the first place.

He took a quick shower and after he was dressed, he went to Ryan's room to wake him up for school. Once he was sure the boy was indeed awake, he told him, "I'll get breakfast, and then we'll go to the bus stop." The little cowboy groggily nodded as he began removing his pajamas.

Tim walked onto the deck behind the house to see the flatbeds returning from the pastures. He was pretty sure he'd lost Matt to the activities at the ranch, so he went inside to finish making Ryan's breakfast and packing his lunch box. Tim hoped he would have time to talk to his lover at lunch because it was going to be a huge distraction until they had some sort of agreement regarding the unexpected windfall.

He prepared a quick breakfast sandwich for the boy before picking up the mug of cocoa made in the new Keurig machine he'd purchased over the weekend, having dumped the old coffee maker he'd hated. He'd tell Matt a white lie about it shorting out or something, but getting rid of it was the right thing to do because it would likely cause a house fire someday.

Slow footsteps on the stairs caught Tim's attention and he turned in time to see Ryan trudging toward the kitchen with his backpack dragging behind him, still appearing to be half-asleep.

He felt bad for the boy. "I'll give you a ride to the bus stop this morning because it's so cold outside, and I don't want you to get sick." Ryan nodded as he ate his breakfast and sipped his cocoa, slowly waking.

"Crap." Ryan was staring at the clock on the microwave. It was nearly time for the bus.

"Come on, Buddy. If you miss it, I'll take you to school." Tim wasn't exactly unhappy to have a little extra time with Ryan if the opportunity presented itself.

They hurried out to the new truck Matt had insisted Tim drive instead of the old rust bucket that had been Uncle Josh's. "I want you safe when you're driving around,

sweetheart. You and Ryan are the most important people
in my world. I'll always worry about you when you're not
with me, but now I'll worry a little less." Tim's heart was
touched, and knowing they hadn't discussed the inheritance yet, Tim decided not to argue.

Tim and Ryan made it to the bottom of the drive just
as the bus was stopping at the Morrow house. Ryan kissed
Tim on the cheek and hopped out in time to flag down the
bus at the end of the driveway.

Tim sat in the truck to watch the boy wave to him as he
reached the top of the steps before the doors closed. As the
bus moved up the hill on its way to school, Tim shut his
eyes and made a Christmas wish of his own... *Please don't
let anything happen to tear us apart.*

After Ryan was safely on his way to school, Tim shifted
the F-150 into reverse, turned around at the end of the drive, and directed the vehicle toward the barn. He stopped,
however, to take a deep breath deciding he wasn't ready to
face Matt and have the necessary discussions, considering
the current bullshit circling their collective drain.

Thankfully, he had to meet Farris March, the designer
Ronni Turnberry had suggested to do his aunt's kitchen,
so he had a solid excuse to leave the Circle C without it
looking like he was dodging Matt.

After he appraised the improvements she made at the Katydid, he'd decide if she was suited to do work at the Circle C. The house desperately needed updating and decorating. He retrieved his phone to send Matt a text as the truck idled at the end of the driveway.

> **I forgot I have an appointment at the farm. I got Ryan on the bus. I'll be back by lunch... I hope. Love u.**

Tim made a detour down the drive toward the Katydid, hoping Aunt Katie wouldn't pitch too much of a fit when his plans interfered with her day. He parked next to the barn and strolled inside, seeing Hank busy cleaning stalls.

"You need help?" Tim was eager for any sense of normalcy in the wake of all the changes in his life of late.

The foreman laughed. "Grab a shovel. The boys are out on the pasture feedin' hay. Josh and Katie are up at the house waitin' on some woman who called to tell 'em she's plannin' to redo their kitchen, but I suspect you know somethin' 'bout that, *millionaire-y*," Hank teased.

Tim looked down at the floor, feeling embarrassed because word at the farm had spread faster than he thought. "I guess Josh told you?"

Hank laughed a little before he walked over to Tim and pulled him into a hug. "Kiddo, you deserve the best. After all the shit you've been through in your young life, none of us would ever say ya didn't deserve anything comin' from that horrible family. We all still love ya. Get a damn shovel and help me out. We're cleanin' out all the sawdust and layin' straw to help keep it warm down here for the horses." Hank's no-nonsense attitude brought a smile to Tim's face because it didn't seem to matter to the man. Hank was truly a role model at the farm.

Mickey Warren walked into the barn with a new mare Uncle Josh had bought. She was pregnant when she'd been purchased, so taking in her large belly led Tim to believe it was time for her to give birth.

"Well, well, look who's finally come around for a visit. You here to observe, or work, or shoot the shit?" Mickey always had a lighthearted attitude that Tim appreciated.

He laughed at Mickey's comment. "I'm here to clean some shit. Is she ready to deliver?"

Mickey led the mare to the birthing stall and released the lead from her halter. "She gives every indication she might be ready, but we didn't really get to watch her through the pregnancy, so I'm just guessin'. It's gonna be cold, ya know, so I brought her in just to be safe. Any objections?"

Tim shook his head, happy the man in front of him was of the same mind as the rest of the people who worked at the Katydid. They all had the animals' best interests at heart.

"Okay, then, I'll get the water while you get the hay. Go up to the house and get us a coupla blankets so we can watch her without freezin' our asses off. Better send a text to your boyfriend that you won't be home unless you're gonna abandon your post," Mickey challenged with a fucking-dare-you grin on his face.

Tim was a little offended by Mickey's comment, so he didn't hesitate to answer. "I'm not going to abandon the post, but I'm going to tell Uncle Josh to come down to check on her. He knows more about these horses than the two of us put together, no offense." Tim headed toward the house.

Mickey Warren was really a great guy, but at times, it seemed that he wanted to challenge Tim's judgment about the well being of the animals at the Katydid. Tim was sure the cowboy was probably savvier than him regarding the welfare of the horses, but Tim wasn't entirely stupid when it came to livestock.

He'd learned a few things over the years, and one of them was Uncle Josh needed to be present when a mare was foaling because he owned all of them. Mickey Warren needed to learn the lesson, too.

Tim ran up to the house, hurrying inside without taking off his boots. Aunt Katie gave him a withering look meant to turn him to salt, but as Uncle Josh walked into the kitchen, Tim said what he came to say. "That new mare, Maisy. She looks ready to foal. Mickey brought her into the barn, and I think you should come check on her." As Tim finished his report, the front bell rang.

"For heaven's sake," Aunt Katie complained as she flipped Johnnycakes on the griddle.

"I'll get it." Tim hurried toward the front door to see a beautiful brunette with a large bag in her arms.

"Farris?"

The woman smiled and nodded. "I'm so happy to get the chance—"

Tim cut her off. "Yeah, about that. My Aunt Katie's likely to be a handful, but *I'm* paying for this so listen to her, but check with me before any permanent decisions are made. She'll probably pick a Kenmore range when a Viking might be preferred."

It wasn't that Tim thought there was anything wrong with a Kenmore. His own mother had always wanted a Viking, and since he couldn't give it to her, he'd give it to Aunt Katie—that was if the stubborn woman would let him.

Farris nodded at him, offering a nervous smile. Tim felt better about the undertaking, so the two of them proceeded into the kitchen to confront the she-beast... Kathleen

Simmons. When he pushed open the door separating the kitchen from the dining room, Aunt Katie bristled.

"Nope. You're not going to complain about this, Aunt Katie. I love you so much, and you *are* going to let me do this for you. Uncle Josh is innocent in this one, so if you want to blame someone and be upset, it should be me, okay? This is Farris March. Farris, this is my Aunt Katie, and she's going to be a pistol, but I want a spectacular kitchen in here, and another one outside. If she gives you trouble, just remind her I'm paying *you* by the hour." Tim pulled the beautiful woman into the room behind him, hauling her books up to the counter.

Farris swallowed before she smiled, so he took her reaction to mean she'd encountered difficult people in her line of work on more than one occasion. He left them to their plans, hoping his aunt would come around.

Tim was certain his uncle had explained the situation to Farris when she'd called to set up the appointment, so Tim kept his fingers crossed that everything would be okay.

The goal was to give Aunt Katie the dream kitchen she'd always wanted but fought against because she refused to justify the expense in her own mind. Those days were over. Tim had it to give, and he was determined to do it.

In his mind, Katie and Josh deserved so much more than a new kitchen for the love and support they'd given him over the years. But—that new kitchen was a damn fine place to start.

Early the next morning, Maisy gave birth to a little filly that Uncle Josh named Daisy. "Not too original," Tim replied sarcastically. It was three in the morning, and he was tired, cold, and cranky.

"She's got a white patch over her eye, so it seems fittin'," Josh said as the three men left the barn and went up to the house to sleep. Tim sent Matt a text telling him Maisy had a filly before he fell into an exhausted sleep.

Of course, he missed his bull rider, but Tim was too damn exhausted to do anything about it. Instead, he sunk into the couch in the living room with a blanket and slept like the dead.

Later that morning, Tim was in the barn with Hank as the foreman trimmed up Josie's mane and tail. "You sure this is the best mount for Ryan? I'd say Chief would be better if he wasn't a stallion, but there's gotta be somethin' better than a damn donkey." Tim chuckled at Hank's complaining nature. The man hated donkeys.

In this instance, Tim agreed, but it was Matt's decision regarding what mount would be the best for his son. "What did Ethan think about her?" Tim held the halter of the jenny, not that she was moving an inch. She'd been through the drill before, and she was very well trained.

Hank exhaled loudly as he trimmed a path behind her ears for the headstall. "He said he wished she was a little bigger so he could ride her because she's a gem. I just can't warm up to the damn things." Hank turned off the clippers and stepped back to observe his work.

"Well, you're not gonna ride her, right?" Tim tied the jenny to a ring outside her stall before he grabbed a broom, shoving it down the hallway to clean up the hair, loose hay, and sawdust.

The roar of a large truck rolling up outside the barn caught their attention. Tim turned to see Matt walk into the barn alley in all his cowboy glory. Ryan wasn't with him, so Tim was a little concerned.

"Hey." Tim glanced at Hank, seeing the man chuckling as he continued to clean up Josie's tail, pretending to ignore the two of them.

"I picked up Ryan's saddle and stuff this mornin'. You didn't have to—why didn't you come home after you finished up with the mare?"

Matt took Tim's hand to lead him to the back door of the F-250. He opened it to reveal a small, leather saddle with matching bridle, breast collar, and a blue and green saddle pad with Ryan's initials hand tooled on a piece of matching leather on the side.

It was beautiful, and Tim knew he'd never be able to pick out anything as great for Matt to use with the horse Tim had bought for him. He wanted to do that beautiful beast justice, so it weighed heavy on his mind.

He wanted Matt to have a grand saddle when he rode in the pastures at the ranch. Maybe he could get Aunt Katie to go with him? She had impeccable taste when it came to things of that sort.

"This looks great, Matty. We can hide it in the tack room until Christmas," Tim offered, seeing the deep furrow of Matthew's brow.

The man didn't waste time responding. "That's fine, but why didn't you come home this mornin'?" Matt gave him a harsh look as they carried it all to the tack room where Tim hurriedly made room for the gifts. Above all else, he was determined for Ryan to have a great Christmas, just as much as he wanted Matt to have one. It was easier to please the boy than it was to please the man.

"Matt, honey, I was simply too tired to drive to your place last night, so I slept here on the couch. There's a

woman at the house annoying Aunt Katie right now because I bought them a new kitchen for Christmas, and
Farris came today to try to set a schedule for the remodel.
I'm sure she'll come stomping out of the house any minute
now because Aunt Katie pissed her off, so if you want to
go back to the ranch to discuss why *you* went to *El Paso*,
I'm fine with leaving." Tim gave the man a stern look of
his own.

Matt froze for a moment before he turned and grinned.
"Well, I guess it's time to finally hash it all out. I'll meet ya
at home, Timmy." The bull rider left the barn and climbed
into the large truck to leave.

Tim walked up to the back porch of the house, listening
to the two women in the kitchen. When he didn't hear any
yelling, he walked down to the F-150 and hopped in. He
took the road to the ranch and when he pulled up next to
the F-250, he hoped the two of them wouldn't be pissed
at each other at the end of the conversation.

Ninety minutes later, Tim continued to listen intently as
Matt explained the total clusterfuck he'd been keeping to

himself. He couldn't believe the shit Mona and Bertie were trying to pull.

Matt explained why he went to El Paso, and he told Tim everything about meeting the family and how surprised he was by the Colonel, Savannah, and her girlfriend.

He mentioned how kind they'd been to him, and how much he'd misjudged Colonel Stanford, based on what Bertie had told him. Tim was glad to hear Matt was learning how to reserve judgment. People surprised you at every turn, so it was best to go into things with an open mind.

The couple was sitting at the kitchen table in Matt's house. Tim had so many things he wanted to say about the situation, but one thing came to mind immediately. He had it in his power to make something great happen, so it wasn't a hard decision. "Okay, it seems the best idea is to just give them the money, so they go away."

When Matt squirmed in his chair, Tim knew he had to put the man's mind at ease. "It's okay, Matty. We have a lot more money they don't know about. Just get... I'll get Ronni to find us a good lawyer if you don't trust Jonathon Wells to handle something like this. We can beat them, I swear." Tim prayed to heaven he was right.

Matt smiled. "I appreciate how much you love us, Timmy, but I gotta do some things for myself. All I need from you is to be by my side, supportin' me in my decisions.

We'll get through this, okay, but we ain't gonna pay 'em off. They'll only come back for more." Matt's tone was reassuring, and his decision was made. Tim respected him, so he didn't offer any more suggestions or arguments. The less he said, the less chance he had of pissing off Matt.

Chapter Twenty-one

Later that afternoon, Tim and Matt were in the carpool lane just as the school bell rang loudly. They were watching for Ryan to come bursting out the door so they could take him shopping for Christmas decorations because the boy was chomping at the bit to decorate the house. He'd only asked about it a hundred times since Black Friday.

Tim had found a tree lot near a big discount store by the highway. He and Matt had decided that after they picked up the decorations and got everything home, they were going to put up the tree. He'd put chili in the slow cooker that morning, just as Aunt Katie had instructed when he'd called her, so they'd have a nice dinner waiting for them when they were ready to eat that evening.

They were scheduled to make the drive to Richmond to finish their Christmas shopping for friends and family after Matt met with his lawyer on Friday afternoon to discuss the custody case Mona had filed against him. Tim was damn worried about the outcome, but after the meeting with Jon Wells, he was hoping they could put all the nastiness and negativity out of their minds until after the New Year.

"There he is," Matt pointed as Ryan walked out of school with a boy who was about six inches taller than him with rich brown skin. Both boys were smiling as they headed toward the school buses, so Matt honked the horn.

Upon hearing the familiar sound, Ryan turned in their direction, so Tim rolled down the window to wave. It was still unseasonably warm in southern Virginia, and they counted every day in light jackets as a blessing.

"Who's the boy he's talkin' to?"

Tim smiled. "Based on the coat, I think it's Rocky Whipple. Ryan's really a remarkable boy, Matty. He's trying to be a good friend to Rocky. For a boy that age, it's really an incredible undertaking."

Just then, a boy bigger than Rocky walked up to the two of them and jerked Rocky back by the hood on the coat he was wearing—the coat Tim and Ryan had purchased for him and left anonymously on the front porch of his home.

They watched as Ryan dropped his backpack and lunch box, turning to the bigger kid and yelling at him. Ryan planted his feet, obviously readying himself for the altercation.

When the bigger boy face-palmed Ryan and shoved him to the ground, Tim rushed to get out of the truck and break it up. He wasn't about to allow his partner in crime to be bullied when he was right there to stop it. Matt grabbed him by the arm, taking him by surprise. "Just wait one second."

Tim looked at Matt like he'd lost his damn mind, struggling to get away. "You can't seriously tell me we're going to sit here and watch Ryan get the shit beat out of him?"

Without turning to look at Tim, Matt pointed. "No, we're not, but this right here is when you decide if you're gonna let a bully run ya. Look at him. Ryan's diggin' in, and he ain't gonna let that bigger boy mess with him or his friend. If we go rushin' up there, we'll embarrass him and set him up to be a target for every bully at this school, Timmy."

Tim turned to see Ryan take off his jacket and push the bigger kid back, knocking him on his ass. Just as the bully was about to charge Ryan, Rocky Whipple took off his coat, tossing it on the sidewalk before he laid into the bigger boy, who was no match for Rocky.

Tim could sense Matt was holding back throwing ghost punches in support, and although he didn't believe in solving any problem with violence, he had to resist the urge to move his arms in support of Rocky Whipple, too.

The two men watched as an adult came to break it up, but before Tim knew what was happening, Matt hopped out of the truck and trotted over to the crowd that had gathered. Tim quickly scrambled to follow.

When Tim ran up to the scene, he heard, "Rocky, I'm going to have to call your mother and make her come to school. This is unacceptable behavior, young man, and if you don't know better, we have a problem." Tim didn't like the way the older woman was speaking to the boy, and that finger she had in Rocky's face was the last straw.

"Mrs. Danbury, it wasn't Rocky's fault. Jerry came up to him and tried to steal his warm coat. Rocky just got it, and we weren't gonna let Jerry take it. He started it, ma'am." Ryan was talking fast as he pointed to the boy with the dirty-blond hair who appeared to be at least three years older than Ryan or Rocky.

"Ryan Collins, you head right to that principal's office as well. Jerry Kelly didn't do anything to start this fight, and you know it. You're an instigator, that's what you are." The snarl on the woman's face had Tim's blood boiling.

Just then, Matt walked up to the little group and gave his best lazy grin. "Hello, Mrs. Danbury. I s'pose you remember me." Matt's friendly greeting was surprising, especially since Tim could see the bull rider's hands were shaking in anger.

The silver-haired woman looked at him for a moment, her confusion quickly morphing into an ugly scowl. "I shoulda put it together, Matthew. It figures your son would be as much of a bully as you used to be." There was a superior tone in her harsh voice.

Tim stepped forward. "Excuse me, but Ryan and Rocky were merely walking toward the bus when this boy came up behind them and jerked on Rocky's coat. Ryan was standing up for his friend, not being a bully, ma'am. You've got it all wrong. We were right over there, watching the whole thing." Tim pointed toward the F-250.

Tim watched as she gave him an up-and-down, scoffing at him. "Who might you be? I don't remember you from school."

Tim had dealt with his fair share of bullies over the years, all of them thinking they were better than him. The woman's attitude didn't put a chink in his armor. He even laughed a little at her, judging her to be a bigger bully than the dirty-blond boy.

"That's because I had the fortune of going to a school where teachers didn't side with bullies. Ryan was defending his friend who, after Ryan got shoved down by this kid, tried to defend him in return." He pointed to the boy who was smirking at the whole thing. "Rocky stepped up to stop it." Tim stepped toward her so she knew he meant business.

The boy, Jerry, moved in front of the woman and turned to face her. "Gram...Mrs. Danbury, I didn't do nothin'. Ryan and Rocky always pick on me." The big kid actually produced a pout.

Just then, a woman of about thirty walked up. She was close to Aunt Katie's height, with a short, brunette bob. She wore wire-framed glasses, and Tim would be hard pressed to say she wasn't attractive. She was wearing a skirt, sweater set, and tights, and she had a cute smirk on her face. "Hello, everyone. What's going on?"

"Rocky and Ryan were picking on Jerry." The older woman pulled the big kid closer to her.

Just as Matt and Tim were about to provide another argument regarding the turn of events, the attractive woman turned to them and smiled. "I'm Miss Blankenship. My stepdad owns the feed store, Mr. Collins."

She then turned to Tim with a welcoming smile. "You're Mr. Simmons' nephew, right? I worked with you setting up the direct link to our order system." She extended her hand to shake Tim's.

Tim laughed. "Tim Moran, Miss Blankenship. It's truly a pleasure to put a face with a name. I'm about to call you again to set up another link from the Circle C to the feed store. I just need to put a few finishing touches on it to make it easier on your end. When are you available to discuss it?"

Matt cleared his throat to get Tim's attention. "Sorry, Timmy, but we kinda have an issue here." He gestured toward Ryan and Rocky before turning his unhappy gaze on the older woman and the other boy.

Miss Blankenship giggled. "No, we really don't, Mr. Collins. See those windows? That's my classroom, and Ryan and Rocky are my students. Every afternoon during the school week, I stand at the window when I don't have after-school duty and watch as my kids go to their buses." Miss Blankenship pointed to the windows directly across from the place where the group was standing.

Miss Danbury scoffed loudly. "Of course, you *would* stick up for *them*." She pointed to Ryan and Rocky, so

Tim stepped behind them, putting a protective hand on each of the boys' shoulders to let them know he was right there for them and that awful woman wasn't going to hurt them if he had any say in the matter.

Miss Blankenship stepped forward. "Polly, Jerry's your grandson, but as we all know, he's not an angel. And by the way, Jerry's in fourth grade, and Ryan and Rocky are in first. Explain to me how those two boys pick on your grandson.

"Take your prejudices back into the school and wait for me in the principal's office. I'm tired of Jerry cornering my students on the playground and hurting them because everyone's afraid to go up against you regarding his behavior. I've spoken with you about it before, but this time, I have parental witnesses whom you can't intimidate." She pointed to Tim and Matt.

"We'll see about this, Cecelia." The older woman stomped off with the bully in tow. Tim wanted to hug the teacher for her big heart, but he was sure it would be inappropriate. He stayed next to the boys, squeezing their shoulders in support.

Miss Blankenship turned to the group and offered a big smile. "I'm sorry I missed meeting you at the open house, Mr. Collins. Ryan is such a great student, and he and Rocky are becoming the best of friends." The teacher brushed her hand over Ryan's hair bringing a giggle from the little cowboy.

Matt's face flushed at her words, and he knew Matt hadn't bothered to go to the open house to meet the teacher. It was too late to worry about it at the time, but it wouldn't happen again if Tim had a say in the matter.

"That's great. When's the school Christmas party? I'm pretty sure Ryan's grandmothers would like to contribute." Tim offered Matthew a scathing glance, daring him to make a comment. Of course, Matt didn't say a word and barely met Tim's eyes as he squirmed.

"Ryan has the schedule in his green folder. He has a solo part in the Christmas concert this year." Miss Blankenship giggled as Ryan's face turned red.

Much to Tim's surprise, Matt cleared his throat and spoke. "That's great to hear, ma'am. We'll definitely be there. I want to thank you, Miss Blankenship, for helping with that mess. I'll talk to Ryan at home." Matt pointed toward the doors of the school where Mrs. Danbury had led away her grandson, the future convict.

Miss Blankenship turned to Rocky and smiled. "Sweetie, go ahead and get your bus. I'll see ya tomorrow, and you and I are going to have our special lunch. You did great on your worksheet, and we have a date, young man. Don't forget to write in your journal tonight." She walked Rocky over to bus number four.

Rocky nodded before he got on the bus, sitting in the front seat behind the bus driver. He waved through the window to Ryan as the bus pulled away, and the little cowboy waved back before he picked up his coat, backpack, and lunch box, staring at his dad for further instruction.

Miss Blankenship led them out of the path of the buses before she turned to Ryan. "Would you mind going back to the classroom to make sure they left the light on in the turtle tank? I'll be in to get my stuff in a minute, but the turtle tank is the class project so I can't really check it myself." She had a big smile as she talked to Ryan.

Ryan looked up at Tim and held out his things. "Can you hold this? He's our turtle, Simon, and we're 'sponsible for him. I'll be right back." Ryan handed off the backpack and the lunch box, pulling on his coat.

Tim nodded with a grin as Ryan ran off toward the building. Miss Blankenship turned to the two of them and exhaled as if she had a heavy heart. Finally, she spoke. "I've been wanting to call you, Mr. Collins. Ryan has been so good for Rocky, sharing his lunch and helping him with this classwork when necessary.

"Rocky should actually be in third grade, but he has a few difficulties. It's really nothing serious, and we're working through them with a psychologist from the Board of Education, but since Ryan has taken him under his wing, Rocky's shown remarkable progress."

Tim saw Matt stand a little straighter and his chest puff up at hearing about his son's amazing capacity for kindness. It was a beautiful thing to witness.

Miss Blankenship continued. "Ryan takes him into the bathroom in the mornings and talks about brushing teeth and washing up. He's brought soap, a toothbrush, and toothpaste from home for Rocky. Nearly every day, I struggle to keep from crying because Ryan's compassion for his classmate is amazing. He must have great role models." She looked from Matt to Tim.

Tim couldn't hold the tears, and when he glanced at Matt, he saw tears in his eyes as well. They had a remarkable boy on their hands. Matt nodded at him and Tim knew the two of them would ensure Ryan wouldn't let go of his tender heart. He'd be supported when he wanted to help someone, and the two of them would always protect him. There was so much to nurture in the boy, and Tim was sure they would, together.

Chapter
Twenty-two

After an unsuccessful trip to the local farm in Holloway to search for a Christmas tree, Matt suggested they wait until the trip to Richmond to shop for a tree and decorations. Once they all agreed on a game plan, Matt dropped Ryan and Tim at the mall in Richmond to do some Christmas shopping before he drove across town to meet with Jon Wells.

He promised his two loves he'd be back in time to shop for decorations, and then they'd get the tree on the way home. He was thankful he'd kept his promise, though the meeting at Jon's office wasn't going exactly as Matt had hoped.

"Your ex? She's truly a royal pain in the ass... well, her and her mother are neck and neck on that account, and their attorney, Janelle Rowland, is no better. Roberta never signed over her parental rights, and she's coming at you for Ryan and a hell of a lot of child support, Matt. Her mother's footing the bill for this litigation nightmare because she wants a cut of the take, as best I can tell. I really think they want the ranch, Matt." Jon glanced through the contents folder on the table between them.

"Yeah, they're both bitches, but I'm not givin' 'em my boy. I figure the ranch is worth about two-million-five with everything, including the stock, outbuildings, and the equipment, so if that's the price, I'll go home and start packin' mine and Ryan's things tonight. I can buy another ranch, Jon. I only have one son." Matt was firm in his conviction.

John sighed and held up a hand. "Look, Matt, I think that's a bit—"

Matt pounded his fist on the arm of the chair. "They're not gonna shut me down with their money-grubbin' greed, so let 'em have it. I have a good life waitin' for me, and those two women ain't gonna get in the way of it."

The handsome attorney chuckled. "You could make things easier for our case by separating yourself from Tim Moran. Just for right now. If they find out about him, they'll have a better leg to stand on against us in court, Matt. This is Virginia, and gay men raising children... It's still a difficult concept for people to accept."

Matt didn't hesitate to respond. "Hell, no. Not gonna happen. I'm not givin' up my son or my man. You gotta find another way, Jon."

Jon lifted his hand to stop Matt. "Based on the discussion we had with the Colonel after Thanksgiving I think..."

Jon outlined a plan to handle the situation, trying to put a quick end to the problem with Matt's ex-wife and her mother: Expose them to the Court as the evil people they tried to hide from the world.

Character assassination had the potential to backfire on their case if Tim and Matt's relationship was used as immorality on their part, but, according to Jon, the two men had many fewer skeletons in their closets than Mona and Bertie.

Their plan had the potential to be successful, but it still had Matt worried. He needed to run it by Tim before he agreed to it, but he wasn't going to say anything until after Christmas. He still needed to get a gift for the sexy man who occupied most of his waking thoughts. The relationship they were building... the family they were making together... was important to Matt so he was going to make certain his guys had a great Christmas.

Later that evening, Matt was under the tree on his belly, trying to secure the large evergreen into the new tree stand. "How's that?" He turned to see Ryan sitting on the floor unwinding strands of lights they'd chosen as Tim plugged them into the socket to test for bad bulbs, neither paying any attention to what Matt was doing at all. They had boxes of novelty lights strewn everywhere in the family room, testing them before they were ready to put them on the tree.

As Matt scanned the sets of lights, he grinned at what they'd chosen. There were strands with horses of different breeds. There were miniature cowboy hats and boots, ropes, and barbed wire circles, along with many strands of multicolored lights. He pulled a bag over to see ornaments of all sorts, including glitter-covered horseshoes.

"I like the way this is goin', guys. Anybody want somethin' to drink?" Matt placed his hand on Tim's knee to help himself up from the floor.

Tim looked up and smiled. "I wouldn't mind a Jack on the rocks." Matt nodded and turned to his son, who was unfurling a plaid tree skirt to look at it.

"This is so cool. It looks like one of Papa Marty's cowboy shirts." The smile on his face had wrapped itself around Matt's heart. He wasn't about to let anyone take the boy away from him, and he wasn't about to hide Tim Moran, either. They were his heart and soul, and last he'd heard, a body couldn't live without either.

"Yep. You want somethin'? That fancy coffee maker does hot chocolate, too."

The old coffee maker Matt had at the ranch died in a quasi-questionable short circuit at Tim's hands, to be replaced by some fancy, single-cup machine Matt had a hard time learning to work. He'd figured it out, but occasionally, he hit the wrong button and ended up with a large cup of watered down coffee, or a small cup of very strong coffee.

"I bought marshmallows at the store." Tim stood with a strand of multicolored lights draped around his neck and twisted gently in one hand.

"*Yummm.* That sounds good. Dad, can you look in my mouth? Somethin' ain't right." Ryan walked over to Matt with his mouth wide open.

Matt had noticed the boy picking around at his cheeseburger when they stopped at the diner for dinner. He felt Ryan's forehead, not finding a fever, which was a relief.

"Sure, little man. Come 'ere." He lifted the boy to stand on the arm of the couch and ducked down a little. When Ryan opened his mouth, Matt chuckled to see Ryan working his tongue over a loose, front tooth in the top row.

"Ah, I wondered when this was gonna start. I'm afraid I have some bad news, son. You're about to become toothless. From now on, we gotta chop up your food in a blender. It'll be like when Papa got his new dentures." Matt couldn't help teasing the boy.

Tim walked over and looked into Ryan's mouth, smiling. "Aw, now, it's not so bad. You get money from the tooth fairy."

Matt snapped his fingers, smiling. "Hey, that's right! I forgot all about that business. So, I don't gotta give ya an allowance this week cause you're gonna get money from the tooth fairy when that tooth falls out. Don't swallow it or you don't get nothin'."

Matt watched his son's face scrunch up in disagreement, and he couldn't hold the laugh. Tim joined him because it was too funny not to laugh, but the boy hopped off the couch and stormed into the kitchen.

When they stopped laughing, Tim told him, "We shouldn't have laughed, but he's so damn cute when he gets pissed. He's saving his allowance to buy Christmas gifts for the family, and he wants to get something for

Gracie so she doesn't feel bad. She told him she bought him something, and he was counting on his allowance to get her a bracelet of some sort. I have the impression we shouldn't tease him about her. He seems really protective of the little girl."

"What's her last name?" Matt was kicking himself for not paying closer attention when Ryan talked about school, which was something that needed to change.

"Umm, Long, I think."

"Hmm. I wonder if she's related to Ralphie Long?" Matt was once again thinking out loud.

"Who's he?"

Matt donned a nostalgic smile. "Ralphie was a kid I went to high school with way back when. He and I played football together, and he got me through biology."

He hadn't hated high school, and some days, he wished like hell he had a do-over to change a lot of shit that had happened in his life since he'd graduated. Unfortunately, he couldn't change his association with Bertie, or he wouldn't have Ryan. *Maybe it's better to leave the past alone?*

Matt saw Tim's face screw up a little before he grinned. "Was he a friend like..." He elbowed Matt in the gut. "Or was he a friend..." He pulled Matt's face down to kiss him.

As Tim started to pull away, Matt pulled him closer and swept his tongue over Tim's soft lips. When the younger man opened his mouth to accept Matt's prodding tongue, the two lost themselves in a needy kiss. No answer was needed to the question Matt made certain. There was nobody like Tim Moran.

Matt thought about Jon Wells' words from earlier in the day. *"You could make things a lot easier on our case by separating yourself from Tim Moran..."*

Matt knew he couldn't do anything of the sort. Tim was too fucking important, and not just to him. He was important to Ryan, and Matt would never do anything to hurt his son. Leaving Tim? It wasn't an option.

When the bull rider pulled back, he smiled at Tim. "I love you, genius. After we get Ryan to bed, we need to have a little talk. I might need your help with somethin'."

Tim nodded as he followed Matt into the kitchen to get drinks for the three of them while they decorated the tree. It was shaping up to be a damn good Christmas.

Matt lifted Ryan up, securing the boy on his shoulders. The gold-robed angel they'd purchased earlier that day held firmly in his little hands. "You got it?"

They'd decorated the tree while listening to Christmas music, and Matt couldn't remember when he'd had a better time.

"Hang onto me." Ryan leaned forward from his father's shoulders, settling the angel on top. Matt glanced up to see it was solid, so he stepped back, saying a little prayer to the heavens for the great life he'd been gifted.

"Hey!" Tim called out to the two of them, catching Matt by surprise. He turned, still holding Ryan on his shoulders as Tim snapped pictures with his phone, grinning happily at the two of them.

Tim looked at Ryan, before he placed his hand on the boy's left shin. "I'll print one off for you to put in your journal for school."

Ryan nodded before Matt placed his son on the floor, turning to look at the Christmas tree. He was pretty sure it wouldn't win any home decorating awards, but it made him happier than he'd been in a long time.

Matt and Bertie had put up a small tree when they were first married, but he'd never felt the joy in his heart when he plugged in the lights as he did that night. It still amazed him how much his life had changed in just a few years.

After drinks and discussions of a visit to Santa, the three of them headed down the hallway to get Ryan ready for bed. After he was tucked in, they read a chapter in their latest mystery book, having a quick discussion about it before they kissed the boy's forehead and left him to sleep.

"I'm gonna build a fire and grab a blanket for us. Will ya meet me on the couch?" Matt pulled Ryan's bedroom door nearly closed.

The boy had a night-light, but Matt remembered being his age and how sometimes, the shadows got the best of him in the dark. He wanted Ryan to know he was safe, just like Marty and Jeri had made sure Matt knew the same when he was a little boy. It was important.

Tim nodded before he hurried down the hallway to the bedroom, which was exactly what Matt hoped would happen. They needed to have a talk about the latest shit hitting the fan, but the two men needed to take advantage of the fact they had some time alone. Matt knew they needed to spend time as a couple, and it wasn't plentiful, so he was going to make sure Tim knew he was special when Matt had the chance.

He went to the kitchen to refill their glasses with two fingers of Jack and three cubes, just as they liked it. He returned to the living room and started a small fire in the fireplace before he turned on some soft music and spread the blanket and pillows on the floor. He slipped down the hall to the bedroom and grabbed a couple of condoms and a bottle of lube to have handy.

He walked into the family room and put the things under the edge of the couch as he heard the bathroom door open. He returned to see Tim in a pair of flannel pajama pants and a long-sleeved T-shirt.

As Tim was trying to slip by him in the hallway, Matt grabbed him to share a kiss. He tasted the minty fresh breath of his lover, and he knew he needed to do a little tune-up of his own before he joined Tim in front of the fire.

"I'll be there in a minute. Maybe poke the fire a little?" Tim nodded and continued down the hallway.

Matt freshened up and went to the bedroom, grabbing a pair of sweatpants because he'd never worn pajama pants in his life. Since he was in high school, he's slept naked, but after he and Bertie married, she didn't like it and he changed his routine, sleeping in shorts so she didn't bitch. Back then, he'd worn a T-shirt to bed, but with the chance to feel Tim's soft skin against his, there was no way he was wearing a shirt. He knew the fire would warm him, along with the welcoming warmth of Tim's gorgeous body.

When he walked into the family room, Matt saw Tim had spread out the blanket and was waiting for him with a tender smile on his handsome face as he sipped his drink. "So, we did a great job on the tree, didn't we?" Tim turned to take in the sight.

Matt sat down on the blanket and lay on his side, plucking his drink from the coffee table as he looked up to gaze into the face of the man he loved. He stared into those hazel-green eyes and exhaled, feeling his cock begin to chub up in definite interest.

Tim wasn't tall compared to Matt, but he had a sexy body and carried himself confidently, which Matt admired. The younger man wasn't bulky, but he had definition. He had an ass Matt was sure was designed by the angels, and the fact it was in the shape of a nice bubble was too enticing for Matt to ignore. It was too fucking hard not to follow the man around with his tongue hanging out, regardless of how fucking humiliating it might be for Matt.

Tim had pale blond hair and Nordic good looks, though Matt didn't know his ethnic history. His shoulders were broad for his slender body, which was hairless except for the trimmed bush around Tim's ample cock. It wasn't unusually long, though it was thick when it was hard, and Matt had learned it warmed when Tim was about to come, along with his sexy balls. Tim had moaned and groaned, enjoying the times Matt went down on him, and he always seemed surprised Matt would do it.

"So, are you going to tell me about your meeting with Jon Wells?" Tim settled next to Matt on the blanket with his head resting on his hand as he stared into Matt's eyes. The bull rider was quiet, but then he took Tim's free hand.

"Well, there are a few things we need to talk about, I expect. Right now, I just wanna sip this whiskey and ask you what you want for Christmas. I know you've shopped for some stuff for Ryan. Maybe tomorrow we can ask Momma to watch him for a few hours so you and me can drive over to Blacksburg Mall. I need to get him some things." Matt finished his drink and placed the glass on the coffee table he'd moved off to the side, so they'd have room to spread out.

Tim's face flushed with the most incredible pink as his eyes cast down toward the floor. "I've got *you*, Matty. I don't need anything else."

It was seared into Matt's heart that he wasn't giving Tim up for anything, and he wasn't going to tell him what Jon Wells had suggested. He didn't want Tim trying to run away from him for any reason. They'd get through the mess Mona and Bertie were trying to create, together.

After they both finished their drinks, Matt took Tim into his arms and pulled his smaller body atop his long frame. He felt Tim's hard cock against his belly as he gently pulled him down for a kiss, and when their tongues entangled, Matt relaxed for the first time that day.

They kissed, lining up their erections through their night clothes. After a few minutes, Tim pulled away, gasping. "I wanna feel you inside me, Matt. Do you think we can make love here without getting caught?"

Matt glanced at the clock on the cable box and smiled. It was midnight, and Ryan was a sound sleeper. "Yeah, baby, I think we can. I brought another blanket and pillows. We need to get those damn sleeping pads, but I'll tough it out for tonight. Maybe tomorrow you can give me a back rub. You know, ridin' a bull all those years takes its toll on a body." Matt winked.

"Let me make that assessment on my own, cowboy." Tim announced reached under the couch where Matt had hidden the supplies. That night, Tim rode the bull rider, and he stayed on longer than eight seconds. He started fast and rough, but when he was near his climax or he sensed Matt was near his, he slowed down and rode the man like a mechanical bull set on slow speed. Matt was about ready to accuse him of cheating, though he knew it wasn't true.

"Fuck, Timmy, *gah*..." Matt couldn't hold the moan as he raised his hips to meet Tim's downward plunge on top of him. His hands were on the smaller man's hips, and as his pubic bone stroked Tim's perineum, Matt's cock stroked his prostate. Matt was enjoying the pressure and the pleasure, and he didn't want it to stop.

"I can't hold back, Matty." Tim gasped as he picked up speed, grinding in circles on the bull rider's hard cock. Matt was meeting him stroke for stroke, and the two of them shot together—Matt into the blasted condom, and Tim on his chest. It had been the most amazing ride of Matt's life.

He pulled Tim down onto his body and held him tight as the two of them caught their breath. Matt listened to hear whether Ryan had been awakened because they might have been a little loud. He didn't hear anything, so he relaxed, happy to feel the weight of his lover on his body. It was a huge comfort.

After the two men cleaned up the family room and Matt closed the doors to the fireplace, they hurried back to the bedroom to climb into the nice, king-sized bed. They cuddled together in all their naked glory with Tim's head on Matt's shoulder, and they both fell asleep.

Matt knew there would be questions the next day because he hadn't really provided any answers regarding El Paso, but as a family, they'd had a wonderful day. He prayed it was one of many.

Shopping for family members was nearly done, and not surprisingly, Matt was the only one who had any shopping left to do because he'd neglected to find anything for his parents, even with Tim's help. Ryan was at the Katydid to work with Ethan Sachs one last time before Josie was moved to the Circle C.

The stalls in Matt's barn were finished, and it was decided Chester would join Josie at the ranch. Tim had suggested adding one more stall 'just in case,' so Matt had four stalls built out for the horses, totaling eight at the barn, counting the wet stalls for birthing calves if necessary. It was all shaping up nicely. Matt considered moving his office down to the barn from its place in the house, but he decided to put it off until after the first of the year.

Matt was busy testing the automatic watering system he'd installed in the horse stalls, so he didn't hear Danny come into the barn until the man cleared his throat. Matt turned to smile at his ranch foreman who'd been around since he'd bought the farm back in the day. They had a great working relationship, or so Matt believed.

Danny had a daughter, Kayley, who was about four or five, though Matt had no idea how the child came to be Danny's. Matt couldn't remember the ranch foreman ever getting married or even talking about a girlfriend. There had never been any discussion of an ex-wife, either. "Somethin' on your mind, Dan?" The man didn't appear to be too happy.

"You know that I know nothin' 'bout horses, Matt. I had a pony as a boy, and we used to feed him grain and peaches from the orchard we had where we staked him out. It's a wonder he didn't die, but he lived long enough to be sold. How many horses do I gotta care for?" Danny's voice was gruff.

Danny Johnson was two years behind Matt in high school, but they knew each other pretty well from playing football. Danny was a running back, and Matt was a defensive tackle, but the team was a tight-knit group.

Danny went into the Army after graduation while Matt went to the rodeo. Danny got injured in a training exercise his first year in and was honorably discharged, while Matt continued to take a beating on the circuit.

When he bought the ranch, Matt tracked down Danny because the guy grew up on a cattle farm and knew more about the day-in workings of it than Matt. They'd been working well together for years.

Getting back to his original question, Matt smiled. "Just Chester, the cuttin' horse of Tim's, and Josie, the little

Jenny. I only built the extra stalls because Tim said it was a good idea. Don't worry, I'll take care of the horses. You keep up with the cattle. How're they doin'?"

"We only have four who are outta sync with our breeding cycles. One of the younger bulls slipped through a fence hole and into two heifers who weren't ready to breed, along with two older cows. I had Stevie and Carl herd him into a little lot we made with cattle panels. He's an Angus-Brahman mix, and he's pretty damn sleek, so the calves oughta be somethin'. Come take a look at him." Danny walked out to one of the Gators they used on the ranch.

Matt followed behind and jumped in, ready to enjoy the ride. When they pulled up next to the makeshift pen the hands had created in a little clearing near a creek, Matt wondered how he hadn't seen the large animal when he'd been out in the fields checking fences. There was a stock tank full of water inside, and it appeared they'd been leaving hay and grain for the bull. He was a big one, Matt saw, and he had an idea about what to do with him.

"He gentle?"

Danny chuckled. "Nary a bit. We've left him alone down here because he's a mean bastard. I'm shocked he hasn't taken down the panels."

"Good. Keep him down here by himself but move him closer to that tree so you can string up a tire. Make sure he has plenty of feed and water but leave him alone. I want you to be the only one to check on him, Danny. He's gonna be a hell of a buckin' bull." Matt observed the bull's reaction when he tossed a few clumps of dirt at it. The damn bull had a fit, bucking and spinning in the little pen. Matt knew he had a winner.

"You gonna register him for rodeo stock?" Danny tossed a few clumps of dirt at the animal as well, both of them laughing as the bull bucked and spun.

"Yep, I am. Somebody's gonna buy him, I can guaran-damn-tee it. His name is Smokey Joe. I'll have Timmy look up his sire and get it all fixed up. Good job, Danny."

A good start in the direction he wanted to take the ranch. He didn't know too much about anything, but he knew bucking bulls, and he had one on the ranch. It was the beginning of the future at the Circle C.

A few days later, Matt drove up to the barn in the Gator after checking fences and counting calves for the year-end inventory to get his taxes in order. Death and taxes were two things a body could count as perpetual, and Matt wasn't immune to the necessity.

Tim had told him he didn't need to do the physical count because they kept immaculate records. For Matt, it was a habit he couldn't shed.

As he walked through the barn, he saw a trailer from the Katydid out front. Tim was in the hallway with Mickey Warren as they were settling Chester and Josie into stalls. It was the day before Christmas Eve, and all Matt had to do was keep Ryan busy enough to stay away from the barn after he got home from school. Josie was Ryan's big surprise, and Matt wanted it to be exactly that.

"I put the saddle in the other stall to hide it, along with my saddle." Tim appeared to be rather sheepish.

"I built a tack room, babe." Matt wrapped an arm around his man's neck to direct him to the room in the barn with new, pine saddle frames. There were hooks for bridles and wooden arms extended from the walls for saddle pads to hang so they'd dry.

Matt had kept it a secret from Tim, and he hoped it was a good space for storing the tack they'd need at the ranch. Matt had decided to move the office from the house to the barn and put it next to the tack room with more permanent fixtures, just as they had at the Katydid. It would just take some time.

Tim turned to stare at him, the surprise evident before he pulled him down for a kiss. "It's so fantastic, Matthew. Where do you want the hay?"

Matt's gaze shot up. "What hay, baby?"

"The bales for... The bales for Josie and Chester. When it gets too cold, they'll need to be inside at night during harsh weather, so we need horse hay. Uncle Josh gave us a hundred bales. We need to order horse feed from the MFA, but I'll call Dean and talk to him about it."

"*Oh!* Shit, I didn't think about that. I guess we can put it over in the corner behind the wet stalls, Naw, that's not a good spot because they'd mold over there. Um, let's put it over by the back wall. There's some crap over there, but I'll get it moved and then we can stack the hay there. How much I owe Josh?" Matt held Tim in his arms.

When Tim grinned at him, he was surprised. "It's an early Christmas gift from Uncle Josh. I'll get Mickey to help me stack it. Go back to what you were doing, babe. I'll see ya later." Tim sauntered out of the barn.

Matt sighed as he watched the attractive ass walk away. It was a sight he always enjoyed.

The bull rider turned to the task at hand—the shit against the wall of the barn. "Well, it ain't gonna move itself, dumb ass," he announced to nobody but Chester and Josie. Matt turned on the radio and began going through the junk that had taken up residence in his barn.

Matt laughed to himself as he assessed the viability of all the crap he'd accumulated since he bought the place—broken chain saws that never got fixed but were kept for a rainy day or parts. Matt didn't know how to fix a chain saw.

Old feed and water buckets with broken handles and holes. A roll of barbed wire left in the rain to rust. He shook his head at the stack as he moved it outside to load into one of the trucks to take to the dump.

As he worked, he knew how his dad felt when he'd cleaned out his barn once he retired from the cattle business and turned it over to Matt. The shit one would keep on a what-if whim was a joke. Cleaning up the junk for a better purpose was a great motivator.

Matt had a pickup truck filled in about an hour, acknowledging the spot by the back wall was the perfect place for hay. It was the best way to start the next chapter of their lives together, cleaning out the old to welcome the new. Matt was truly looking forward to the new.

Chapter
Twenty-three

Tim walked into the house at the Katydid on Christmas Eve, glancing around to take in the pure beauty before his eyes. Aunt Katie always loved Christmas and had, once again, gone above and beyond with her decorations. The ambiance automatically reinforced the holiday spirit Tim had coursing through his body, flooding his heart.

The holidays hadn't been a great time at his home but were even less so after the death of his mother. He'd been in the barn office working on updating the farm's records, becoming more aware they probably needed someone else part-time on staff to do it daily, though he wasn't about to suggest it to Uncle Josh. He just needed to figure out a better way to manage his time so he could handle everything at both places.

Aunt Katie had tried over the years to encourage him to embrace the holiday spirit, but Tim never really bought into her bill of goods, learning to be excellent at faking it so he didn't ruin her holidays. Christmas, she always said, was when she missed Shane the most because there was nothing like having your children home for Christmas.

Finally, Tim understood what she'd meant by her observations because he was looking forward to seeing Ryan's face on Christmas morning. He firmly believed his aunt was right.

Ryan only had half a day of school, so Tim planned to take him shopping in town for his few remaining gifts. Waiting in the back of the truck was a large, red, crushed-velvet bag full of gifts for Cindy and Rocky Whipple to be covertly left on their front porch, just as they'd done with the coat after Thanksgiving.

The personal gifts for Cindy were purchased with the aid of Jeri and Katie, while Farris March helped Tim arrange for the delivery of a new stove and refrigerator scheduled for that afternoon at the Whipple home, along with the installation of a new hot-water tank and an up-dated electric bill so the small family could have heat and hot water.

There was no trace of who it was coming from, but Tim was taking Ryan by the house, hoping they could see any proof the Whipples were okay. They'd also arranged for food to be delivered to the home in time for dinner that night.

Tim hoped it wasn't overkill, but Ryan had been the one to tell Santa what he wanted when Tim and Matt had taken the boy to Roanoke to do more shopping and visit Santa. It was Ryan's *Christmas wish*, as he'd told them, so they honored it. When Santa and his elf, Snowflake, started to cry as the boy explained the situation, it brought tears to Tim's eyes as well.

"See, I don't need nothin', Santa, but I got this friend, well he's my best friend, Rocky Whipple. I think you mighta lost his address since he and his momma had to move, and maybe you don't know how hard it is for them now 'cause you get busy this time of year. See, she's real sick and she can't work. They had to move from their good house to a bad house, but his mom made it real nice. Trouble is, the stove don't work, and sometimes, the hot water thing don't either so he has to take a cold shower and he don't like it so he skips it more than he should.

"For my wish, I want Rocky and his momma to have a nice place to live that's warm and has lots of food and hot water. I want him to have clothes that fit him...well, I bought 'em...actually, Tim bought him stuff to wear, but we're gonna make it out like you did 'cause I know you prolly don't know his size since he hit a growth spurt. Anyway, I want his momma to get better so they can do stuff together again like they used to since he don't got a dad. I'm lucky 'cause I got two dads who take care of me really good, so I wanna use my Christmas wish for Rocky and his mom. That's okay, right?" Ryan asked as he finished his request.

Tim and Matt were standing off to the side, and when Matt reached up to wipe his eyes, Tim couldn't help himself. "We have an amazing boy," he told Matt, who leaned down to kiss his cheek. It was an incredible moment, and there wasn't a dry eye among the crowd who was within earshot of Ryan's visit with Santa.

In search of sustenance, Tim headed into the farmhouse kitchen where Aunt Katie was at the stove cooking up a storm, which didn't surprise him at all. He was, however, surprised to see Mickey Warren in an apron with a knife in his hand chopping carrots.

"Well, well. Another cook-in-training at the knee of Chef Kathleen Simmons," Tim teased, slapping Mickey on the ass before he went to the fridge for a glass of sweet tea.

Aunt Katie laughed before she walked over to give him a kiss on the cheek. "Hello, Timothy. Stan Hanson called. He'll be here about one o'clock to deliver that stallion. He said you promised him cash for a saddle?"

Tim smiled. "Oh, wait until you see him, Aunt Katie. He's a magnificent beast, and I'm sure Matt would be willing to breed him to some mares here at the farm if you and Uncle Josh were interested. He's a beaut," he told his aunt excitedly. Tim couldn't wait to see the stallion in the barn at the Circle C. Seeing the bull rider on the back of the large horse would make his day.

Aunt Katie pulled Tim into the dining room with a somber look on her face he wasn't exactly thrilled to see. "Tim, hon, what if this gift is *too* much? What if Matt didn't spend as much on you for Christmas? You've only been together for a few months, you know, and he might not think you'd give him something so expensive for your first Christmas together. You don't want him to be embarrassed at your extravagance, do you?"

Tim knew her to be the head of reason, but in his heart, he knew he'd done the right thing by purchasing the animal. The stallion was a gift given with love. That had to mean something.

He took a calming breath before he spoke because he knew she was only thinking of him. "Aunt Katie, please don't worry about it. I told Matt I wanted a Kenny Chesney CD for Christmas, and I meant it. I don't care about him reciprocating, trust me. I've got him and Ryan, so I'm all set with gifts," Tim explained with a splitting grin on his face. He meant every word.

He went back down to the barn, leaving Mickey and Katie in the kitchen with their cooking chores. The Christmas Eve celebration was set to be at the Katydid. Christmas Day was scheduled to be at Jeri and Marty's house, after Matt, Tim, and Ryan spent the morning together before joining the families. Tim had offered his lover time alone with his son, but...

"So, uh, I was thinking maybe I should stay at the Katydid on Christmas Eve to give you and Ryan time alone on Christmas morning. He might appreciate it being just the two of you, and then I'll see the two of you later," Tim suggested as the two of them were working in the office in the house one day in early December.

Matt glanced up from the computer screen where Tim was teaching him how to go about updating the website in the event of changes on the ranch if Tim was unable to handle the task himself. The look on the bull rider's face wasn't exactly happy.

Matt pushed the chair away and pulled Tim into his lap, staring deeply into his eyes. "Why do I gotta learn this shit? You're not goin' anywhere, right? We said we'd sit down and discuss how much I owe you for the work you've done here at the ranch after the first of the year. You ain't gonna leave us, right?"

Tim was alarmed by Matt's inquisition, so he hurriedly answered, "No, Matty, not at all. I just wanted to make sure you could. I was thinking about a 'what-if' scenario. If I was hit by a bus, could you continue to maintain the system here and keep things up to date? That's all, baby. I'm not goin' anywhere."

"Well, that ain't exactly true now, is it? You don't wanna be here when Ryan opens his gifts on Christmas mornin'. I still don't understand why?" Matt bemoaned before he pushed Tim off his lap and hurried to stomp down the hallway.

Tim followed after him, finding him in the kitchen pouting like Ryan. The man looked so sad and adorable. Tim wanted to smack himself for hurting him. "Okay, stop pout-

ing. I'm sorry, Matty. I just wanted to give you and Ryan this holiday together because I know he's been gone for these last few Christmases, and I thought the two of you would want time together without me. I love you both so much, and I honestly don't want to be away from either of you, but I don't ever want to infringe on your father-son time."

Matt set his jaw before the large man took Tim's face into his hands and stared into his eyes, mesmerized. "I've told you I love you. You've told me you love me. We fuck like rabbits when we can get a hot fifteen minutes because we love each other and want to show each other how we feel, right? Is there somethin' I'm missin'?"

Tim laughed. "No, baby. You're right about all of it. I'm sorry." No more talk was had about Christmas plans. They were set and they included the three of them living at the Circle C.

Tim ended up in the barn office trying to catch up on a little work while he waited for Charlie-the-stud to make his appearance. He was excited about the arrival of Matt's gift, so he pushed Aunt Katie's words out of his mind and prayed he wasn't making a big mistake by purchasing the huge stallion for the man he loved. God knew he wasn't exactly confident in his choices all the time.

When Hank knocked on the door of the office, Tim saw a smile on the cowboy's face. Tim hurried from behind the desk to meet the man on the step and eagerly asked, "Is he here?"

"If you mean a huge black stallion with four white socks and a long mane and tail, then he's here. There's also a man here who's expectin' a little cash," Hank told him. Tim went back to his coat and grabbed the envelope from the pocket because he'd taken out a few thousand dollars as backup.

He walked out of the office to see Uncle Josh chatting with Stan Hanson. Tim walked up and smiled, shoving his hand toward Mr. Hanson. "Pleasure to see you again. How's Charlie?" he asked as he walked to the side of the trailer where the stallion was standing patiently.

"He's doin' just fine. I was gonna have him shod for ya, but I talked to Josh, and he told me Matt's a farrier, so I just had him perdied up a bit. I got him vet checked before I brought him over, so here's the health certificate along with the registration transfer papers. You can sign 'em and send 'em to ASHA. Where do ya want him?"

Tim looked at Uncle Josh, who chuckled before he responded. "It's the American Saddlebred Horse Association, which y'all will wanna do if you're gonna breed him. We got stall three ready for him." Tim followed Stan to the trailer. When the large horse backed out, Stan handed Tim the lead rope.

He froze for a second, but he remembered not to allow himself to show fear around the stallion. Horses picked up on nerves and reacted in kind, as Uncle Josh had explained to him more than once, so Tim took a few calming breaths before he turned to the stallion, rubbing his right hand along the horse's neck. "Well, Charlie, welcome to the Katydid. Your home is gonna be at Circle C, but that will take a few days," he whispered to the gorgeous animal as he moved to brush his hand over Charlie's face and nose.

The horse snorted, but he didn't move an inch, which made Tim relax even more. He'd made a wise and wonderful purchase.

Thankfully, when Tim walked down the hallway with the large stud horse following behind, there was no uprising amongst the other occupants of the large barn. As Tim looked around for the first time that day, he could see there weren't many horses in the stalls, not full as it had been the day before when he was helping. He turned to Josh and spun his finger. "What gives? Where's everybody else?"

Uncle Josh chuckled. "You're bringin' a huge stud horse in here and some of the boarder mares are in season. I don't want him takin' down my barn to get to 'em." His uncle wore his usual smart-ass grin.

"Shit, am I going to have to worry about that with Josie?" Tim asked, not having thought about the female donkey who would be residing at the Circle C after the holidays. He'd considered the stalls in Matt's barn, and they weren't bad. They were solid, but if the stallion really wanted out, he doubted the cedar boards would contain him.

"Since you brought it up, I'll just tell ya. In the future, it *will* be a problem, but that stallion can spend a lot of time out in the pasture over the winter if he has a blanket on him. He'll grow his winter hair, and he won't give a shit about the cattle.

"Now, when it gets icy, Matt needs to bring him inside, so he doesn't fall and break a leg. Just keep Josie at one end of the barn and Charlie at the other or take her up to Marty's for a few days when she's in season. She gives off a different scent, and she's too small to breed to that stud. It should be fine, son," the wiser man explained.

Tim looked at Uncle Josh and took a deep breath. "Did I make a mistake buying Charlie for Matt? I mean, if he and Ryan can't go riding together, why'd I buy him the horse?" At that point, he felt totally defeated about his Christmas surprise, but he'd made his bed, and it was time to lie in the damn thing. Josh didn't offer him an answer about making a mistake before Stan and he left the barn to go to the house for coffee. It only made Tim feel worse.

After Stan Hanson left the Katydid, Tim walked down the hallway of the barn to stall number three where Ebony Prince Charles seemed to be getting acclimated to his new surroundings. The stall was much larger than the one at Stan's farm. Tim was happy the horse seemed to be at ease with his new digs.

"I know you're a big stud, but so is my boyfriend, which is why I thought the two of you would be well-suited. I didn't take into consideration the fact you're used to getting lucky on a regular basis but that won't be happening too much for you in the future unless I can come up with an idea to find you a little company. I suppose I didn't think things through very well." Tim felt like a total failure about finding the appropriate gift for the man he loved.

Tim jumped when he felt a hand on his back, turning to see Mickey Warren standing beside him. "He's a prime piece of horseflesh, that stallion. I'd bet Matt Collins would be thrilled to have such a fine animal to ride." Mickey joined Tim at the stall door.

They could see Charlie was perfectly calm as he grazed on the hay Mickey had left for the horse earlier. He took a drink from the water fountain mounted in the stall before he lazily walked over to the door, hooking his head over the top and snorting at the two of them.

"Dude, that's just gross," Mickey teased as he wiped the snot off his jacket onto Tim's coat.

"Stop it," Tim whined as he moved away before he felt a tug on the back of the hood on his zip front hoodie. He turned to see Charlie had snagged it in his mouth, pulling Tim back to the stall door.

Mickey laughed. "Oh, seems he likes ya, Tim. He doesn't want you to get away."

"I'm guessing he wants to know what the hell he's doing here with somebody as lame as you looking after him," Tim teased in return.

They both laughed as they headed toward the office for coffee after Tim freed himself from Charlie's teeth. How he and the stallion would get along, Tim wasn't sure, but he hoped and prayed buying that horse for Matt was a good idea.

Aunt Katie had given him doubts, and it made him sick to his stomach. He was only trying to do something for the man he loved, but suddenly, he wasn't so sure of his choice.

The two men walked to the house together, but before they went inside, Mickey stopped him. "I gotta thank ya for all the support you gave me with Josh and Katie. I doubt they'd have given me a shot if you and Matt hadn't been in my corner. I hope we'll become better friends in the new year. I'd like to hang out with you guys sometime if that's possible. You didn't know me from anyone, but you gave me the benefit of the doubt and I wanna prove to you your trust wasn't misplaced."

When Mickey enveloped him in his strong arms, Tim didn't hesitate to return the grip. He knew the man hadn't been off the farm since he'd been jilted by his former lover, Jackie, and Tim was sure Mickey had missed physical contact, even of the innocent type. He'd be glad to help a friend with an affectionate hug when needed. Everybody needed a hug now and again.

Tim sat in his F-150 waiting for Ryan to come out of Holloway Elementary. He'd heard the bell ring, but he was so excited to take the boy to the Katydid to see Charlie and ask his opinion regarding whether Matt would appreciate the stallion, he was fidgeting in his truck seat.

Tommy Morrow ran out of the building toward the bus, and Tim knew Ryan wasn't far behind their neighbor because Tommy's classroom was next to Ryan's. When

Rocky Whipple walked out of the building alone, Tim worried. As far as he knew, the boys were best friends, and Ryan was dutiful about walking his friend to the bus to ensure nobody messed with him, even though Rocky was much larger than Ryan.

He noticed Miss Blankenship walked out of the building to wave goodbye to her students as the buses pulled away, and he felt an uneasiness in his gut. He still hadn't seen Ryan, so he pulled out of the carpool line and parked in the visitor parking lot. He hopped out of the truck and dodged the buses, trying to catch the teacher before she returned inside. When he touched her shoulder, she turned to him and smiled brightly. "Merry Christmas, Mr. Moran. Did Ryan forget something?"

Tim's blood ran cold. "Did Matt pick him up? He was busy at the ranch, and I had some things to do this morning, so we didn't exactly catch up."

They hadn't explained their relationship to the teacher, and standing on the sidewalk outside the elementary school didn't seem the right time to do it, so Tim remained vague. He knew a lot of the parents thought he and Matt were just good friends, and Tim was fine with it, opting for whatever caused the least number of problems for Ryan at school.

"His, uh, his mother and grandmother picked him up. They said Mr. Collins was running late due to a problem, so she agreed to pick up Ryan since they were having an old-fashioned, family holiday at the ranch. It sounded like they were preparing for an exciting holiday," Cecelia Blankenship explained.

Tim felt his stomach fall into his boots before it attempted to creep back up and cause him to lose his lunch. "Okay. Do you remember, uh, what time did she pick him up?"

The woman stared at him with concern on her face. "Did I do something wrong, Mr. Moran? Mrs. Collins showed me the papers to verify she had joint custody of Ryan, and I didn't question them. She and her mother picked him up an hour ago, just as our holiday party was ending."

Tim could barely contain his stomach, but he simply smiled at her and offered a reassuring nod. "I'm sure things are fine, Miss Blankenship. Merry Christmas," he told her before he sprinted to the F-150 and climbed inside.

He made a hasty U-turn in the parking lot and gunned it out to the ranch. He prayed the boy was home and his mother and grandmother were there waiting to ambush Matt for whatever past indiscretions they deemed him guilty.

Unfortunately, Tim's gut kept telling him that wouldn't be the case, and he knew this was a horrific turn of events. It was going to be bad, for sure, but he prayed it wasn't the worst-case scenario he imagined—the two women taking Ryan away where they could never find the boy.

Tim grabbed his cell from the console where it was charging to call the ranch, disregarding the law against talking on one's cell while driving. "Circle C." Danny answered.

"Hey, it's Tim. Is Ryan around? I was supposed to pick him up from school to do a little last-minute shopping, but I think he forgot. The bus should have dropped him off by now," he explained to the ranch foreman.

Danny answered too quickly, in Tim's opinion. "Naw, the bus came by but didn't stop. Are ya sure he isn't at the school?"

Panic seized Tim's chest, but he tried to tamp it down and keep his shit together. "Is Matt around?" He left no room in his voice for confusion regarding the severity of the situation.

"He's on his cell phone right now. Hang on for a hot minute." Danny put the call on hold.

The various scenarios running through Tim's head were too much for him to contemplate as he drove out to the ranch. Bertie and her mother weren't supposed to be in Holloway, much less picking up Ryan at school on Christmas Eve without any notice. The sooner he got home to see the boy in the house, safe and happy, the better.

"Hey, babe. What's wrong?" Matt asked, not waiting for Tim to respond. "I've got a cow in labor right now on Christmas Eve. How weird is…" the cowboy joked.

Tim broke in. "Matty, is Ryan home?"

"No. You told me you were pickin' him up for his last round of shoppin'. Is somethin' wrong?" Matt suddenly sounded concerned. Tim knew it wasn't something to explain over the phone, so he didn't.

"I'll be there in a few minutes." His heart was pounding out of his chest because he had visions of a repeat of three years prior when Bertie Stanford took Ryan away from Matt. Tim wasn't sure how the man would recover from the pain once again.

Tim was kicking his own ass for not giving the watch he'd had made especially for the boy as an early Christmas gift. He thought maybe he was being paranoid because it had an embedded GPS chip, which really seemed fucked up as he thought about it.

He'd had a feeling something bad was lurking around the corner and would take them by surprise since he'd heard Matt's story, so he ordered the watch to be on the safe side. It had Raphael, Ryan's favorite Ninja Turtle, on its face, but Tim worried Matt wouldn't be happy with him for the gift after he explained its value. He didn't want to upset Matt, so he'd held off giving it to Ryan early.

Just another day and they could have found the boy quickly, without any trouble. Second-guessing himself would never happen again.

As he approached the Circle C, Danny and Matt exited the barn, both on their cell phones. Tim stopped the truck and hopped out, sprinting over to Matt and taking his arm to stop his pacing.

"Thanks, Rob. They were at the school at eleven-thirty, or so Ryan's teacher told me when she called. I appreciate anything you can do to help. I have no fuckin' idea where they went, but I'll try to think of a place and call ya back." Matt said goodbye to the person on the other end of the line.

"Matty, I'm so sorry. I just didn't..." Tim offered before he totally lost his shit and started to cry. He felt as if it was his fault for not giving Ryan the watch as he'd wanted to but hindsight was twenty-twenty.

Tim wasn't sure what else he could have done to avoid the situation. Long before he'd shown up at the school to pick up Ryan, they'd already taken him.

Matt engulfed him in strong arms. "Baby, it wasn't your fault. They were gonna do what they were gonna do. We just gotta get him back. His teacher called me after you left the school so upset, and she told me what happened today. I decided to call the Colonel. He's got access to resources I'm sure we don't even know about, and he said he'd look into it."

Tim swallowed and stared into the bull rider's azure eyes, trying hard to regain his composure. Falling apart and crying like a fucking baby would do no good. It was time for calmer heads to prevail.

"I have money, Matty. I can find us some more resources, I swear. I'm sure Uncle Josh, or maybe Ronni, knows people who can help us.

Matt leaned down to kiss his lips softly. "I love you, Timmy. We'll get our son back, I swear."

Chapter
Twenty-four

Early Christmas morning, the doorbell rang as Matt sat at the kitchen table with two fingers of Jack chilling over three ice cubes in an old juice glass with Bam-Bam Flintstone on it. They were old jelly glasses he and Jeri had collected when he was a boy, and he remembered his mother giving him the set with all the Flintstones characters on them as a gag gift the Christmas after he and Bertie were dreadfully wed.

The thought struck him funny as he emptied the glass, so he chuckled, hearing footsteps approaching. He turned to see a large man following Tim into the kitchen, and he smiled. He didn't know the man, but if he was a friend of Tim's, Matt knew they'd be friends quickly.

"This is DB Jeffers. DB, this is Ryan's father, Matthew Collins," his lover introduced. Matt stood unsteadily, bracing himself against the kitchen table before he extended his hand to the stranger.

"What can I do for ya?" he asked with an unattractive slur to his voice as he took in the man's size. He was as big as a fucking refrigerator, and he had a gold tooth, which Matt found funny for no reason that made sense, but he was able to keep from laughing.

The man was shorter than Matt, and his skin was a deep brown. He was dressed in a pair of dark jeans and a red sweater with a gray, wool-tweed, driving cap on his head. He had a set of diamond studs in his ears, and he was wearing black, horn-rimmed glasses. He was a good-looking guy, but Matt had no idea why the man might be at his house.

"I spoke with Colonel Stanford last night and he sent me to help ya out with this situation. I was under him at Bliss before I got out last summer. Tell me what happened, sir," the man requested as he took the seat Tim had offered.

Matt looked at his lover with a cocked eyebrow as Tim stood next to him, hand reaching out. "I'm gonna take this and make you some breakfast. DB, are you hungry?" Tim removed the empty whiskey glass and bottle, swatting Matt's hand as he tried to grab them.

"Matthew, we need you to sober up so we can explain what happened to DB. I'll try to start telling him the story, but you know more of the details than me," Tim insisted, which didn't exactly make Matt happy.

He just wanted the pain to go away again. It had worked the last time Bertie took the boy, drinking to block the pain. Why not use a tried-and-true method?

After Matt hung up from his call with Rob the afternoon before—the day his son had been abducted—he went to the cabinet and pulled out the bottle just as he'd done when he came home to find his home empty and his three-year-old son missing.

They should have been sitting at his mother's house where Ryan would be tearing through the gifts his parents and the Simmons' had bought. Matt would have already taken Ryan to the barn to show him how Josie had settled in, and the saddle would be on the gate with a big ribbon on it, along with the bridle and saddle pad. It would have been so perfect.

Matt felt the tears leak and unlike earlier, he didn't stop himself. He turned to the handsome stranger and pulled the wallet from his jeans' back pocket, flipping it open to show him Ryan's school picture. "That's our boy. He's gonna be eight this summer. He just lost a front tooth earlier in the month."

Matt became too overwrought with emotion to continue speaking. His heart had blown apart, and he didn't know if there was enough left to try to fix it—ever.

He sobbed as Tim cleared his voice. "DB, I'm sorry. He's been drinking all night, and I shouldn't have let him do it, but I can't make him do anything he doesn't want to do. After I feed him and get him into bed, I'll tell you everything I know about this situation."

Tim wrapped his arms around Matt's shoulders and held him tight to his body. The bull rider did the same and sobbed into Tim's stomach like he'd never stop crying for the rest of his life.

It was unbelievable to think Bertie could be so goddamn hard-hearted that she'd take his son, his reason for living, for the sake of money... yet again.

Matt looked up at Tim, "He should be here openin' his gifts. He... The fuckin' cops are full of shit and worthless," Matt huffed out between sobs.

Tim pulled a tissue from the box and handed it to him. He blew his nose and tried to compose himself, but the whiskey and the circumstance had him hamstrung and an emotional mess.

DB pulled a small bottle out from his jeans pocket and addressed Tim. "Put this into a glass of warm water," he instructed.

"What is it?"

"It'll sober him up pretty quick. We're wasting precious time here instead of getting the boy back. The trail is cold after a day, and I'm not about to let this get away from me," DB insisted. Matt watched as Tim did as he asked, placing the glass in front of him.

"Drink it, Mr. Collins. You ain't gonna wanna let too much more grass grow under our feet if you want your son home." The man's voice was serious.

Matt did as instructed. It went down quickly, tasting a little bitter.

"Where's the bathroom?" DB asked.

"Oh, it's just up the stairs and down the hall. The door is open."

DB grabbed Matt's hand and hauled him out of the kitchen. He instructed Tim to make some very strong coffee as they climbed the stairs.

The next thing Matt knew, he was on his knees, feeling as if he was going to die as his stomach expelled the half bottle of bourbon he'd consumed while looking through the pictures on his phone of Ryan after the local police told him there was nothing they could do before they left his ranch.

They reminded him Bertie still retained joint custody of their son, and the agreement made no distinction regarding which of them had primary custody. They wouldn't be looking for his son at all.

Matt truly wanted to throttle his attorney, Jon Wells, for suggesting Bertie could be enticed to bring Ryan home if Matt was to acquiesce regarding a joint custody agreement the first time she took the boy, which he hadn't been happy about giving. It worked, but at what price?

Matt climbed out of the icy-cold shower he'd inflicted upon himself in hopes of sobering up and quelling the puking. His teeth were chattering enough to rattle his whole body, so he reached down to feel his balls had left the sack, likely returning to the spot in his belly where they'd resided before he hit puberty.

When the bathroom door opened, he was surprised to see his father walk in with a large mug of steaming something. "Drink this. Why the fuck didn't you call me and your mother last night? We'd have— Well, Matthew, he's our grandson, ya know? You're not the only one who missed Ryan when that bitch took him last time." His father's face mirrored the pain in Matt's soul.

Matt sighed, knowing he should have called them the previous night before the idea of getting drunk sounded so fucking great. He'd been so devastated by the fact Bertie took his son again, and he couldn't think straight. He guessed Tim wasn't thinking straight either.

They were both a mess, and Matt was instantly pissed at himself for the way he handled the situation. It wasn't what he should have done as a father because he should have been actively pursuing a strategy to find his son, not drowning his sorrows as if the boy was going to be gone for another three years.

"I'm sorry, Daddy, but I guess we weren't thinkin' straight last night. I'd have thought Danny woulda called ya." Matt glanced at his father to see the worry.

"We went to dinner at the steak house with Katie and Josh after Tim called to say y'all were gonna stay home. We decided y'all just wanted more time together since it was your first Christmas, so we went out for dinner. Danny called and left a message at the farm, but we didn't check them 'til this mornin'. That man out there is a big bastard." Marty pointed his thumb over his shoulder.

Matt chuckled, not feeling any humor in the situation. "Yeah, he is. I wish he'da beat me to death rather than give me that shit in that little bottle."

Matt wrapped a towel around his waist before taking the cup of coffee from his father. His head was still groggy, but between the puking and the cold shower, he was sober enough to have his common sense kick in and give him ten kinds of hell.

You fuckin' idiot! You shoulda started tryin' to follow 'em. No, you gotta just sit in this fuckin' house again and drink yourself into a stupor like ya did the last time she took him!

He slugged down the burning hot liquid and looked at his father with a new resolve. "Can you have Tim bring me another cup while I get dressed? I'm sorry, Dad for not bein' the best father I can be, but that's about to change." Matt opened the bathroom door.

Marty grabbed his arm and looked into Matt's eyes. "You're a good father, Matthew, you just don't know what to do about things like this, though none of us really do. How often does someone have to handle their child being taken?

"You've gotta learn to deal with some pretty crazy shit as Ryan gets older because he's gonna try your patience, I swear, but you'll love him regardless. Get dressed. I'll send Tim back with the coffee."

Marty stopped and turned to look at Matt who was heading to the dresser to retrieve some underwear. "Matthew, son, Tim blames himself because he was pickin' Ryan up from school, and he feels like he shoulda been there earlier. He had no way of knowin' what was gonna happen, but it don't stop him from blamin' himself. Maybe talk to him?" Without waiting for his response, Marty turned to leave the room with the empty cup.

Matt pulled on boxer briefs and went to the closet to grab jeans and a sweatshirt. He slipped on a pair of suede slippers his mother had given him for Christmas the year before, relishing the comfort of the wool lining on his frozen feet. He pulled on his jeans and the sweatshirt before he went to the bathroom to brush his teeth, praying not to gag.

After he finished, he combed his wavy hair and returned to the bedroom, seeing Tim sitting on the bed looking so fucking guilty it was sad. There was no reason for the handsome man to blame himself. He hadn't done a damn thing wrong.

Matt walked over to sit down next to him, pulling his smaller body onto his lap. "I love ya, Timmy. Thank you for lettin' me wallow last night and thank you for takin' care of me. I'm so sorry this happened, but we're gonna get our boy back, I swear."

Tim pressed his forehead to Matt's shoulder while he sobbed. It was definitely Tim's turn to cry because Matt had cried damn near all night, but it wasn't getting them closer to getting Ryan home.

After a few minutes, Matt reached for a tissue from the box on the nightstand. He tilted up Tim's handsome face and wiped his eyes. "We gotta get our shit together because this ain't gettin' him home. I love ya. Let's go talk to that big bastard in the kitchen. What the fuck did he put in that glass?"

Tim giggled a little as he wiped his eyes. "Ipecac. It makes you vomit, which you did for a long time. How's your throat?"

Matt swallowed, feeling a tightness. "I'll live. Come on, we got a little man to rescue." The two of them rose from the bed and walked down the hallway, then down the stairs where everyone was waiting for them in the kitchen.

Matt noticed the tree wasn't on, and he decided it would stay dark until Ryan was home, irrespective of how long it took. It wouldn't be Christmas without his son at home, but they would bring him back.

The doorbell rang again as Matt sat in the family room, discussing things with his parents and Tim's aunt and uncle. DB Jeffers and Tim had gone to Matt's office where they'd been for two hours. Matt had no idea what they were doing, but they'd seemed determined when they left so he chose to give them privacy.

His mother rose to answer the door, but Matt decided he should make himself useful, so he walked down the hallway to open the front door, ecstatic to see the Stanford family, along with Andy, Savannah's girlfriend, smiling at him. Obviously, they'd given up their holiday to come to Holloway. It touched Matt's heart.

"God, you guys. Please come in. I'm so glad you came, but I'm sorry your Christmas was ruined." The Colonel shook Matt's hand and pulled him into a hug.

"Now, son, you're a part of our family as well, and my grandson's been taken. That's a reason to come here to support family and do everything we can to get him back. Anything yet?" Rob asked as he walked in with DeAnne behind him, hugging Matt. Savannah, Andy, and Robby followed. It was nice to have them there, ready to help Matt though they barely knew him.

Matt showed them into the living room where everyone was discussing the best way to handle the situation as they saw it. His parents had never met Robert Stanford, and he was sure his mother knew Bertie had no love for her father, so when his mother bristled, he regretted keeping his family out of the loop about why he'd gone to El Paso.

Things had happened so fast with Ryan's disappearance that giving an explanation for why Matt was in touch with Colonel Stanford had just slipped his mind. As they all stood in the living room staring at each other, Matt knew an introduction was long overdue.

"Momma and Dad, this is Colonel Robert Stanford, his wife DeAnne, their daughter, Savannah, her girlfriend, Andy, and their son, Robby. Everyone, this is my mother, Jeri, and my father Marty. These are our good friends and Tim's aunt and uncle, Josh and Katie Simmons. Tim's back in the office with DB." Matt glanced at the Colonel.

After hands were shaken, Rob turned to Matt and smiled. "Let's go see how far they've gotten. DB can work miracles, Matt, so let's hold off on worrying right now. He was in Delta Force."

Rob turned to DeAnne and grinned. "Honey, maybe you can make some tea? I think it might help everyone relax a little. This problem will be solved quickly, and when we get my grandson home, I want him to be thrilled everyone's already acquainted."

DeAnne smiled and gestured to Jeri and Katie. "Would you mind showing me to the kitchen?"

Matt got the idea. "Dad, why don't you and Josh take Savannah, Andy, and Robby down to the barn to show 'em Josie. She's a Christmas gift for Ryan."

The Colonel squeezed his shoulder. Matt glanced at the man, who gave a subtle nod before the two of them proceeded down the hall to see if there was any progress on finding Ryan.

Rob stopped Matt just outside the door and turned him, staring into his eyes. "Matthew, I don't plan to lose my grandson. I'll do everything I can to bring him home, rest assured."

Matt nodded and led the man into the room, feeling a little hope creep into his soul for the first time since he'd learned what those women had done. Taking his son for a second time had Matt seeing *blood* red.

Chapter Twenty-five

Tim listened to the large man behind him on his phone. "It's me. Find me a cell number for Roberta Stanford Collins. Try any iterations of the name, okay? Also, find me the address of Ramona Stanford. Start with Colorado."

He didn't know to whom the man was speaking, but Tim didn't hesitate to begin his own search using the parameters DB had instructed the person on the end of the line. Tim proceeded to hack into a lesser-known *unofficial* cell phone directory and set up a search of the things DB had described.

Tim held up his hand and pointed to his screen, happy to see the search had produced exactly what DB had requested. "Never mind." The large man ended the call and leaned over Tim's shoulder.

"I didn't know you were a hacker, Tim." Tim laughed at the man's teasing.

They'd gotten to know one another a little while Matt was puking his guts out after DB had conned Tim into slipping his man a drug that would make him throw up everything Matthew had eaten as a small child.

Initially, Tim had been pissed about the deception. DB *had* apologized for not being forthcoming regarding what the bottle was filled with and what it would do. He had, however, asserted how necessary it was to get Matt sober so they could have coherent answers. It had worked, and Tim wasn't about to hold a grudge.

"I'm a man of mystery, DB. I'll widen the search to Colorado, Utah, Arizona, and Nevada for Mona, but I don't know where Bertie lives in Canada." Tim pecked away on his keyboard.

DB laughed out loud, showing his gold tooth. "Oh, that's perfect. If they try to take him over the border it becomes— Uh, let me make a call about it. Narrow in on Mona because she likely has a phone we can track. If Bertie's is issued out of Canada, we'll need a little help," DB told him.

There was a quick knock before the door opened and Matt walked in with a tall, majestic-looking man behind him. The man stood ramrod straight and he had a military haircut, for certain, so Tim figured him to be Bertie's father. He was good-looking, probably in his fifties, or so Tim deduced.

As the search engine continued its job, Tim stood to address the man. "Colonel Stanford, it's a pleasure to meet you, sir. Matt has told me about your family, and I've been anxious to meet all of you. I appreciate you coming to support him during this mess. Of course, you remember DB." Tim pointed to the man standing behind him on the phone speaking French. Tim could tell it surprised all three of them.

"Merci beaucoup!" DB signed off the call and turned to look at them with a smile.

DB walked over to the Colonel, extending his hand to shake before he pulled Rob Stanford into a one-armed, man hug. "It's good to see you again, sir. I'm glad you called me about this. I was able to change my flight to Hawaii until after the New Year, but I'm guessin' it ain't gonna take us that long to find your grandson."

Rob nodded and turned to Tim. "I'm assuming you're Matthew's partner. I've heard a lot about you, young man. I'm glad you're here." Colonel Stafford shook Tim's hand.

Tim slumped into his chair, still feeling guilty. "Sir, I believe it's my fault."

Matt squeezed Tim's shoulder and placed a hand on his cheek to gently turn his head. "It's not your fault, baby. I'd have never imagined they'd come here to Holloway." Tim's computer chimed.

Tim quickly turned back to the desk, checking the screen for the last tower Mona's cell phone had pinged. It was in the small town of Christiansburg, Virginia, not more than forty miles from Holloway.

"She's off 460 in town. It's only four minutes from Virginia Tech, so it's on the Blacksburg side." Tim pointed to the cell towers where the phone was continuing to hit.

There were a handful of hotels and motels in the area, but they needed to narrow it down because there were too many to search every one of them. "How do we find an exact location?" the Colonel asked.

"Give me a minute." Tim went to work, hammering on the keys without glancing up. The three men were talking behind him, but Tim wasn't listening.

He picked up the location finder app on Mona's phone and hacked it, finding her exact location. "Got it. She's at the Hampton Inn. It's on Arbor Drive. Shall we?" Tim jumped up and followed the other three men running down the hallway, ignoring the others in the house.

They all grabbed coats and headed out the front door. Tim had his cell in his hands, having honed his signal to Mona's so he could guide them to where the woman was located. Of course, they had no way to know if she had Ryan with her, but it was the best lead they had so it was worth a try.

They hopped into a big Lincoln Navigator, Tim in the front seat next to DB while the Colonel and Matt were in the back seat. Tim gave DB directions from the GPS on his phone, and when they pulled up to the hotel half an hour later, they all looked at each other.

"So, how do we get in without her knowing it?" Matt was vibrating with nerves.

Rob cleared his throat. "I'll go in. I have my military ID, and if she registered under her married name, that's so much the better. I'll just say I'm here to meet her and our daughter. Tim, give me your cell number, and I'll text you the room number after I get the key. Meet me there."

The three of them nodded in agreement before the Colonel exited the vehicle and casually strolled inside. Tim happened to see movement out of the corner of his eye, so he turned his head to see Ryan with a woman he didn't recognize. The little cowboy was walking a small dog on a leash, and the woman was on a cell phone.

He pecked DB's forearm that was resting on the console, directing the man's attention toward the passenger window. "That's our son. Is that Bertie?" Tim glanced at his lover in the back seat.

"That fuckin bitch!" Matt swore as he reached for the door handle. Suddenly the door locks clicked, keeping Tim and Matt inside.

DB turned to look at Matt, brooking no patience for an argument. "Look, cowboy, we don't wanna go to jail. What's good for the goose is good for the gander as they say. You've got joint custody, right?"

"Yeah, but..." Matt's voice was shaky.

DB cut him off. "I'm gonna go get your boy and the dog. Get the Colonel outta that place immediately so we can haul ass because we don't want to worry about cops comin' into this shit. Let 'em come to the ranch after us." DB opened his door and hopped out.

The man adjusted his hat and looked at Tim. "How I look?" DB gave time a wink and a toothy smile.

"Quite handsome." Tim returned the grin.

"Hey, you're already spoken for." Matt reached over Tim's seat and tapped his man on the shoulder. Tim climbed over the console to sit with his cowboy as they watched DB stroll to where Bertie was standing with the boy and the dog.

Tim quickly sent a text to the Colonel to return to base, and when the man walked out of the hotel lobby, Tim saw him observing the area as he guessed a military man would do before his eyes set on his daughter and DB in an argument, which became the direction the Colonel headed.

DB had Ryan and the dog within reach, both of whom were struggling to get away. Matt reached over the seat to unlock the doors of the SUV, and they hopped out to run to Ryan, happy tears streaming down their faces.

"Daddy!" Ryan gasped as Matt picked him up, apparently much to Bertie's surprise, based on the look on her face. She'd been arguing with DB, not paying attention to her surroundings, but when she saw Ryan in Matt's arms, she cursed.

Matt hugged his son before handing him off to Tim, who clutched the little cowboy tightly, vowing to never let him out of sight again. Tim ignored everything around him, feeling the tears continue to rush down his face. He wasn't at a place of gratitude yet, but it was coming soon.

Ryan pulled away from Tim, smiling at him as his own tears fell. "I'm sorry she took me, but she said we was goin' to the ranch because her and Daddy had decided to share me. She told me she was movin' to Holloway with Nana Mona, and she had a dog for me. She said Daddy told her it was okay for me to have a dog. I wanted it to be true, Timmy." Ryan continued to dry the tears on Tim's face.

"I know, little man. We all want our wishes to come true, and when they do, it's hard to see beyond them. It's okay, now. We've got you back." Tim continued to hold the boy tightly.

"Who the fuck is that asshole holding my son? Give me my son, goddammit."

The woman's voice carried her complaints on the breeze.

Ryan squirmed out of his arms. When Tim put him on the ground, the puppy wiggled over to Ryan, shaking all over with happiness.

"This is Corky. He's a—"

Suddenly, Matt was yelling. "I'll fuckin' kill ya, you hear me? He's my son, and you left him behind for the money the first time, Bertie. Leave us alone."

Tim saw Ryan turning his head, and he couldn't have the boy hearing how ugly things had gotten between his parents. The Colonel and DB were minding Matt, so Tim was going to mind Ryan. "What kind of dog is he?"

"Uh, I think he's a mutt. Momma said she got him at a dog shelter, and she thought I'd like him. She lied to me, didn't she? She just wanted to take me away from Daddy again, right?" Once again, Tim saw the boy was wise beyond his years.

Tim decided it wasn't worth breaking the boy's heart to tell him his mother was a cold-hearted, money-grubbing liar. He bit his tongue as he thought about what he wanted to say before he spoke.

"Well, maybe she wanted her equal time with you, but she could have gone about it a better way. Let's go get in DB's SUV. Wait till you meet him. He was in the Army with your Grandpa Rob. Oh, wait till you meet *him* and your aunt and uncle. This is gonna be the greatest Christmas ever."

The dog broke away from them and ran back into the excitement, barking and jumping around. It wanted in on the excitement, obviously.

"This ain't over, you motherfucker!"

Tim wasn't taking any chances, so he put Ryan in the far back seat of the Navigator. He turned to see Matt had the dog in his arms, and Bertie was pounding on his back before her father peeled her off him, taking her by the arms and telling her something that seemed to rile her up more.

When Matt hopped into the back seat and handed Ryan the anxious puppy, Tim saw the smile on his face. "He wanted to come with ya back to the ranch. He can sleep in your room, I reckon."

DB and Rob Stanford got into the SUV without a word, and the group began the trip back to Holloway. Tim sent a text to his aunt confirming they had Ryan so the people at the house could stop worrying. He was determined it would be a Christmas they'd never forget, and not because of the attempted kidnapping.

Tim knew those two women were going to take Matt to court eventually, but he had a suggestion for how to deal with the situation he'd give more thought to and maybe discuss with Ronni when the time was right.

When they arrived back at the ranch, everyone released a collective sigh. Since Christmas Day was a Friday and it was already shot to hell, they all decided they'd celebrate the holiday on Saturday.

They decided to have pizza at the ranch that night and Ryan finally got to meet Grandpa Rob, Grandma DeAnne, Aunt Savannah, and Uncle Robby. The family from El Paso was happy to be there, and Tim was glad to have them around.

Everyone loved the dog, and when the Stanford's went to the Holiday Inn by the highway, Tim's and Matt's parents walked out behind them. Uncle Josh pulled Tim aside as the others hugged and kissed.

"You want me to sneak Charlie into the barn in the mornin'? I'll make sure he's got feed and water 'fore I leave to go back home."

Tim considered his offer for a minute before he spoke. "Do you think I should give Charlie to Matt, or should you keep him and use him for breeding stock? This is all… Well, everything got so fucked up, Uncle Josh. I'm worried it's just too much." Tim was whispering, trying to remain calm.

Josh closed his eyes for a second, smiling slowly before he opened them. "If this whole situation hadn't happened, would you give him the horse?"

"Well, Aunt Katie said it might be too much of a gift."

Josh chuckled. "The first stallion I owned was a gift from Kathleen. I was embarrassed because my girlfriend made more money than me, and I put up such a fuss. That's why she mentioned it, Tim.

"I got over it eventually, and Scout helped us buy the land we have now. I was too proud to accept a gift I couldn't afford to give *her*, but I learned to allow someone I loved to give me something and appreciate it. Give Matt that same chance, Tim." Josh gave a confirming wink.

It all made perfect sense to Tim, so he nodded. He greatly appreciated his aunt and uncle for their unyielding love and compassion. Aunt Katie's words were based on something that happened earlier in her life when she felt she'd made the wrong decision, and she was only trying to save Tim the same heartache.

Tim was pretty sure Matthew Collins would appreciate his gift—that beautiful stallion. It was given with love, after all.

Chapter Twenty-six

After everyone left the ranch that night, all promising to return the next morning to celebrate Christmas, Matt and Ryan played with the little puppy while Tim found a box in the basement to make it a bed. He told Matt he was hoping to save them from a massive cleanup the next day by not allowing the dog to roam the house freely until it was potty-trained.

The three of them finally took the dog for its last walk and when it was time for bed, Ryan asked to sleep in a fort like they'd made at Thanksgiving. Of course, Matt couldn't say no.

The bull rider built a small fire while Tim turned on the Christmas tree. Holiday music was softly playing in the background as the three of them held each other tightly, dozing off. Corky was next to Ryan's feet, and thankfully, he settled down right away in his temporary, cardboard bed.

His boys, as Matt thought of them, dozed as quickly as the dog, but every time Matt closed his eyes, images of Ryan missing from his life appeared, startling him awake. He needed to call Jon to come up with a more permanent solution to keep Bertie from having any claim to Ryan. It was essential she'd never be allowed to take the boy away again.

Matt woke at six in the morning, having seen the clock on the cable box turn over to four before he finally dozed. He was pretty sure he was lucky to have slept the two hours he had all things considered.

He slipped upstairs to the bathroom to shower and dress for the day because the work on a cattle ranch didn't stop simply because the owner failed to get a good night's sleep. He thought he'd heard Danny's truck passing the house on the way to the barn earlier, and he really wanted everything set up for Josie before Josh brought her over. When Ryan finally made it to the barn to see her, Matt wanted the boy to be happily surprised.

He slipped on his old boots and checked his phone, seeing it was an unseasonable fifty degrees outside, so he skipped the coat and went out the back door toward the barn.

When he arrived at the door, it was open, which worried him. Danny didn't open the barn doors when he arrived. He always went directly to the machine shed.

"*Whoa!*" The shout came from inside the barn.

Matt wished he'd brought the shotgun that was locked up in his office because he didn't recognize the voice. If someone was trying to steal from him, he was about to take out all his pent-up anger for Bertie on someone's unsuspecting face.

When Matt walked into the barn, there was a tall guy standing next to one of the stalls where a huge black horse was tied. The guy was brushing him and attaching a ribbon to the mane.

"What the hell?"

The man turned around and smiled. "Well, hey now, bull rider. This is supposed to be a surprise. You best get outta here, so you don't ruin Tim's fun." It was Mickey from the Katydid, and Matt started laughing because he was wearing a Santa cap atop his cowboy hat.

"Where in the hell did that horse come from?" Matt approached the beast, seeing it was one of the most beautiful stallions he'd ever laid eyes on.

Mickey stopped what he was doing to turn to Matt. "Look, I was told to drop him off here along with a saddle and fix him up a little. What're you doin' down here?"

"I came to do the same for Josie. You comin' over later?"

Tim had bought Mickey a gift and Matt hoped the guy would come for the celebration. He knew Tim thought of the guy as a good friend, and he wanted Mickey to feel welcome in their home. Maybe he could help Matt talk Tim into finally moving in permanently so Mickey could have Tim's bigger room at the Katydid? It wasn't exactly a bad idea.

"Yeah. Josh insisted Tim wanted me to come. I also got a message from your father-in-law. Quote, 'Tell Matthew he better make Tim believe this stud horse is the best gift he ever received. Tim's worried he won't like it, and Matt better love it, or I'll come over and kick his ass until he figures it out.' Unquote. I don't know nothin' more than that to tell ya. I'll fix Josie up for ya, too. Just get outta here so you can fake your total surprise. I'll make it nice I promise." Mickey gave him a big grin.

Matt nodded and hurried out of the barn and back to the house, leaving his boots on the back deck so he could sneak inside and start the coffee. He heard the dog whining, so he rushed to the family room to get him before he woke Tim or Ryan.

He grabbed the pup and took him out into the back yard along with a couple of paper towels to pick up the waste because he didn't want the backyard to become a shitty mess. He put the puppy down and watched it sniff and wander all over the backyard, heading toward the fence separating the yard from the cow pasture.

"Ho! Hang on, bud." Matt caught the dog just before he went under the fence. He wished he'd brought the damn leash, but luckily, he'd averted a disaster.

After the dog did his business, Matt cleaned it up, mildly complaining, before he carried the little dog into the house, putting him just inside the back door after stopping in the garage to open a big trash bag to put the dog crap and paper towel inside.

Matt would need to decide what to do with the little *presents* the mutt would leave behind because he didn't want it being stepped in and brought into the house. There would have to be new rules for boots because now they had cow, horse, *and* dog shit to worry about being dragged inside. Cleaning those floors wouldn't be anything Matt looked forward to doing.

He glanced at the clock, seeing it was six forty-five in the morning, which he determined was late enough. He grabbed his cell and hit the contact information for Jon Wells. He pressed the button to call him and chuckled to himself, sure the man wouldn't answer. It rang twice.

"Wells," Matt heard his attorney answer. Clearly, he'd awakened him, and it brought a big grin to his face as he considered how much he was about to fuck up the man's holiday weekend.

"I oughta sue ya for malpractice, ya prick." Matt was joking, but maybe not entirely? If Jon hadn't suggested the damn joint custody clause in the first place, Matt wouldn't have lost his son for the thirty-six hours it took to get him back.

"Who the fuck is this?" Jon Wells didn't sound very happy.

"Can't you read? I know you have my number in your cell."

Matt had lost a lot of sleep because he couldn't shut down his imagination regarding all the scenarios which could have occurred when Bertie took his son. It seemed fitting Jon Wells should suffer a little bit as well since he'd been the one to leave the door open for Bertie to take the boy in the first place.

"Aaron? What the fuck, man? You know what time it is? I thought you and Ricky were well on your way to St. Kitts for your honeymoon. The roaming charges will eat you up, man." Jon chuckled, which brought a laugh from Matt as well.

Matt heard someone in the background. "Get off the fuckin' phone, Jonny, and fuck me."

The voice was soft, but it was definitely low-pitched. Matt had never asked about Jon's personal situation, having assumed the man was straight. Obviously, his gaydar was for shit.

"It's me, Matt Collins. Because of your fuckin' joint custody clause in the divorce papers, my ex-wife kidnapped my boy from school on Christmas Eve. I had to get a goddamn Special Forces soldier to help me get him back because the cops wouldn't do a goddamn thing about it. You said to put it in the papers so we could get the fuckin' thing over with faster, and the cops told me I didn't have a goddamn leg to stand on when it came to gettin' him back.

"Now, you're gonna fix that shit, Jon. I ain't gonna have my son taken from me again, so I'd suggest you think on it and come up with a fix so it doesn't happen again." Matt's words were harsh, but not unjustified.

There was a quiet "*Oh shit!*"

Yeah, you better be worried, you pricey motherfucker!

"Tell me what happened. I can't do anything today, but Monday, I can file a TRO and a motion for sole custody," Jon suggested.

"I don't know what the fuck that is, but you better file somethin'. That joint custody shit shoulda never happened so you better fix it. Rob and his family are here, so you might wanna come out and pick his brain about how to handle Bertie and her mom because he used to be married to the woman. I don't wanna give 'em money, but if it's all I can do, then so be it.

"We're celebratin' Christmas today, so I know Rob and DeAnne will be here. Come talk to him cause I ain't flyin' your ass to El Paso again on my dime. You fucked it up by not wantin' to drag out the divorce. Well, I paid ya an assload of money to handle it, but this is a clusterfuck, as I see it. Time you started earnin' that big check." Matt hung up.

He didn't dislike Jon Wells, but he felt the man deserved some of the blame for the agony he and Tim had endured while they tried to find Ryan. It was time to do something about it once and for all.

As he made himself a cup of coffee from the fancy machine, Matt heard the delightful giggle of his son. "Stop, Corky. My feet are ticklish."

Matt laughed as he filled the side tank on the coffee maker with more water and put in a small foil-covered cup to fix a coffee for the man he loved. He continued to listen to Ryan laughing, which was a fucking great sound to hear, considering Matt, at one point, wasn't sure he'd ever hear it again.

As he'd told Ryan about Tim more than once, the sound made his heart happy.

After Tim's coffee finished, Matt made hot chocolate for Ryan. He went to the cookie jar his mother had put on his counter and pulled out a handful of sugar cookies, putting them on a plate. He grabbed a big baking pan to use as a tray, putting the mugs and the cookies on top to carry them into the living room.

He saw Ryan and the dog snuggled together with Tim watching the two of them as they appeared to be dozing.

Matt smiled. "Merry Christmas, baby." He sat, juggling the pan. He held it out for Tim, who sat up to take his cup of coffee and a cookie.

Suddenly, Ryan's eyes popped open. "Is that hot chocolate I smell?"

"Yeah, but before you get it, go to the john and then get your dog some water. I'm gonna call Papa Marty to pick up some dog food for Corky. We fed him ham last night, but he can't eat a steady diet of it. We'll get him a proper bed and stuff on Monday, so he doesn't have to stay in the box.

"When you take him out to do his business—and he is *your* dog so you're gonna be responsible for him—you need to put him on a leash until we can get a different kind of fence around the back yard so he can't get to the cow pasture. The cows would step on him and hurt him. We also need to get him an appointment with Doc Grant to check him out. I'll call on Monday. Now, scoot. The grandparents will be here at nine."

Ryan gave him and Tim smacking kisses on their cheeks before he ran up the stairs with Corky stumbling up behind him. Matt scooted into the fort next to Tim and kissed his cheek. "How'd you sleep?"

Tim yawned and smiled. "Okay, but we gotta get those damn sleep pads. This hardwood is hell on the back."

Matt thought for a minute and decided to pursue a line of questioning he never imagined he'd consider. "Would you rather have carpet in here? I mean, we can get carpet if you want, or do you wanna redo the whole place? We can paint or put new tile in the kitchen. We can get new furniture, too, Tim. Whatever you want.

"I want this to be a home you want to come home *to*. I love you, Timmy, and I want you to live here with us. Please, move in."

It wasn't really in Matt's DNA to beg for anything because he was used to being an alpha male where things came easily to him. Recent events taught him it was smart to appreciate the people in his life, and after all, Tim had come through for him in spades more often than Matt could have ever anticipated.

The shit he did to bring Ryan home was beyond Matt's comprehension, but he knew Tim loved the boy as much as he, and Matt wanted the three of them to share their lives. It was *Matt's* Christmas wish.

"Keep your eyes closed," Matt told Ryan as he carried the boy down to the barn on his shoulders. They'd left the dog in the laundry room for a few minutes because he'd likely scare the horses, who were already trying to adjust to their new home. Matt knew Corky would have to get used to the animals on the ranch, but that would come with time. Right now, it was the moment for great surprises.

"Where we goin'?" Ryan asked, excitement evident in his voice as he held his hands over his face as he'd promised.

"Don't you worry about it. Just keep your eyes closed. Santa made a special trip to deliver your gift last night, so let's be grateful."

Tim looped his hand through Matt's crooked elbow as the three walked up to the barn. Tim opened the door and glanced in, turning to smile at Matt and Ryan.

They all walked into the barn, and Matt stopped in front of Josie's new stall. He reached up and took Ryan down from his shoulders, holding him against his hip. He saw the boy's nose wrinkling as he sniffed, and he was pretty sure Ryan was onto the surprise, so Matt said, "Open 'em."

Ryan dropped his hands and climbed from Matt's arms onto the gate to see the little female donkey inside with a red and green bow tied around her neck. She was eating from a grain bin Matt had hung low on the stall wall. Ryan looked at Matt and Tim, and then back to Josie as if he didn't believe it was true.

"Oh, Daddy!" he gasped as he threw himself back into Matt's arms and hugged him tightly. Matt felt tears on his neck, and he gave a watery smile of his own. It was exactly as he hoped it would be.

They all heard a snort behind them, so they turned to see the huge stallion Matt wasn't supposed to know about.

"What the hell is... Where'd that come from?" Matt tried hard to keep a curious look on his face.

"Surprise?"

Tim's half-hearted response was nervous as the three of them stepped over to the stall. The stallion walked over to Tim and swung its head over the side of the gate, whinnying softly as Tim stroked his head.

"Matty, this is Ebony Prince Charles. I've been calling him Charlie, but you can call him anything you want. He's a Kentucky Saddler, and Uncle Josh says he's an amazing ride. I haven't ridden him yet because he's yours. Merry Christmas."

Ryan looked at Matt and grinned, announcing, "We both got horses, Daddy. This is the best Christmas *ever!*" Matt had to agree.

The rest of the day was full of surprises for the family. Somewhere along the way, Tim had the foresight to ask Aunt Katie to drop off the gifts for Cindy and Rocky Whipple on Christmas morning. She took footage on her cell phone and showed it to them later that afternoon.

Rocky opened the front door, running back inside, and returning with his mother, who started to cry as she saw the red, crushed-velvet bag. There weren't many dry eyes among the group as they all watched the scene unfold on the cell phone screen.

Ryan took great pride in taking his new grandfather, Rob, down to the barn to show him Josie and his new saddle. Matt smiled at the fact Ryan hadn't opened all his gifts because he wanted to wait until the next day when he could be alone with his dad and Tim so they could add to their family traditions. It brought a sentimental smile to Matt's face.

Matt took great pride in showing off the stud horse Tim had given him for Christmas. The horse was magnificent, and Matt was anxious to take him out into the pasture. The saddle wasn't fancy, but it was broken in, which was exactly what Matt loved about it.

Tim explained to him his desire to commission a fancy saddle for Matt, but he quickly dissuaded his lover from pursuing anything of the sort. Matt wasn't the "fancy-saddle" kind of guy, or so he told Tim. The old rough-out was perfect for him in every way.

Tim's face glowed with happiness when Matt took him downstairs to show him the vintage *Pac-Man* video game he'd managed to buy from the guy who owned the pizza place in town. He explained to the man he loved how he planned to have the basement finished to make a game room, along with two bedrooms and a full bath. He told Tim they'd thank themselves when Ryan got older because he'd have a place to entertain his friends, and Matt and Tim could have some peace in other parts of the house. The passionate kiss he received in return made his blood roll through his veins from his quickly beating heart.

As everyone stood in the living room with drinks later that afternoon, Matt whistled to get everyone's attention. When they all turned to look at him, his heart was full. There were family, old friends, new friends, but at the center of all of it stood Tim and Ryan with joy shining on their faces. Of course, there was a mangy little mutt running around pissing on the hardwood, but time would cure all ills.

"I'd like to thank all of you for joining us to celebrate the first Christmas of our new family. As I look around, I see a lot of family and people who are gonna become family. I have a lot to be grateful for this Christmas, and I wanted to thank all of you for supporting us through the trials and the blessings. Merry Christmas." Matt lifted his glass in a toast.

He pulled Tim close and kissed him before he picked up Ryan to hug him as well. In Matt's opinion, the holiday had started out rocky, but it ended up being the best Christmas he'd ever had in his life. He said a silent prayer that it was the first Christmas of many to come.

Epilogue

"Quit fussing with it." Tim straightened Matt's tie for the umpteenth time that morning. They were heading to court for the hearing regarding Bertie's surrendering of her parental rights. She had agreed to give Matt full custody and renounce her rights to Ryan with no explanation, but Tim smiled because never was there a more important check written than the one that he'd given to Matt's ex-wife.

"I still don't know what the fuck that bitch is playin' at." Matt ran a hand over his freshly trimmed hair.

Tim smiled as he finished tightening the knot under Matt's chin. Matt was the most handsome man he'd ever seen in his life. The bull rider was still in shape and seeing him atop Charlie riding in the pasture at full trot was a gift from the gods. The man was sexy as hell, but on that grand stallion, he was like a marble statue.

"She's not playing at anything. I truly believe she's seen the light. According to what Jon told us, she called and volunteered, right?" Tim couldn't look his lover in the eyes.

It wasn't exactly the truth, but it was the letter of the contract Ronni Turnberry had prepared for Tim and presented to Bertie Collins. After he offered her five-hundred-thousand dollars to walk away and never return, she quickly abandoned her mother's idea of fighting Matt for Ryan's custody.

Ronni flew up to Toronto and explained things to Bertie, getting her to offer an affidavit stating her mother wasn't fit to have custody of Ryan due to her history of drug and alcohol abuse, as well as signing over her paternal rights to the boy for the check Tim was offering.

It was sad someone had set the price of a little boy for half-a-million dollars to a mother who should have rejected the idea immediately when it was offered, but Tim was grateful. He'd have paid every penny he had to secure the same agreement.

"Yeah, well, I think it's a bunch of bullshit. I guess we'll see." Matt pulled Tim into his body and kissed his lips gently. The adjustment to moving in had been a little difficult, but it was only because they were doing a few things at the house to make it more welcoming.

Matt refused to handle the updates and changes, so Tim went for a homier, lived-in approach as the style, unlike the way he viewed it the first time he walked in to fix Matt's computer.

There were pictures of family everywhere. There was comfortable furniture the three of them picked out together, and they had a large dining room table seating nearly everyone in the family at one time.

The Moran-Collins family was large, and it seemed they added more members all the time. Tim was grateful for it. Before he showed up in Holloway, he barely had any family at all.

"There. That looks perfect. We need to get going, babe. Jon's supposed to meet us at the courthouse."

Matt nodded, following Tim out of the bedroom, holding tightly to his hand as Tim hoped he would for the rest of their lives.

An hour later, they were sitting in the family courtroom, waiting for the judge to hear their case. "Your Honor, I submit the affidavits in support of quashing the Motion for Custody submitted by Mona Stanford, the grand-mother of the minor. Her own daughter has renounced her parental rights and agreed to give full custody to the boy's father having determined he's better fit to raise the child.

"Exhibit Two is an affidavit submitted by Colonel Robert Stanford, the minor's grandfather who was mar-ried to Mrs. Stanford, attesting to the fact his former wife is unable to care for the boy based on her documented history of drug and alcohol abuse. Her daughter has also submitted an affidavit in support of Colonel Stanford. It's a travesty to take up any more of this court's time on the matter. We ask that sole custody is granted to Matthew Collins, the boy's father." Jon took a seat next to Matt.

Tim turned to glance at the horrible woman, Mona Stanford, as she rose from her chair with her right fist in the air and an ugly scowl on her face in protest of Jon's statements. Mona had only contacted Bertie to try to hop on the gravy train of the money she thought Matthew had stashed away. She didn't want anything to do with Ryan, as Bertie mentioned in her affidavit.

Mona had been dating someone she thought had money, who thought she had money as well. In the end, they were both disappointed to learn each of them was as poor as a church mouse. It was truly when two grifters met, and now, Bertie had shut her out of the windfall she'd received.

Matt's ex was settled into a new life with some ex-convict from Canada. She didn't really want to raise Ryan, as she'd admitted to Ronni during their meeting in Toronto.

Of course, if there was money, she'd sell out her own mother—which she'd done without a second thought. It didn't matter to Tim. They had a good life waiting for them and a lot of money to pursue the things they'd enjoy. If they didn't have Ryan, there wouldn't be enough money in the world to make either of them happy.

An angry squeal caught everyone's attention. "They're fags! They have no business raising that boy!"

Mona Stanford's screams could likely be heard through the courthouse. The judge banged the gavel and looked at those in attendance until the room quieted.

He glanced through the papers in front of him for a few minutes before he leaned forward to speak into the microphone in front of him. "Based on the evidence and the affidavits submitted in support of Mr. Collins' testimony, I have no choice but to find in favor of the Respondent. Sole custody is granted to the father, Matthew

Ryan Collins, and a Permanent Restraining Order is hereby granted against Mona Stanford, who is so ordered to cease and desist with contacting the minor child in any way.

"Violation of the Order will result in incarceration, Mrs. Stanford. The transcript of these proceedings is hereby entered into the record. This court is adjourned." The judge slammed the gavel on the desk, and everyone rose as he left the room. When the door to his chambers closed, they all cheered and hugged each other.

Matt's parents and Tim's aunt and uncle had accompanied them to Richmond for the hearing, along with Mickey Warren. They all went out to have lunch to celebrate after the hearing, and the gathering was lively. It was a great day for the family, one Tim doubted they'd ever forget.

Tim stood in the hallway of the barn, saddling Chester at the ass crack of dawn. It was spring, and they were planning to move, vaccinate, and well-check the cows and calves, along with cutting out some of the larger feeder calves to ship to the auction.

Matt walked into the barn with a big grin for Tim, setting his heart ablaze. "We have a little bit of time before everybody's ready. Have I shown you the new hayloft?"

Tim giggled as he put down the curry comb. "Why, Mr. Collins, I don't think you have."

Matt walked over to him, kissing him silly once again. It was incredible to feel the man's arms around him. The winter had been spent having some work done around the place, along with forming a routine for their new family and even creating more new traditions for Ryan.

They had many nights of sleeping in the fort after Jeri and Marty bought them a huge air mattress for Christmas, and it was their favorite thing to do on cold nights. Matt would build a fire, they'd make camp-style food and eat in front of it, and then Ryan, who was above grade level in his reading and comprehension skills, would read books to his father and Tim. Both men would state unequivocally it was their favorite way to spend a Saturday night.

Of course, the other nights, Matt and Tim shared the king-sized bed in the primary bedroom, but truth be told, they only needed about a third of it because they slept so closely entwined the rest of the bed was empty. It was shaping up to be a lovely life.

"Well, baby, allow me," Matt told him as he tossed Tim over his shoulder and hurried up the ladder. When they got there, Tim was surprised to see a thermos bottle, a flannel blanket atop a bed of hay, and a bottle of lube.

He giggled as he was lowered from Matt's shoulder. "Seems you made a little party here, cowboy." They both laughed at Tim's teasing comment.

Matt pulled him close and looked into his eyes, causing Tim to sigh like a lovesick teenager. Tim could see the love in those big blues, and it warmed his heart. "Yeah, I wanted us to break in the hayloft the old-fashioned way. Can I interest you in a little vanilla coffee with a splash of cream?" Matt picked up the thermos.

Tim took it from his hands and smiled. "How about *after*?" He took Matt's hand and sank down onto the bed his man had made for the two of them.

They'd made love many times. Sometimes loudly when Ryan wasn't home. Sometimes quietly when Ryan was sleeping in his room, and sometimes in the heat of passion in a dark corner of the barn or in the office of the Katydid.

They had a great romance, and they loved each other. The passion was usually pretty difficult to contain when they were within arm's reach.

"I— We have our tests back. Can we skip the condoms?" Matt leaned forward to kiss Tim, taking his breath away once again.

When they broke apart, all Tim could do was nod. They made quick work of their clothes, and when Tim put himself on all fours on the blanket with the hay reinforcement, he gasped as Matt licked his balls... his perineum... his hole.

When Matt's tongue penetrated him, Tim nearly melted. It felt so incredible, and Matt had never done anything like it in the past.

"*Baby*, that feels so *goooood*." Tim felt it to the bottom of his soul.

"Good enough to make ya wanna stay here forever so I can do it every night?" Matt was taunting him between licks. Tim felt a slick finger enter him, and he was nearly speechless.

"*God, yessss.*" He hissed as he felt the second finger breach his entrance.

When number three joined the party, Tim was out of his mind. The intrusions abruptly left his body before a much larger invasion took place. When Matt's thick cock entered him, his body became liquid.

"So fucking good." It was hard to speak when one's mind was being blown.

When Matt pulled out, Tim felt the emptiness. "*Whyyy?*"

"Roll over, baby. I wanna look into your eyes." Matt's voice was demanding, so Tim did exactly as he asked. He'd gladly do it because he loved the man and looking into those bright blue eyes as Matt took him to the clouds was a wonderful experience.

Once he settled on his back, he felt Matt enter him again, gently that time. Matt covered his body and offered a happy gasp as he sank inside Tim's channel. When he didn't start moving, Tim stared into those blue orbs. "Are you okay?"

"I love you." Matt's eyes teared up.

Tim's body stiffened. "Are you breaking up with me? Is this a goodbye fuck?"

Matt chuckled. "*Hell* no. I wanted to have ya pinned in one place to ask ya if you'll marry me? It's legal, ya know?"

Without waiting for an answer, Matt moved seductively inside Tim. The love they made brought the most amazing feelings Tim Moran had experienced in his life. It was hard to really think about the fact that his biggest dream might come true. Matt was his first everything, and maybe he'd be his only and his last?

They moved together in perfect sync, which made it easy for Tim to answer. "I'd love to marry you. I love you, bull rider."

They raced to the climax, and when they each shot off, they both had stars in their eyes. It had been ecstasy, and they'd arrived at another crossroads.

Matt broke the silence. "There's no hurry, you know, to get married. If you wanna wait a while to be sure this is what you want, I'll wait for you." He kissed Tim's neck, face, and lips.

Tim chuckled. "I might be pregnant, you know. This is the first time we've done it without protection."

Matt laughed before he got very serious as he dipped his face into Tim's neck, kissing the flesh there before he pulled back and gazed into Tim's eyes, giving him a serious look. "Well, baby, if that's the case, I'll live up to my responsibilities and make an honest man of ya. I love you, Timothy Moran."

"I love you, too, Matthew Collins." Tears leaked from Tim's eyes as his heart overflowed with joy.

Matt smirked. "Good. All that's left is to find the preacher, sign the papers, and have the party."

Tim later laughed to himself as he thought about the moment while his head rested on the sleeping bull rider's chest. "Who knew?" Tim whispered to himself, smiling as he settled into the man he loved.

Life was full of big and small disappointments, along with big and small surprises. Tim Moran got two very big surprises in the form of Matthew and Ryan Collins, and he knew he'd never have found his heart's desire if he hadn't taken a chance... For the Love of the Bull Rider.

About Sam E. Kraemer

I grew up in the rural Midwest before moving to the East Coast with a dashing young man who swept me off my feet. We've now settled in the desert Southwest where I write M/M contemporary romance. I also write paranormal M/M romance under "Sam E. Kraemer writing as L. A. Kaye." I'm a firm believer that love is love, regardless of how it presents itself, and I'm proud to be a staunch ally of the LGBTQIA+ community. I have a loving, supportive family, and I feel blessed by the universe and thankful every day for all I have been given. In my heart and soul, I believe I hit the cosmic jackpot.

Cheers!

Other Books by Sam E. Kramer/L.A. Kaye

Books by Sam E. Kramer

The Lonely Heroes Complete Series

RangerHank

GuardianGabe

CowboyShep

HackerLawry

Positive Raleigh

Salesman Mateo

Bachelor Hero

OrphanDuke

NobleBruno

Avenging Kelly

ChefRafe

On The Rocks Complete Series

Whiskey Dreams

Ima-GIN-ation

Absinthe Minded

Weighting... Complete Series

Weightingfor Love

Weightingfor Laughter

Weightingfor a Lifetime

May/December Hearts Collection

A Wise Heart

Heart of Stone

Whatthe H(e)art Wants

A Flaws & All Love Story

Sinners' Redemption

Forgiveness is a Virtue

SwimCoach

Men of Memphis Blues

Kim& Skip

Cash& Cary

Dori& Sonny

Perfect Novellas

Perfect

2Perfect

Power Players

TheSenator

Holiday Books

MyJingle Bell Heart

Georgie'sEggcellent Adventure

The Holiday Gamble

Mabry's Minor Mistake

Other Titles

WhenSparks Fly

UnbreakHim

TheSecrets We Whisper To The Bees

ShearBliss

Kiss Me Stupid

Smolder

ADaddy for Christmas 2: Hermie

BOOKS by L.A. Kaye

Dearly and The Departed

Dearly & Deviant Daniel

Dearly& Vain Valentino

Dearly& Notorious Nancy

Dearly& Homeless Horace

Dearly& Threatening Thane

Dearly & Lovesick Lorraine

Dearly and The Departed Spinoffs

The Harbinger's Ball

The Harbinger's Allure

Scotty & Jay's First HellishAdventure

Scotty & Jay's Second HellishAdventure

Other Titles

Halston's Family Gothic - The Prologue

The Mysteries of Marblehead Manor

Mutual Obsessions

Milton Keynes UK
Ingram Content Group UK Ltd.
UKHW040817141124
451205UK00001B/14

9 798227 234407